Maia was n... where Bren... beneath the mistletoe, and her heart executed a series of hops and skips.

And then, suddenly, he was there. He and Channing approached from the other side of the arena, the two of them talking quietly.

At that same moment, TJ spied Brent and took off stomping through the soft dirt.

"TJ! Come back." Maia went after him.

She wasn't fast enough, and he reached Brent well ahead of her. A string of gibberish followed as TJ hugged Brent's knee.

"What's up, pal? Here to see Santa?" Brent bent down and lifted the small boy into his arms without a trace of awkwardness.

Maia came to a standstill and stared as TJ put his face nose to nose with Brent's and said, "Be doo doo."

TJ hugged Brent around the neck, and Maia's heart dissolved into a puddle.

This was the kind of man she'd hoped to find. But would he stay?

Dear Reader,

Sometimes, a story takes a completely different direction than what I had planned. *A Secret Christmas Wish* originally had a hero I described as a horse trainer who was hired on part-time at Your Perfect Plus One. He'd been saddled (pun intended) with some expensive medical bills and needed extra income. At his first job, a wedding, he'd meet my heroine, Maia, a competitive trail rider and single mother who also worked part-time for the same company. The book was going to be light with a touch of humor.

While there are still moments of humor—nothing like an adorable toddler's antics to make you smile—a different Brent took shape on the pages when I started this book. For a long while now, I've been wanting to write an outwardly strong character with a hidden disability. Brent is that character. His private battle with depression has brought him to a low point in his life, largely because he's in denial. A possible future with Maia gives him a reason to get better, but alas, that's easier said than done.

I hope you enjoy reading Brent and Maia's journey, not only of love and growth but also of healing and understanding, as much as I enjoyed writing it.

Warmest wishes,

Cathy McDavid

PS: I love connecting with readers. You can find me at:

CathyMcDavid.com

Facebook.com/CathyMcDavidBooks

Twitter: @CathyMcDavid

Instagram.com/CathyMcDavidWriter

HEARTWARMING

A Secret Christmas Wish

—

Cathy McDavid

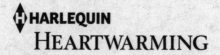

❖HARLEQUIN
HEARTWARMING

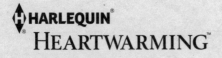

HARLEQUIN®
HEARTWARMING™

ISBN-13: 978-1-335-42647-5

Recycling programs
for this product may
not exist in your area.

A Secret Christmas Wish

Harlequin Enterprises ULC
22 Adelaide St. West, 40th Floor
Toronto, Ontario M5H 4E3, Canada
www.Harlequin.com

Printed in U.S.A.

Since 2006, *New York Times* bestselling author **Cathy McDavid** has been happily penning contemporary Westerns for Harlequin. Every day, she gets to write about handsome cowboys riding the range or busting a bronc. It's a tough job, but she's willing to make the sacrifice. Cathy shares her Arizona home with her own real-life sweetheart and a trio of odd pets. Her grown twins have left to embark on lives of their own, and she couldn't be prouder of their accomplishments.

Books by Cathy McDavid

Harlequin Heartwarming

Wishing Well Springs

The Cowboy's Holiday Bride
How to Marry a Cowboy

The Sweetheart Ranch

A Cowboy's Christmas Proposal
The Cowboy's Perfect Match
The Cowboy's Christmas Baby
Her Cowboy Sweetheart

Visit the Author Profile page
at Harlequin.com for more titles.

This book is dedicated to everyone who's struggling with depression or has struggled in the past. You aren't defined by your illness, you should never be judged by it and, most importantly, you aren't alone.

CHAPTER ONE

STARING AT AN attractive cowboy across the way while on a date with someone else probably wasn't considered good manners. Maia MacKenzie imagined her mother rolling her eyes and announcing she'd raised her youngest daughter better than that.

But, Maia rationalized, this wasn't a real date. Yes, technically she'd arrived with the man sitting to her left. And, like all the guests at Wishing Well Springs wedding barn, she waited for the familiar strains of "Here Comes the Bride." But at the end of the reception, they'd part ways and never hear from one another again.

Her date—Kenny Haselhoff, she reminded herself—seemed nice, if a bit nervous. She sent him her best you've-got-this smile. He fidgeted in response, his knee bobbing up and down.

According to the bio she'd been provided, Kenny worked as a project manager for a large flooring company, liked to golf and jog, was a newly divorced father of two and had season tickets to the Arizona Cardinals games. In the story outline he'd created, they'd been seeing each other for the past two months and weren't yet serious.

In truth, Maia had just met Kenny for the first time thirty minutes ago. In the rear parking lot of Payson Feed and Hay, of all places. He'd chosen the discreet location, insisting they not be glimpsed by anyone attending his cousin's nuptials. As Maia had learned this past year working for Your Perfect Plus One, people were funny when it came to weddings. They had no problems going solo to any other activity. Nightclubs. Parties. Sporting events. Movies. But somehow, arriving alone at a wedding screamed *loser* with a capital *L*.

Which explained why her older sister's wedding-and-event-date company had doubled in size since opening and why Maia was busy most weekends. Weddings were big business in this tourist town. More than ever since Wishing Well Springs had opened its doors. Getting hitched or hosting a family reunion in a glamorously rustic barn with an adorable Western-themed miniature town next door appealed to a lot of people. Particularly over the holidays.

Personally, Maia wouldn't want to get married on Thanksgiving eve, but to each their own. The turkey with all the fixings dinner reception at Joshua Tree Inn next door did promise to be delicious. She had that to look forward to at least.

Her gaze traveled again to the attractive cowboy in the pew across the aisle. He looked vaguely familiar, though not in an I-know-you way. More like an I've-seen-you-somewhere way. Hmm. Maybe his name would come to her before the end of the wedding.

"Who are you looking at?" Kenny whispered.

Caught off guard, Maia swallowed a groan. Busted. She was here as his date and a representative of Your Perfect Plus One. He was entitled to her undivided attention for the duration of the wedding and reception.

She pinned a pleasant expression on her face and turned toward him, vowing to do better. It was unlike her to slip. She prided herself on her four-point-eight-star client-satisfaction rating.

"The decorations," she murmured. "They're lovely."

She wasn't lying. Not about that. The wedding barn had been transformed to reflect the fall season and Thanksgiving. Shades of gold, orange, yellow, deep browns and reds abounded. At the end of each pew hung a cluster of tiger lilies tied with a satin ribbon. On the table behind the altar, a festive array of pumpkins, gourds and dried rainbow corncobs spilled from a wicker cornucopia flanked by vases holding enormous bouquets of fall flowers. Multicolored dried oak leaves were scattered on the carpet leading to the altar, left there by the flower girl.

The effect was magical. Maybe Maia would consider a Thanksgiving wedding after all.

"When I introduce you to my cousin," Kenny said, "don't forget to say we met at a golf tournament where you drove me around in the VIP van."

His nerves were showing again.

"I won't."

Maia wasn't sure about the necessity of adding a VIP van to the story. But whatever. Her job was to go along with the role the client chose for her. Many of which were far removed from her often-boring real life as a hardworking single mom to a young toddler. On some of her more memorable wedding dates, she'd been a cemetery-plot salesperson, a phlebotomist, a fish-hatchery technician and a travel blogger. That last one had been something she wouldn't mind trying in real life. The traveling part.

Your Perfect Plus One was *not* a matchmaking service and certainly *not* a hire-for-the-evening service. Maia's assignments lasted only for the wedding and reception or event, during which she'd sit beside her date, show interest in him and engage in friendly, casual conversation with the other guests. She'd leave at the end with people convinced he'd found a nice gal. What he told his friends and family later about their fictitious breakup wasn't her concern.

Music started, and everyone shifted as one to watch the bride and her father proceed down the aisle. A small lump formed in Maia's throat. It happened every time, regardless if she knew the couple or not. Something about witnessing the happiest day of two people's lives brought out her sentimental side.

The moment was also a small reminder of her own thwarted wedding. She no longer pined for her former fiancé. Hardly! She more often wanted to boot him from here to the next county for all but ignoring their son. But she'd once almost been this stunning bride, and the memory strummed those tender heartstrings.

After the ceremony, the newlyweds practically floated down the aisle. They were followed by the wedding party and close family members. One by one, the pews emptied. When their turn came, Kenny took Maia's arm.

"This okay?" he whispered.

"Of course." She smiled. "I'm looking forward to meeting your family."

Minimal, appropriate and respectful touching was allowed. Also dancing. Again, respectfully. Only once had Maia's date gotten a little handsy with her. She'd politely and firmly reminded him of the client contract terms, and he'd backed off. He'd even given her and the company a glowing review. Good thing. A bad review could reflect negatively on her sister's fledgling business.

Outside, Maia listened with half an ear while Kenny chatted about both the fun and trouble he and his cousin had gotten into as teenagers. She couldn't shake the sensation that someone was staring at her. As she and Kenny entered the receiving line, she glanced behind them— and immediately locked eyes with the attractive cowboy. He grinned.

Wow! He'd donned a tan Stetson that showed off his navy Western-cut suit and emphasized his ruggedly handsome features.

She spun back around, her insides fluttering and her cheeks growing warm.

"You ready?" Kenny said as they took another step forward.

What? Right. The receiving line. "Yes."

Focus, she reminded herself. She had a job to do and company policies to uphold. No flirting or romantic fraternizing with any of the guests topped the list. That would be the end of her lucrative part-time job, and she needed the extra

CATHY McDAVID   13

money. Winning the Diamond Cup without a
new competition saddle would be difficult, and
they didn't come cheap.

Besides, the cowboy was with somebody.
Maia had caught sight of a turquoise dress and
blond hair. His wife or girlfriend, no doubt.

Steeling herself, she silently counted to ten
and smiled at Kenny. "Sounds like you two had
a great childhood."

He looked at her strangely. "I was talking
about my dog."

Was he?

"Murphy. My goldendoodle."

Maia nodded. "Your cousin gave him to you
as a puppy."

"His mom did. My aunt. For my kids."

She ground her teeth together. What was the
matter with her? She normally didn't botch
dates.

"I'm sorry," she said. "I won't mess up again.
I promise."

And she didn't. When the receiving line
advanced, and they greeted the bride and
groom, she offered a warm handshake, made
the appropriate comment about where she and
Kenny had supposedly met—which earned
him a fist pump from his cousin, the groom—
and, lastly, expressed her very best wishes for
the newlyweds.

"Thanks," Kenny said in a low voice once they'd moved away.

"Did I pass?" she joked.

"With flying colors."

They gathered in front of the wedding barn with the other guests milling beneath the yellow, orange and green crepe-paper bells strung in the branches overhead. Maia slipped into the velvet wrap she'd been carrying. Payson could turn cold in late November. Rain wasn't uncommon. Today, the elements had cooperated and gifted the newlyweds with unseasonably mild weather to go with a shimmering blue sky.

She and Kenny made small talk while they waited. To be honest, Kenny did most of the talking with Maia chiming in now and then and always sticking to the script. A few times, the cowboy drifted into her line of vision. She diligently avoided eye contact.

Okay, maybe not that diligently. The petite blonde clung to the cowboy's arm, her grip borderline possessive. Funny, mused Maia, they didn't look like they belonged together. Not that a person could tell from appearances. But they gave off an undeniable vibe of being mismatched.

"You simply must check out the miniature

Western town around the corner," a middle-aged woman in Maia's circle commented.

"It's adorable," she replied. "I love the jail and the general store."

The woman's glance flitted between Maia and Kenny. "I thought Kenny said you were running late and didn't have a chance to see it."

Beside her, Kenny tensed.

"I…um…" Oops. Maia thought fast. "I attended a friend's wedding here this past summer."

She'd actually attended six weddings here during the last year, not to mention several dozen more at different locations, some as far away as Phoenix. All in the role of a client's date. Her sister was extremely careful and usually sent Maia on weddings for nonlocals, minimizing the risk she'd be recognized and have some explaining to do.

"Yes," the woman in her circle agreed. "Wishing Well Springs is very popular."

Whew! Kenny must have experienced the same relief, for he relaxed.

Not long after that, the bride and groom announced that everyone should head on over to the inn across the way for the reception. They and the rest of the wedding party would be along once they'd finished with the photographer.

Maia and Kenny rode the short distance in his car. He didn't say much until they were in the parking lot searching for an empty space.

"That went okay," he conceded.

"I'm sorry I got distracted."

"Yeah."

Was he accepting her apology or just acknowledging her admission? She let the subject drop. No sense rehashing her blunder. Better she spend the remaining two hours being the best wedding date possible. Surely in that short amount of time, and in a space the size of the dining room at the inn, she could avoid the cowboy.

She and Kenny met up with some of the other guests during their stroll inside. On a credenza to the right of the dining room entrance, they located their meal tickets and table assignment. He led the way, weaving in and out of the growing throng of people and pausing periodically to say hello to someone.

Midway across the room, he pointed. "There we are. Table eighteen." After covering the few remaining feet, he pulled out a chair for Maia.

"Thank you," she said and lowered herself onto the plush cushion.

Removing her wrap, she looked up—right into the compelling hazel eyes of the attractive cowboy sitting directly across from her.

BRENT HAYES HAD arrived in Payson a little before eleven that morning, driving straight through from Tucson where he'd been staying with an old rodeo friend. He'd left at the crack of dawn, pretty sure his friend had been happy to have his couch back after three weeks and not unhappy to see Brent's truck backing out of his driveway.

He had that effect on people, the last couple of years, anyway. He'd worn out his welcome at more places than he could count, including his mom's and cousin's.

In the two hours since he'd hit town, he'd met with the owner of Your Perfect Plus One and completed the required paperwork. He'd taken a preemployment drug test three days earlier while still in Tucson, the same day as his on-line interview and background check. The drug testing company had forwarded his results to Your Perfect Plus One, and Brent had received the official offer via phone call yesterday.

Are you sure you can handle this? the owner had inquired after giving him a brief orientation and set of instructions.

Yes, ma'am. He'd flashed his winningest grin. *I'm a fast learner. I won't let you down.*

I hope not.

By the way, is there somewhere I can change?

She'd escorted him to a dressing room where

he traded his jeans and faded work shirt for his one good suit. After that, she'd sent him off with a worried smile, admitting she was in a bind and didn't have much choice.

Brent had driven straight to the prearranged meeting location where Bobbie-Ann waited. The two of them had then headed to Wishing Well Springs, arriving in plenty of time despite her concerns they'd be late.

She was a talker, which was fine with Brent. He hadn't expected to know any of the wedding guests except Bobbie-Ann, and had no problem with her taking the lead in their conversations.

Another benefit to sitting quietly was Brent could people watch. It remained a favorite pastime from his days on the rodeo circuit.

The woman with the mink-brown waves and even darker eyes had caught his attention from the second she'd walked into the wedding barn. No denying her prettiness, but it was her animated expressions that had kept him seeking her out. She spoke volumes without saying a word, and he was listening. The guy with her didn't stand a chance. She clearly wasn't into him.

Brent and the woman sitting across from each other at the reception had been a stroke of good fortune, and his long-dormant interest was piqued. Not that he'd ditch Bobbie-Ann.

No way. Or be less than the attentive and affable companion his job required of him. But his obligation to her extended only until the end of the reception.

"Hi. I'm Bobbie-Ann and this is Brett," Bobbie-Ann said, greeting the two new arrivals and using the fake name Brent's new boss had selected for him. "Isn't that cute? Bobbie-Ann and Brett. We sound like a singing duo. Are you on the bride's side or the groom's? She and I roomed together in college."

"Groom's," the guy answered. "He's my cousin." He indicated himself and then his companion. "Name's Kenny and this is Marla."

"Nice to meet you," Brent said, speaking to the guy but looking at Marla. Funny. She didn't look like a Marla.

Introductions continued with their four tablemates, and conversation flowed. The women discussed the wedding ceremony, the bride's dress, the elaborate multitiered cake in the corner and the newlyweds' honeymoon plans. The men stuck to sports and Kenny's new Lexus sedan.

Brent replied when asked a direct question. Otherwise, he listened and fulfilled Bobbie-Ann's need of the moment—fetching her a drink from the bar, locating her a fresh linen napkin when she dropped hers and making sure the server got their correct meal tickets. In between, he studied Marla.

"We've been dating a couple months," Kenny answered in response to another guest's question. "We met at a golf tournament. Marla was the VIP driver who took me around."

"That's cool," the young man said.

"Yeah. It is." Kenny's gaze went to Marla.

She smiled in return. A platonic smile, though Brent doubted anyone else noticed.

"You must meet a lot of interesting people driving for events," Brent said.

"Um, no." Marla shook her head, sending her long brown waves into motion. "I... It was a one-time job. A friend convinced me." She laid her hand on Kenny's arm. "Which turned out well for us."

"What's your regular nine-to-five?" Brent asked and then gave himself a swift invisible kick when Bobbie-Ann stiffened.

He really needed to keep his mouth shut. Except he hadn't enjoyed himself this much in months. No, longer than that. Certainly not since before the National Finals Rodeo two years ago, when he realized his bull- and bronc-riding career had tanked with zero possibility of him rebounding.

Marla blinked, hesitating. Her glance cut

quickly to Kenny. When he and everyone else remained silent, she finally answered.

"No one wants to hear about me."

"Yes, we do," the women nearest her insisted.

Bobbie-Ann remained uncharacteristically quiet.

Marla let out a long, indecisive breath. "I'm a competitive trail rider."

"No fooling!" Brent didn't know a lot about the sport, other than it required a tremendous amount of athleticism, strength and hard work on the part of both horse and rider. "That's impressive."

"Not really," she said, attempting to dismiss her accomplishments.

But Brent observed a slight squaring of her shoulders he could only describe as satisfaction or pride.

"Have you won any events?" the woman asked.

"A few. Not in a while, though. I took a break from competing. Life got in the way. I just recently returned."

"Good for you." The woman smiled approvingly. "I admire anyone who can return after a setback."

Brent did, too. He knew firsthand how hard that was, having tried himself and failed. He liked to think he was at long last moving out of the dark place and that life would improve in Payson. At least he was getting out of the house, seeing new sights, meeting new people, trying new things. A definite improvement.

As was landing gainful, permanent employment. Working sporadically for these last two years had drained his bank account. The full-time wrangler job at Mountainside Stables was right up his alley. A wedding date for hire? Not so much. Still, he couldn't complain. The part-time gig paid well.

"I'm trying to get Marla to take up golf," Kenny said, and then went on to describe a nine iron he'd purchased the previous week.

Marla appeared relieved to no longer be the center of attention.

Kenny's lengthy description of his new golf club was thankfully cut short when the servers materialized with their food.

Brent savored every bite of his delicious turkey dinner, which would be the closest he'd come to celebrating Thanksgiving. If he wasn't working tomorrow at Mountainside Stables, he'd spend the day staring at the walls. Much the same as he'd done last Thanksgiving. And Christmas. And every other major holiday.

The remainder of the reception progressed as expected. After their meal, toasts were made and the cake cut. A DJ took to the small stage, and guests joined the bride and groom on the dance floor.

Brent turned to Bobbie-Ann. "Would you like to dance?"

"Yes!" She jumped to her feet.

They hit the floor a total of six times—Bobbie-Ann more often than that, pairing up with friends and participating in the boisterous line dances. Brent took advantage of the breaks to resume people watching or engage in casual chatter with other guests at the table. Sadly, Marla didn't return, Kenny apparently keeping her busy elsewhere.

Just as well. She had a boyfriend. And, besides, Brent wasn't in any kind of emotional place to consider a relationship, committed or casual. Hopefully, that would change along with his new jobs and new address.

It was time he got his act together. Past time. Problem was, he had almost no motivation. What had once been easy for him now required tremendous effort. Brent didn't like labeling his problem. Men didn't suffer from depression. Especially big, tough, physically strong men like him. Men who rode bulls and broncs for a living. In his mind, he should be able to just shake it off. Except he couldn't.

He woke up most mornings with little desire to crawl out of bed. When he eventually did, he dragged through his day as if wearing a hundred-pound chain around his neck and cement shoes. The idea that he might need professional help often occurred to him. His ego refused to let him seek it.

Instead, he put on happy face and pretended everything was fine. Maybe one day, he'd start to believe it and feel better for real.

Sometime later, the DJ announced the last dance. Bobbie-Ann found her way back to the table, her complexion glowing from mild perspiration, her eyes bright and a grin stretching from ear to ear. The wedding had been winding down for the past forty-five minutes, but not Bobbie-Ann.

"One final spin?" Brent asked.

"Love to."

The DJ played a slow number.

"Guess it's time to go," Bobbie-Ann said on the way to the table.

"Guess it is."

She glanced toward the door and then back at Brent, her eyes hopeful. "I don't suppose we could go somewhere else?"

The owner of Your Perfect Plus One had prepared Brent for just this possibility, and he let Bobbie-Ann down gently. "I wish I could. I have an appointment at five."

"Another wedding date?"

He said nothing, neither denying nor confirming. There was a limit to how much personal information he'd reveal.

"Got it." She nodded resignedly.

Brent kept a lookout for Marla while crossing the room toward the exit. She wasn't anywhere to be seen. Neither was Kenny. They must have left. Brent snuffed out the slight stab of disappointment.

He and Bobbie-Ann drove to the shopping center where they'd met up and where Brent had left his truck.

"It was nice to meet you," he said reaching for the door handle. "Happy Thanksgiving."

She surprised him by leaning over and throwing her arms around his neck. "Thanks. You were a great date. Really wonderful."

"You take care, Bobbie-Ann."

"You, too."

ONCE IN HIS TRUCK, he called Your Perfect Plus One and reported in to the owner, who was pleased to hear the date went well. Next, he plugged his destination into the GPS app on his phone.

While he followed the voice's directions, he mentally prepared for his second job interview today. Mountainside Stables was located on the grounds of Bear Creek Ranch, a four-star resort north of Payson. And while situated on the resort grounds, the Stables was independently owned and operated. Brent had talked with the owner of the trail-ride outfit twice already on the phone, and the man had assured him today's interview was a formality. Brent had the job if he wanted it, which he did.

But first, he needed to escape the exhaustion pulling him down and down. The long day of driving, combined with the wedding and his constant battle to present a cheerful front, had worn him out. One more hour, he told himself, then he could surrender to the depths until tomorrow.

Twelve miles north of Payson, he spotted the monument sign for Bear Creek Ranch. As he executed the turn, the GPS voice informed him that he'd arrived.

Though not yet five, the sun had already dipped beneath the nearby mountains. The sky hung in that drab place between dusk and nightfall. Brent related. He felt that way most of the time. Though, there'd been a bright spot today: sitting across from Marla during the reception.

He exercised care on the long, winding dirt road. Sharp bends could easily hide people on foot, riders on horses and nocturnal critters in search of food. He crossed a narrow bridge traversing Bear Creek, the origin of the ranch's name, according to their website. Every building at the hundred-year-old vacation lodge was constructed of logs, from the main office to the dining hall to the quaint guest cabins.

Arrows pointed the way to the stables, and he followed them. A red barn appeared at the bottom of the hill, off to the side and nestled against a stand of tall pine trees. Horses of varying sizes, colors and breeds ate contentedly in the large enclosure beside the barn, their noses buried in three communal feed troughs. Brent parked next to the hitching post and got out. A man he judged to be in his early sixties emerged from inside the stables.

"Evening," he called. "You must be Brent."

"Ansel?"

"In the flesh. Welcome to Bear Creek Ranch."

The two shook hands. Ansel's roughened palm and weathered cheeks belonged to a man who'd spent his life outdoors rather than tied to a desk. His amiable grin put Brent instantly at ease.

"A pleasure to meet you, sir."

"Channing speaks highly of you. It's on account of his recommendation I'm offering you the job."

"He and his family are good people. I've known them a lot of years. Competed against

Channing on the rodeo circuit. He won more than I did."

Ansel chuckled and went on to explain the requirements of the job as guide for the mounted trail rides. In addition to weekly wages, Brent would be given a bed in the employee bunkhouse and three squares a day. He'd be up with the sun and work until it went down, five days on followed by two days off. If there were no customers to take out on the trails, he was expected to clean tack, make repairs, train the livestock, run errands and whatever else Ansel required of him. Brent's free time was his to spend how he saw fit.

"I like to stay busy," Brent said. Staying busy kept his mind occupied and kept him from sinking into the dark place.

"Trust me, that can be arranged." Ansel chuckled again.

Before he could continue, a figure emerged from the stables, the two-story building casting her in shadows. She'd changed from her pale gold dress into jeans, and it took Brent a few seconds to recognize her. When he did, his pulse spiked.

Marla!

She recognized him, too, her brown eyes widening with surprise.

"Brett?"

"Hi."

"You two know each other?" Ansel asked.

"We met this afternoon," Brent said. "At a wedding. And the name's actually Brent."

"Oh. I apologize." She looked chagrinned. "I must have misheard."

He didn't explain the use of a fake name for his wedding-date side gig.

A movement drew his attention, and he realized Marla wasn't alone. A child, a boy of one or maybe two, stepped out from behind her. After giving Brent a cautious once-over, he tipped his head way back and lifted his arms to Marla.

"Mama. Up. Up."

Mama? Well, thought Brent, that was unexpected.

"What are you doing here?" she asked him, her tone curious rather than alarmed as she stroked her son's head.

"He's our new wrangler," Ansel said and turned to Brent. "Maia's my daughter. And this here young whippersnapper is TJ, my grandson."

"Mama. Up."

"Maia?" Brent asked. "This is embarrassing. I thought *your* name was Marla."

She laughed. "It's Maia. But sometimes

Marla. It's a long story." She bent and lifted the boy into her arms, settling him on her hip.

He grinned, his previous exhaustion vanishing. This new job of his suddenly held much more appeal.

CHAPTER TWO

THE COWBOY WHO had distracted Maia at the wedding and the new wrangler her dad had hired were one and the same. What were the odds? She'd thought her eyes were deceiving her when she first stepped out of the stables and saw Brent. He'd discarded the tailored suit jacket he'd worn earlier in favor of a fleece-lined denim one and swapped out his tan felt Stetson for a weathered straw one. But there'd been no mistaking that engaging smile and those intense hazel eyes.

She noted he appeared more relaxed in these surroundings than at the wedding. Like he wanted to be here. Like he belonged.

"This is probably going to sound strange…" Maia hesitated and then blurted, "Have we met before? Other than at the wedding?"

"Don't think so." His voice took on a husky quality. "I'd remember you."

"I, ah, meet a lot of people because of work. I…guess you remind me of someone."

Brent's smile widened. "I get around. I suppose it's possible we've crossed paths."

She jostled TJ to quiet his fussing and her own mild disconcertion. Brent had attended the wedding with a date. Maia couldn't forget that very important detail. He and Bobbie-Ann were serious for all she knew, and she'd never infringe on an established relationship despite a mutual attraction.

Besides, between caring for TJ, working at Mountainside Stables—her parents' horse-rental outfit that catered to Bear Creek Ranch's year-round guests—and her demanding training schedule, she had zero free time for a man. More important, she wasn't about to get derailed again. Making a good life for TJ and winning a competitive trail-riding championship were her priorities. Not dating.

Real dating. Your Perfect Plus One didn't count.

"We have only one ride scheduled tomorrow because of Thanksgiving," her dad said to Brent. "You leave at eight sharp, which means you'll be saddling up at seven thirty. Which also means you need to be here by six for feeding and chores."

"Yes, sir."

"Maia, you go with him tomorrow. Show him the ropes."

She'd expected as much; she and her dad had discussed it before Brent arrived. But that was also before she'd learned Brent was her dad's new hire. Showing *him* the ropes added a whole new element to the ride.

"Mama, Mama." TJ leaned in, and, putting his face in front of hers, patted her cheeks with his pudgy hands. "Firsty."

"Hold on, sweetie."

Glad for the distraction, she reached into the fanny pack at her waist and extracted a baby bottle of apple juice she'd brought for exactly this occasion. Uncapping the bottle with a flip of her thumb, she handed it to TJ and then re-pocketed the cap. TJ watched Brent as he drank, his cherubic features reflecting a mixture of wariness and interest.

"How long is the ride?" Brent asked.

"This one is ninety minutes," Maia's dad explained. "We offer everything from an hour to a full day that includes a box lunch. My wife, Lois, Maia's mom, manages the reservations and the money. All our horses are dead broke, though a few can get testy now and then. You'll learn their different personalities and to match the horse to the rider based on their experience."

He spent the next several minutes detailing Mountainside's daily operations.

"Think you're up to the task? The days are long and the work hard."

Brent nodded. "I'm used to long days and hard work."

Maia's arms had grown tired, and she shifted TJ to her other hip. "You ever trail ride before?"

"Once or twice. When I was younger."

"You'll learn," her dad said. "I figure anyone who can score 91 in bronc riding can surely handle one of our fat, lazy horses."

Bronc riding! Of course. That was where Maia had seen Brent before. He used to compete at the Rim Country rodeo arena in Payson. If she remembered correctly, he was chasing a world title. Though, now that she thought about it, she hadn't seen him at the arena for quite a while.

"Aren't you friends with Channing Pearce?" she said, naming the rodeo arena manager.

"Guilty as charged."

"Channing's the one who recommended Brent for the job," her dad said.

"I see."

Only Maia didn't see why a professional bronc and bull rider would hire on with a horse-rental outfit. She loved Mountainside Stables and hoped to take over from her parents one day. But a wrangler/trail guide did seem like a step down for Brent. The qualifications weren't many. Her dad often employed high school students during the summer tourist season.

She supposed Brent had his reasons, and she didn't ask. Later, she'd pump her dad for information.

"Remind me, aren't you from Oklahoma?"

"Kansas. I grew up in Wichita." Brent's expression brimmed with aw-shucks charm. "Most of my family's still there."

It was on the tip of her tongue to ask how he knew Bobbie-Ann if he wasn't from the area. She refrained. He had one friend in Payson: Channing Pearce. Obviously, he had another—this one a lady. Perhaps several lady friends. Handsome professional rodeo cowboys rarely lacked for companionship.

"I'd take you out myself tomorrow," Maia's dad said, "exceptin' I have plans."

"He volunteers at Payson Rescue Mission." Maia was proud of her dad and bragged about him every chance she got. "They put on a really nice holiday dinner for the residents. Dad's specialty is baked sweet potatoes."

"I like to pay it forward when I can. This community's been good to me and mine over the years."

Brent's smile lost some of its exuberance. "I'm sure the residents appreciate it. The holidays can be hard when you're alone and away from home."

He spoke as if from experience.

Her dad apparently had the same thought, for he said, "You should join us for dinner, Brent. That is, if you aren't busy."

"I'm not, but—"

"We'll sit down to eat around three, after I get back from the shelter. Arrive early. Lois puts out a bowl of homemade apple cider that's lip-smacking delicious."

"Thank you, sir." Brent shook his head. "I couldn't impose."

"No imposition. The more the merrier. My other daughter and her family will be there. A few of the neighbors. You'll fit right in."

"I'll just grab a bite at the dining hall or in town."

"Nonsense. I insist. Maia will give you directions to the house."

She'd expected Brent to say he was busy with Bobbie-Ann. Since that wasn't the case, she added a little arm twisting of her own. Why not?

"We invite all the new hires. It's kind of a tradition."

With a soft sigh, Brent relented. "Okay. For a little while."

Maia's dad clapped him on the shoulder.

"Glad that's settled. Now, Maia, honey, take him to the bunkhouse while I finish up here for the night."

She held back a protest. Was her dad matchmaking? It wouldn't be the first time since her almost marriage. Ansel MacKenzie was progressive enough to believe a woman should have the same opportunities as a man and traditional enough to think he wanted his daughters married to, in his words, *a good man of sound character.*

"Fine. Will do, Pops." Time for her to hit the road, anyway. Her mom, who babysat TJ while Maia worked or trained, had already fed him dinner. But he was an early-to-bed and early-to-rise baby and would tire soon. Then he'd become whiney and cranky, sort of like his mother when she got tired.

Her dad sauntered over, kissed her on the cheek and ruffled TJ's pale brown hair. "Night, little man. You behave for your mama."

TJ crinkled the fingers of the hand not holding the bottle. His version of a goodbye wave.

"I'm parked on the other side of the stables," Maia said to Brent and tilted her head in that direction. "I'll meet you out front, and you can follow me."

"Okay."

At her SUV, she loaded TJ in the car seat, her

mind still on Brent. She didn't quite know what to make of him. He gave off an air of mystery that intrigued her. The only personal information he'd revealed was that his family hailed from Wichita. And he'd required considerable persuading before agreeing to attend Thanksgiving dinner—which struck her as strange, as he hadn't been the least bit antisocial at the wedding. Then there was the noticeable change in his mood at the mention of the holiday.

She motioned to him as she pulled onto the bumpy dirt road. In the back seat, TJ babbled and pointed out the darkened window. She had no idea what caught his interest, possibly his own reflection. At fifteen months old, his intelligible vocabulary was limited.

As she drove, a notification appeared on her vehicle display informing Maia of a text message and asking if she wanted to read or ignore it. The number of the sender belonged to her sister, Darla.

Maia hit the Read button and the vehicle's mechanical voice recited, *Call me. Smiley-face emoji.*

She hit Reply and said, "Later. Still at work."

The voice responded with, *Your message has been sent.*

Maia would phone her sister on the drive home or tomorrow morning. For now, she wanted to concentrate on Brent. Not on *him*, she silently correctly herself. On getting him situated in the bunkhouse. As her dad had asked.

She mulled over what little she'd learned of him. He hadn't been competing professionally for a while. He was agreeable to working at a job beneath his qualifications. He didn't talk a lot about himself. The air of mystery surrounding him deepened, and she was admittedly curious.

Approaching a sign saying Employees Only Past This Point, Maia turned right. A hundred yards beyond that, she stopped in front of a small cluster of private buildings—the largest two being bunkhouses, the smallest a storage shed. Brent pulled into a small clearing behind the bunkhouses where employees parked. She then opened the rear door, unbuckled TJ from the car seat and lifted him out.

After setting him on the ground, she took his hand in hers. Brent rounded the corner of the bunkhouse, a duffel slung over his shoulder, the pair of dress boots he'd worn to the wedding tucked under his arm and an undeniable spring to his step. Seemed whatever came over him at the stables had vanished during the short drive.

Must have been a momentary flash of homesickness, Maia decided. Well, she'd do her best to make him feel at home here. Strictly as a co-worker, of course.

She had to remind herself of that twice more as he neared, his gaze not once wavering from hers.

DURING THE DRIVE to the bunkhouse, Brent had managed to vanquish the gloom that abruptly descended on him at the stables. It was often like that. He was struck down with no warning, the sensation like a sofa falling on him from a third-story window. Unlike tonight, he usually needed a day or two to crawl out from underneath the wreckage.

A desperate desire to not embarrass himself in front of Maia had given him the boost he needed.

"Hi." He put on a smile, the one he hid behind.

At his approach, her young son reached out his arm and gave Brent the same curling finger wave as he'd given his grandfather earlier.

"Hey, partner." Brent winked.

The kid uttered some gibberish in return that Brent translated to mean hello.

"This is the men's quarters," Maia said. "Next door is the women's."

The two buildings appeared identical, save the wrought-iron cowboy figurine mounted above the door on the men's building and a matching cowgirl figurine above the door on the women's.

Maia knocked and waited for a response. Getting none, she dug in her pocket for a ring of keys and unlocked the door.

Sticking her head inside, she called, "Anyone home?" When there was still no response, she entered.

TJ remained rooted in place.

"Come on, sweetie." She took his hand in hers.

He snatched it away and, pointing to Brent's boots, uttered more gibberish.

"Like those?" On impulse, Brent offered the kid a boot. "Maybe you can carry this for me. Be careful. It's heavy."

TJ clutched the boot awkwardly to his chest, his face alight with joy as if he'd won a prize.

"Wow." Maia stared at her son. "He's usually shy with strangers. You must have a knack with children."

"Not a knack. A little experience."

"Kids of your own?" Maia asked.

"What? No. I have some friends with kids."

"Nieces and nephews?"

"Not yet, and probably not for a while."

His younger brother and sister were still teenagers. A product of their dad's second marriage, they lived with him and their mother on the other side of Wichita. Brent seldom saw them.

His parents had divorced twenty-three years ago after a bitter falling out that had to do with his dad's chronic need to control. Sides had been drawn, and Brent, being only six at the time and having no choice, went with his mom. He and his dad saw each other once or twice a year, but the rift created by the divorce was too great to breach. His dad's constant attempts to tell Brent how to run his life rubbed him wrong. As a result, neither of them made more than a token effort.

If he ever had a family of his own, he was determined to be a better husband and give his children the kind of loving upbringing he'd missed out on.

"I think he likes my boot more than me," Brent said, referring to TJ.

Proving he was right, TJ shouldered his way past Maia into the house, dragging the boot behind him.

"TJ, don't," Maia chased after him. "You'll scuff it."

"He's fine," Brent assured her and followed them inside. "Let him have his fun."

Maia stopped and turned to face him, a question in her voice. "You sure?"

"That boot's been through far worse treatment than one little kid can inflict."

"O…kay." She winced as TJ inserted his entire leg into the boot. "I hope you don't regret it."

Brent doubted he would. Watching TJ's comical attempt to walk across the floor only made what had been his best day in a long time even better.

He looked around the bunkhouse. "Nice setup."

"Obviously, this is the communal kitchen and dining area." Maia gestured to a kitchenette complete with three-burner stove, microwave, refrigerator and four-person table and chairs. "There's the living room." A sofa and recliner faced a wall-mounted TV. "Internet's available, though the signal's not always the best out here. That door leads to the bathroom, and then there are the beds."

Six narrow beds sat perpendicular to the walls, each with its own nightstand, lamp and three-drawer dresser. Brent tried to remember the last time he'd slept on an actual mattress.

"Nothing fancy," Maia observed.

"Are you joking? This is great."

She tilted her head. "Looks like that bed over there's available."

The neatly tucked covers and a lack of any

personal items cluttering the nightstand and dresser top supported her assumption.

Brent walked over and tossed his duffel bag onto the bed, set his cowboy hat atop the bag and his remaining boot on the floor. "Where is everyone?"

"Rowdy, he's our other wrangler, went to Show Low. He's spending the holiday with his girlfriend and her family. You'll meet him tomorrow when he gets back. Your other bunk mates all work in the dining hall. They won't return until late—they're prepping for the Thanksgiving dinner tomorrow. Sorry, but you'll have to make your own introductions."

"Are they expecting me?"

"Dad told them."

"I'm surprised Mountainside employees are allowed to stay in the bunkhouse," Brent said, "seeing as it's separate from Bear Creek Ranch. The owners don't mind?"

"Dad had that included in our contract with the owners. Some of our wranglers are nomads, for lack of a better word. No permanent roof over their heads."

Like Brent. "Does your family live here, too?"

"Wouldn't that be nice, but no. They have a house in town. Dad keeps his personal horses at the stables."

"I noticed a lot of vehicles on my drive through the ranch. I'm kind of surprised there are so many guests here. Don't most people visit family and friends over Thanksgiving?"

"Bear Creek Ranch is booked to capacity *every* holiday, including Christmas. People like to get away for all sorts of reasons."

Brent thought if he had the money, he'd spend the holidays somewhere fun rather than alone at home. Not that he called any particular place home and hadn't since he'd hit the rodeo circuit at nineteen.

"Like Dad said," Maia continued, "you get three meals a day. Just go the kitchen entrance behind the dining hall. Breakfast starts at five thirty. One of the staff will make you a plate. No limit on coffee, iced tea or soda, so don't be shy. There's also a coffee maker here." She indicated the counter. "If you have personal food you don't want to share, either put your name on it or store it in your dresser. Bunkhouse rules are posted on the wall by the bathroom. You'll find the guys friendly and respectful as long as you're the same."

"I spent the last ten years on the road, eight of those competing professionally. For most of that, I had to share a room with other guys. I think I can get along with everyone."

Her gaze cut to TJ, who was now pushing

Brent's boot across the floor and making engine sounds as if the boot were a toy car.

"I suppose we should get going," she mused. "Let you settle in."

He didn't want to be by himself. Not yet. He wasn't ready for the gloom to creep slowly in and smother him. If he sat at the kitchen table, would they stay?

Pulling out a chair, he dropped into it. "Have you known Channing a long time?"

His ploy succeeded. She joined him, albeit hesitantly. "Most of my life. My family attends a lot of events at the arena. What about you? Known Channing long?"

"I started rodeoing shortly after he did. Like you, I've been to Rim Country more times than I can count."

She waited, perhaps for Brent to elaborate. When he didn't, she said, "I bought my competition horse from his girlfriend, Kenna."

"I've met her. A talented trick rider."

"She originally used Snapple for performing, but he didn't work out."

"Is he better at trail riding?"

"Not bad. Actually, in all fairness, Snapple's fantastic most of the time. Strong. Young. Athletic. Fast. Sure-footed. Amazing lung capacity. A real beauty. Everything I want in a competition horse. Problem is he has one bad habit.

The same bad habit Kenna had with him and why she sold him. I hate giving up and selling him, not without first trying every technique I can think of. And if I did sell him, I'd have to start over again with a different horse. That would set me way back and undo all the progress I've made."

"What's the bad habit?" Brent removed his jacket and draped it over the chair beside him.

"Horses are judged on more than speed of recovery and endurance in trail riding. Good manners are a big part. Snapple sometimes reacts when a person or another horse gets too close to his lower left flank. He was bitten there as a yearling, and it left a nasty scar. He used to bolt and run away on Kenna. I've trained that out of him, but he shuffles sideways or dances on his front feet. Once in a while he bucks. Just a small hop. If that happens during a competitive ride, I'll lose points or risk disqualification."

"Maybe I can help."

Maia studied him. "You have a special technique to correct bad habits like Snapple's?"

Brent shrugged, keenly aware of her scrutiny. Rather than feel uncomfortable, he returned it. "I've ridden a lot of reactive horses."

"Rodeo, right. Bucking broncs. But last I checked, cowboys encourage the broncs to buck. Not to behave."

"You aren't wrong. But I was part of a crew that broke and trained wild mustangs rounded up by the Bureau of Land Management. The mustangs deemed adoptable were then sold or auctioned off."

She sat straighter in her chair. "When was that?"

"Last year." Before she could ask for more details, he said, "The job was seasonal." He didn't admit to quitting. She might think he'd quit Mountainside Stables, too. Which he probably would at some point when the funk he refused to label as depression prevented him from performing his job. "I learned a few tricks."

"Okay. Worth a shot. Might help and probably can't hurt. Let's talk more tomorrow before the ride."

She slanted him a look. Something of a flirty look, if he wasn't mistaken. At the very least, an I-find-you-interesting look. His pulse spiked before he could caution himself to keep cool and not respond.

Except, like at the wedding today, he smiled back. It felt good, normal, to be talking with a pretty girl. Brent could forget for a few moments and just be his old self.

He took the flirting one step further by saying, "I could use something to fill my days off.

Can't think of anything better than spending time with you."

"What about Bobbie-Ann?" she asked, a hint of reservation in her voice.

"Bobbie-Ann?"

"Doesn't *she* fill your days off?"

He chuckled. "She's not my girlfriend, if that's what you're asking."

"She's not?"

"Nope." He leaned forward. "I'm single."

Maia's smile returned, and she also leaned forward. "Me, too. Single, that is."

This piece of news cheered him more than it should, considering she could do a whole lot better than a flat-broke, has-been cowboy with little to show for himself.

Then he remembered. She hadn't attended the wedding alone. "Will Kenny object?"

"We're… It's nothing. Very, very casual. In fact, I doubt I'll see him after today."

"No?"

"Definitely no," she reiterated. "We were never going to last. I just agreed to be his wedding date."

Huh! Another crazy coincidence. Brent wasn't just cheered, his mood soared. Fate, it seemed, was smiling down on him for once.

He forgot all about being cautious and about

being a lousy catch. "It's the same with me and Bobbie-Ann. Was the same, I should say."

"Really?"

"To be honest with you, I only just met her today."

Maia drew back, her expression incredulous. "You did? You just met her and she asked you to a wedding?"

Brent debated how much to reveal. He felt funny admitting his new side gig as a wedding-and-event date for hire. On the other hand, he wanted Maia to know beyond any doubt there was nothing between him and Bobbie-Ann. "Don't know how you'll take this, but here goes. She hired me. Besides Mountainside Stables, I also work for Your Perfect Plus One. They're a—"

"I know what they are." Maia blinked at him in disbelief, her smile dimming.

Did she think badly of him or the service the company provided? "Look, it's completely aboveboard."

"My sister owns the company. I work for her, too. Kenny hired me to be *his* date."

Now it was Brent's turn to draw back. The difference was his smile grew. "No fooling!"

"Working for her is how I pay for my competitive trail-riding costs."

"Small world. I plan on using the money to

pay for extra costs, too." Okay, to pay down his maxed-out credit cards and the money he'd borrowed from his cousin. But those were technically extra costs, right?

"Darla doesn't usually send two employees to the same wedding or event," Maia said, a frown creasing her brow. "She must have been in a bind."

"She mentioned that when she hired me."

Darla's bad luck had been Brent's good luck. He shouldn't be happy. He had no business encouraging Maia or believing he was ready for a relationship. Except he was happy. This felt like exactly what he needed to lift himself out of the dark place he'd been living in for too long.

She suddenly stood, the frown expanding to include her mouth. "It's late. Come on, TJ."

It was getting late, though Brent didn't have much to unpack.

Maia went over to TJ. When he refused to abandon Brent's boot, she lifted him into her arms. He immediately burst into outraged tears.

"Shh, sweetie." She propped him on her hip and started for the door.

Brent went with her. "Look, I realize we only met today, and, well, I don't want to jump to any conclusions…?"

Maia blew out a long breath. With each passing second, Brent's stomach sank further. Had he completely misread her signals?

"We work together," she said at last.

"Yeah."

"Your Perfect Plus One has a strict no fraternizing policy."

"I swear, Bobbie-Ann and I aren't seeing each other."

"Not you and Bobbie-Ann. *You and I* can't see each other. The company's no-fraternizing policy also extends to coworkers, for obvious reasons."

"It does?" If he'd read a clause in the employment contract about coworkers not fraternizing, or Darla had told him, he didn't remember.

"Yes."

He struggled to form a response. A low humming had begun filling his ears and interfered with his ability to think straight.

"I am glad that Dad and my sister both hired you," Maia said, sounding twenty feet away rather than two. "And I'm looking forward to any advice you have for my horse." She opened the door with the hand not holding TJ and stepped outside onto the stoop. "See you in the morning."

"See you."

Had Brent spoken? He wasn't sure.

His last sight of Maia before he closed the

door was of her hurrying to her vehicle. A few minutes later he heard the sound of her engine starting. Eventually, that faded, and Brent was left alone.

He had more items in his truck to unload. A briefcase containing his personal papers, tablet and phone charger. A footlocker for shoes, boots and his buckle collection. A wheeled suitcase holding more clothes and a plastic crate with miscellaneous items. He didn't go after them.

Instead, he shuffled across the floor to his bed, removed the duffel bag and dumped it on the floor. After stripping off his shirt and removing his belt, he threw them on top of the bag. He then kicked off his boots and peeled off his socks before crawling beneath the covers.

There, Brent closed his eyes and listened as the humming grew louder and the familiar heavy weight pressed down on him.

Tomorrow. He'd wake up and face the day. Do what needed to be done. For now, though, he'd just lie here.

He was still awake when his bunk mates arrived a few hours later, but he didn't get up. That required too much effort. Instead, he peeked his head out and muttered hello. Claiming he had an early morning, he rolled over and pretended to go to sleep. What they thought about him, he didn't care.

CHAPTER THREE

WHEN BRENT'S ALARM went off at 4:50 a.m., he was already awake and had been for most of the night. He quickly silenced his phone and scanned the darkened bunkhouse, noticing one of his bunk mates up and roaming the kitchen area. From their prone positions and soft snoring, the rest appeared to still be asleep.

Throwing back the covers, Brent sat up and swung his feet onto the floor. The thick cotton batting filling his head began to pulsate as blood moved through his veins. He shoved his fingers into his hair and massaged his temples. He would have liked to blame insufficient sleep for the lack of mental clarity, but he knew better. The reminder that he had nothing to offer someone like Maia—who deserved more than a guy the likes of him—was responsible for his fogginess.

With each high, he hit a little harder on the inevitable low and took a little longer to recover. His motivation dwindled, the road to recovery stretching further and further ahead. If not for friends like Channing—who'd given Brent a swift kick, along with a helping hand—it was anybody's guess where Brent would be today. Crashing on someone else's couch? Living in his truck? Staying at the shelter where Ansel volunteered?

He'd been given a chance to turn his life around and, by God, he wouldn't waste it.

Drawing on his slim supply of energy, he pushed to his feet, the effort akin to emerging from a pool of quicksand. Rummaging through his duffel bag, he extracted clean clothes for the day and his toiletries kit. With a mumbled, "Good morning," to his bunk mate, he ducked into the bathroom.

Twenty minutes later, he reentered the world, a shower and shave having marginally revived him. The smell of freshly brewed coffee also helped.

"Mugs are in the cabinet to your right," his bunk mate said in a low voice. Short, with jet-black hair, he sat at the table and scrolled through his phone.

"Thanks." Brent selected the largest mug and filled it to the brim.

"Name's Javier." The other man put his phone down. "Not sure I caught yours last night."

"Brent. Brent Hayes." He sat in the chair

where his jacket still hung, his glance cutting to the other four men lying in their beds.

"Don't worry about them." Javier looked over his shoulder. "They can sleep through an earthquake."

"Sorry I wasn't more companionable when you came in. I had a long day. Drove up from Tucson and then—" he stopped short of admitting he worked for Your Perfect Plus One "—went to a wedding."

"It's cool. You hungry?"

"I could eat."

Brent's last meal had been at the reception around four. Too early to be called dinner.

"Dining hall opens about now."

"I can drive," Brent offered. "Just give me a few minutes."

"You got it, amigo."

While Brent finished his coffee, he attempted to tidy his bed and then checked his phone for texts and emails, answering only those he deemed urgent.

One of those happened to be a notice of past-due payment on his most overburdened credit card. With a few swipes of his finger, he processed the minimum payment. It was enough for now to keep the wolves away from his door. With room and board provided, Brent's monthly expenses would drop. And the money from his second job would soon make a dent in his debt.

He scanned an email from Darla, Maia's sister and his boss at Your Perfect Plus One. She'd forwarded the positive client satisfaction survey from Bobbie-Ann and asked Brent if he was available the Saturday after Thanksgiving for a wedding in the neighboring town of Green Valley. He answered yes.

Too bad Maia wouldn't be there. Then again, her absence was for the best.

He tried to focus on the positives. He had a new job—two new jobs—and would be helping Maia with her horse. His days had a purpose after going months and months without any. He put Thanksgiving dinner at the MacKenzies' out of his mind rather than risk his mood plummeting again.

"Are there a washer and dryer around here?" he asked Javier as they exited the bunk house.

"In the storage shed. That building on the end. Gotta provide your own laundry detergent."

"I read that in the rules."

Javier laughed as he buckled his seat belt. "Don't let them intimidate you. We're not sticklers here. We all live and work together. Might as well get along."

"When does your shift start?"

"Nine. I'm the lunch prep cook, though I assist with other meals when needed."

Brent checked the dash clock which read 5:32. "I need to be at the stables by six."

"I'll catch a ride back or walk."

"You sure? I can drop you off."

"Trust me, I'm sure."

Shortly after Brent pulled in next to the dining hall, he saw why Javier was in no rush to hurry breakfast. A tiny redhead in jeans and a bulky jacket jogged over as they approached the kitchen's rear entrance. She kissed Javier's cheek before linking arms with him.

"Hi. You must be the new wrangler. Javier told me Ansel hired someone. I'm Syndee." She then recited the unusual spelling of her name. "I work in housekeeping."

"I'm Brent. Nice to meet you."

Clearly, Bear Creek Ranch didn't have the same restrictions regarding coworkers fraternizing as Your Perfect Plus One. Not that it made any difference, Brent reminded himself.

Inside the kitchen, he was met by the enticing aromas of baking biscuits, frying bacon, grilling hash browns and tangy fresh-cut fruits. His stomach growled as they gave the prep cook their requests from the employee menu. Brent chose a side of pancakes to go with his scrambled eggs.

He, Javier and Syndee sat at one of the three scarred and rickety wooden picnic tables behind the dining hall reserved for staff. They were soon joined by several more employees, too many for Brent to remember all the names thrown at him. Everyone ate with speed, their meals growing cold because of the chilly morning temperature.

"Brent's taking his first group of riders out this morning," Javier said, repeating what Brent had told him on the drive. "Maia's going with him."

"Oooh. Maia." Syndee peered at Brent over her cup of juice and waggled her brows.

She couldn't be much more than twenty—the same age as Javier. Brent wondered if she resided in the women's bunkhouse then decided no. She and Javier would have come to breakfast together.

"Ignore her." Javier bit into a piece of toast. "She's always trying to fix up couples."

Syndee kissed his cheek again. "I just want everyone to be happy like us."

"Maia seems happy," Brent said in what he hoped was a neutral tone.

"She is." Syndee propped her elbows on the picnic table, fully embracing the conversation. "Now. She wasn't happy after sending her fiancé packing three weeks before the wedding."

Brent half expected Javier or someone else to caution Syndee about gossiping. No one did, and she continued.

"The sleazeball cheated on her. Not just with one woman but two. Two!" She held up her first and second fingers for emphasis. "Poor Maia had no idea. His sister found out and told Maia. Caused a real problem with his family, too. The sister did the right thing, though, if you ask me. Maia deserved to know. Soon as she found out…" Syndee exhaled a long breath. "It wasn't pretty."

"That's a shame."

Brent had his faults. Betraying the trust of someone he supposedly loved wasn't one of them, and he had no respect for those who did. His parents' failed marriage was the result of deep-rooted and irreconcilable differences, and he often felt his dad had bailed too soon. But there'd been no infidelity on either his mom's or dad's part.

"Yeah, Maia took it real hard," Syndee said. "She was super down in the dumps."

The observation earned her several murmurs of agreement from others at the table.

"And then, a week later, she learned she was having a baby. Can you imagine? Things went from bad to worse after that. Her sleazeball ex wanted nothing to do with TJ. I mean nothing.

What kind of guy refuses to take responsibility for his child?" Syndee made a sound of disgust. "Maia's way better off without him. TJ, too."

"We don't know everything that happened between them," Javier cautioned.

"We know she had to take him to court to get child support. We also know he cheated on her with two, *two*, women," Syndee emphasized again. "And she's raising that sweet little boy on her own. No wonder she was a wreck for so long. She only started being her old self when she got back into trail riding."

Brent felt uncomfortable listening to his new coworkers discuss Maia despite his avid curiosity. She had a right to her privacy and might not appreciate people discussing her personal life or him listening.

He'd been the subject of many conversations when he'd left rodeo after finally admitting defeat. The pitying looks and well-meaning platitudes and attempts to bolster his flagging spirits had worsened his funk rather than improved it.

Grabbing his paper plate and plasticware, he stood. "Nice meeting y'all."

"See you at lunch?" Javier asked.

"Probably not. I have somewhere to be."

Syndee elbowed Javier in the ribs. "I'm sure he's got plans. Don't pressure him."

Brent didn't admit Ansel and Maia had invited him to Thanksgiving dinner. The way the employees talked, they would surely have a field day with that information.

"Catch you later," Syndee called, her good-bye echoed by the rest.

Brent returned his plate and silverware to the kitchen, offered a wave and then made a beeline to his truck. The chronic pressure eased as he started the engine. He wasn't sure if the change was because he'd left rather than stick around listening to more gossip about Maia or because he was about to see her again. Probably a little of both.

Would she be there waiting for him? If not, he'd poke around on his own. At the sight of Maia's truck, Brent smiled to himself. Climbing out, he activated the door lock, pocketed his keys and phone and jogged toward the stables.

She was in the horse pen, tossing hay from a wheelbarrow into the feed troughs. Brent entered through the gate.

"Sorry if I'm late."

"Morning. And you're not."

Her congenial smile contained not a single trace of the flirting from last night. Okay, they were going to be friends. Strictly friends. That was all right with him.

As he helped her with the hay, their glances connecting often, a thought occurred to him.

If Maia shared his interest, and if his new purpose got him out from under the black cloud constantly hovering above, maybe he could quit Your Perfect Plus One. Then, they'd be free to see where things went.

His cheer lasted all of three seconds before he remembered his exorbitant debt and the payment he'd made this morning on his phone—just enough to save his credit rating from sinking below sea level.

Nope, he needed both jobs if he didn't want to put his entire financial future at risk and alienate his buddy who'd fronted him a loan. That meant he and Maia maintained the status quo. Now and for the foreseeable future.

"LET ME INTRODUCE YOU to Snapple," Maia said when she and Brent had completed the morning chores.

"Lead the way."

He accompanied her to the feed trough where the big Appaloosa polished off the remaining morsels of his breakfast. She was eager to hear what Brent had to say. He had a lot of first-hand experience. Though others had offered their opinion of Snapple and his bad habit, they hadn't rehabilitated wild mustangs for the BLM, which elevated Brent a notch or two in her opinion.

All at once, Snapple swung his head around and tried to nip his nearest neighbor, an overweight bay mare who'd dared to cross an invisible line.

"He's not mean," Maia said, rushing to Snapple's defense. "He just likes to guard his food."

"Is that the same behavior he exhibits when someone or another horse gets too close to his scar?"

"No. Then he's nervous and fearful rather than aggressive."

"Okay." Brent rubbed a knuckle along his chin and continued to study Snapple.

Maia studied Brent in return. She still couldn't put her finger on what made him tick. Initially, he'd seemed happy to see her this morning. Now, however, he'd withdrawn. No, that wasn't the right word. He'd put up an invisible shield, not dissimilar to what had happened last night after they'd discovered they both worked for Your Perfect Plus One.

There it was; she'd answered her own question. She'd made a hasty retreat, letting him know there'd be no acting on their mutual attraction. As a result, he was respecting her boundaries. She should be appreciative. And she was.

The twinge of disappointment she felt was something she'd have to get over. She needed her side job at her sister's company and wasn't about to lose it for some cowboy who'd happened to wander into her life and might wander right back out.

"You free Saturday afternoon?" she asked. "We have two rides scheduled, both short. The last one finishes at four. We can work with Snapple after that."

"I have a wedding but not until the evening."

"Me, too. Not a wedding, a corporate holiday party."

"That won't give us much time. An hour, tops."

"I realize I'm being pushy," Maia admitted. "Problem is, I have only five months to train Snapple, and myself, for the Diamond Cup. That might sound like ample time, but most serious competitors train up to a year for a big event like this one."

"An hour's long enough for me to assess him."

"Thanks." She released a sigh of relief. "I should finish showing you around before our customers arrive. I need to leave as soon as we're done to pick up TJ."

"He's a cute kid."

"And a handful. A typical toddler intent on conquering the world. Mom works out of a home office and babysits for me while I'm here or training. Which is no small task. I couldn't manage everything without her."

"He seemed pretty mellow last night."

"He was tired. He starts running out of steam by dinner. Thank goodness. I'd never get the laundry or dishes done otherwise."

"My buddy and his wife just had a baby girl. He tells me she keeps them awake all night."

Maia stopped herself from gawking. Here was the first bit of personal information Brent had revealed about himself. "Lucky for me, TJ is a good sleeper." She waited for Brent to elaborate about the friend with the new baby. When he didn't, she gave up. "Ready for the grand tour?"

She showed Brent the stables, pointing out the tack room, the equipment shed, the enclosure where they stored the grain, the first-aid supplies—both human and equine—and Mountainside's two ATVs parked beneath an aluminum awning. They ended the tour at the small office, a room barely larger than a broom closet. Maia brought out a three-ring binder containing maps of the various trails and gave it to Brent.

"People have the first right of way," she explained. "Horses are next, and vehicles last. But don't automatically assume drivers will yield to you and the riders. Always take extra precautions."

"Got it."

"You can borrow this for a few days if you want." She handed him the binder. "Study up. Though we always send out at least two wranglers on every ride, in case there's an emergency. You'll either go with me or Rowdy. Sometimes Dad. If the rides end early enough, I'll train even if only for an hour or two. I also train on my days off, of course."

"You go out alone?"

"Usually. Most people can't or don't want to keep pace with me, either because their horse isn't capable of it or they're not. Why?" She grinned. "You thinking of coming along?"

"I'd like to see how Snapple reacts on the trail when another rider closes in on him. Is there a horse in your pen out there with enough gas and grit to match Snapple even for a mile?"

"Hmmm." She considered a moment. "Possibly Lone Star. He's half Thoroughbred. If not him, we could ask Channing to borrow one of the arena horses."

"I'd hate to trouble him."

"Oh, he won't mind. My dad and his dad are good friends and on the city council together."

The sound of an approaching vehicle alerted them their customers had arrived for the trail ride. Brent stood nearby and watched while Maia conducted a brief conversation with each individual—a mother, father, two kids, ten and twelve, a friend of the kids' and Grandma and Grandpa. She chatted about their level of experience while jotting down notes on the questionnaires they'd completed.

Then, while the family waited and petted the horses, she and Brent went into the pen, nine halters split between them.

"Let's use Shorty over there for the grandmother." Maia pointed to a stubby black gelding. "He's lazy as they come and a good match for someone who's nervous and hasn't been on a horse in years. We'll put one of the boys on Astro over there and the other on Golden Boy."

Brent collected the bay and palomino. Once they'd saddled all seven horses for the riders, they selected their own mounts. Brent chose Lone Star, and Maia approved. The two should get acquainted before going on a practice ride with her.

"You're not using Snapple?" he asked.

As usual, the Appaloosa had been following Maia around the pen like a devoted puppy dog. She hugged his neck, her heart filling with love. She had to find a way to correct his bad habit. Parting with him wasn't an option.

"He's strictly for competition," she said. "I can't risk injuring him on a nontraining ride. Neither do I want to confuse him by holding him back with these slowpokes and then pushing him for speed the next time."

Before long, they were mounted up and heading down the road away from the stables with Maia in the lead. She conversed with the group over her shoulder, reminding them of the rules—no galloping, no jerking on the reins, no kicking the horse, remain with the group, no venturing off the trail, no roughhousing. Upon learning the group was from Phoenix, she also shared interesting tidbits about the area and the history of Bear Creek Ranch.

She periodically checked on Brent way at the back of the single-file line. He looked good in the saddle. Tall and confident. She had to force herself to look away.

Hopefully, he was paying attention to her chatter as he'd be giving this same talk when it was his turn to lead a ride. Though, that would be a while. Until then, he'd learn from Maia and Rowdy.

The family appeared to enjoy themselves, laughing when they had to duck their heads to avoid being struck by a tree limb and gushing over the spectacular mountain views when they crested a hill. Pictures and videos were taken with phones, the boys teased the girl, and Grandma shrieked when Shorty stumbled while walking along the creek bank. Maia relaxed as her horse, a well-seasoned veteran of these trail rides, plodded along with almost no direction from her.

It was a far cry from when she rode Snapple. Then, she spent every second on high alert. This morning, she enjoyed the contrast between the chilly air and the sunlight filtering through the fragrant pines to warm her face.

Someday in the not too distant future, TJ would be old enough to accompany her on these shorter rides. She took him out occasionally around the stables on their most reliable horse, sitting him securely in the saddle with her. He loved it and cried when she lifted him down.

Turning east onto Nine Stones Trail, Maia led the group on the return trip to Bear Creek Ranch. At the stables, the riders dismounted. The adults complained their joints ached. The kids complained the ride wasn't long enough and asked to go again tomorrow. Dad complained about the cost but ended up saying he'd see.

When they'd gone, Maia and Brent unsaddled the horses, returned them to the pen and put away the tack.

"Well, what do you think?" she asked.

"About the ride? I enjoyed myself." A hint of the flirty smile that had gotten her attention at the wedding yesterday appeared. "What do *you* think? Have I got what it takes to be a wrangler?"

"You made the cut." Feeling the effects of his smile clear to her toes, she almost returned it before stopping herself at the last instant. Seriously, she needed to control her reaction to him if they were going to continue working together.

"Is that yours?" he asked, eyeing her competition saddle, with its distinctive design, on the rack.

"For now." She returned the saddle Grandma had been using to its designated spot. "I'm having a custom one made. It should be done after the first of the year."

"Nice."

"It is nice," Maia agreed. "And expensive."

She'd put half down when she'd placed the order for the saddle and set aside a portion of every paycheck from Your Perfect Plus One to cover the balance. If not for her part-time job, she'd be competing in her old saddle.

Granted, races weren't won or lost solely because of a saddle or any piece of equipment. But a custom saddle could make the difference between the competitor's legs giving out two-thirds into the race and making it comfortable to the end. Ninety miles in one day over rough terrain was no small feat. Every advantage counted.

When they were finished and the stables in order—her dad would return after Thanksgiving dinner for the nightly feeding—Maia and Brent walked to their vehicles.

She unlocked her SUV. "See you at dinner."

"See you."

His response lacked enthusiasm, leaving her to wonder if he'd back out at the last minute. She followed him up the road as far as the turnoff for the bunkhouse. She kept going, leaving Bear Creek Ranch and heading south toward Payson. She'd collect TJ at her parents' house and take him home where they'd both get ready for dinner. Her mom needed a break. Hosting twenty-four people was hard enough without TJ underfoot. Besides, she missed her little boy when away from him.

Voice activating her phone, she placed a call to her sister.

Darla answered with a huff. "Finally!"

"Sorry I didn't call back last night," Maia said. "TJ kept me busy. And I'd have called earlier, but I know how you like to sleep in on your days off. And then I was giving Brent a tour of the stables. Speaking of which, did you know he was Dad's new wrangler when you hired him?"

"That's why I called you last night." Static caused by the Bluetooth garbled her sister's voice. "To give you a heads-up. I didn't have a chance before the wedding."

"We figured it out after we met at the stables."

"Probably just as well you didn't know at the wedding. No awkwardness."

If she had known Brent worked for her sister, she might not have been initially attracted to him. On second thought, knowing or not knowing wouldn't have made a difference.

"Him working for Dad is a plus," Darla continued. "I figure he's more likely to stay, if only so Dad doesn't give him grief. I've had real trouble keeping guys on the payroll. Why they seldom stay and gals remain is a mystery to me. And according to my client, he did great yesterday."

"I think so, too. From what I saw, she appeared happy."

"It's his cowboy charm and good looks, which I'm sure you noticed."

Maia didn't reply. Her older sister had been teasing her from the moment she'd learned to talk. If she discovered Maia liked Brent... Well, suffice it to say Maia would be hearing about it forever.

"Why the long silence?" Darla asked. "Is there a problem?"

"Nope. I was just thinking. You and Dad both hiring him was too much of a coincidence."

"Your friend Channing recommended Brent to me *and* Dad."

That made sense. "Why does he need a second job?"

"Why does anyone need a second job? But you'll have to ask for the specifics. I don't divulge an employee's personal information."

Maia wouldn't ask. Brent's need for extra money was his business.

"He's coming to Thanksgiving dinner."

Darla hesitated. "He is?"

"Dad invited him." *So did I.*

"O…kay."

"I get that you prefer to keep your personal and professional lives separate."

"It's easier that way. My clients need to trust me and feel confident I respect their privacy. Me socializing with employees could affect that trust."

"You socialize with me," Maia countered.

"You're my sister. That's different."

"Brent's new in town and had nowhere to go."

"And Dad has a soft spot for people down on their luck."

Maia heard the softening in her sister's voice. "Brent said he wouldn't stay long." The exit came into view, and Maia flipped on her right blinker.

A high-pitched screech sounded in the background, and Darla groaned. "Gotta run. The girls are at it again."

"Love ya," Maia said.

"Love ya, too."

She disconnected, turning in the direction of her parents' home and her own house a mile farther down the road.

Her sister worried dinner might be awkward, which Maia understood. She, on the other hand, looked forward to it. Holidays at the MacKenzies' were a big, happy and frequently raucous occasion.

Okay, yes, Brent would be there. Of course, he had nothing to do with the excitement building inside her. That was entirely due to her anticipation of seeing family and old friends and TJ having fun with his cousins.

Except it was Brent's face continually coming to mind as she drove the remaining distance.

CHAPTER FOUR

BRENT ARRIVED EARLY to the MacKenzies' home for Thanksgiving. Not for the hot apple cider, as Ansel had suggested, but to make points with his new boss. Brent had driven three miles out of his way to find a grocery store open and had purchased a bouquet of flowers for Maia's mom. His wallet complained about the loss of another twenty-dollar bill, but he didn't feel right about arriving empty-handed.

He found a place to park on the jam-packed country road—how many people were invited today?—and strode up the walkway leading to the MacKenzies' front door. He spent a full minute breathing deeply and letting the moment sink in before ringing the doorbell. For the first time in two years, he wasn't spending a holiday by himself. That had to be a step in the right direction.

One downside—he'd be sitting across from Maia again and reminding himself of all the reasons she was off-limits. On the upside, it was good practice. He'd never turn his life around if he didn't learn to navigate difficult and uncomfortable situations.

Besides, was seeing Maia outside work really that terrible? He liked her and enjoyed her company. She had a way of putting him at ease, and he sensed no judgment when she looked at him. Then again, she didn't know his full story.

As if hearing his thoughts, she, and not one of her parents, answered the door.

"Happy Thanksgiving." She beamed at him.

"Um, thanks," he muttered, her dazzling smile momentarily short-circuiting his brain.

She nodded at the flowers. "Those are beautiful."

"They're…for your mom."

"She'll love them." Maia turned and motioned to him over her shoulder. "Come on in. I'll introduce you."

In the large great room, with its vaulted ceiling, roaring fireplace and holiday music playing in the background, at least twenty people sat or stood in small clusters. Four children of varying ages tumbled about in the center of the floor. Brent recognized the youngest one, Maia's son TJ. Most adults held a glass or bottle of some beverage. Brent's mouth watered at the enticing aromas wafting from the kitchen.

"Hey, everyone," Maia called out. "I want you to meet Brent Hayes, our new wrangler."

The introduction was met with a chorus of hellos and nice-to-meet-yous.

Brent raised his hand in greeting. "Howdy. Happy Thanksgiving."

"You know Dad, of course. And Darla. Her husband, Garret, is around here someplace."

Maia's sister stepped out from around Ansel. "Good to see you again, Brent."

Was it good? He couldn't tell if the owner of Your Perfect Plus One was okay with him being at her family's celebration or not.

"Same here. And thanks again for inviting me, Ansel," Brent said before Maia whisked him off to the kitchen where her mom was readying dinner with the help of three other people.

"Mom, this is Brent."

"A pleasure, ma'am."

Lois MacKenzie wiped her hands on her apron and then reached out to Brent. Before he could shake her hand, she pulled him into a warm embrace.

"I'm a hugger. You'll have to get used to it."

Brent tried to recall the last time someone had hugged him with such exuberance. Lois was the first one to let go.

"Ansel told me your ride went well this morning." Her lively eyes resembled Maia's. Actually, there was a lot about Lois that resembled Maia, including her mannerisms.

"The customers didn't complain, I hope."

"Not to me."

He gave her the flowers. "These are for you."

"Oh, my," she gushed and accepted the bouquet. "Aren't they gorgeous." She then handed the bouquet to Maia. "Can you put these in water for me, sweetheart?" To Brent, she said, "I look forward to chatting later. For now, I have a turkey to carve and gravy to make."

"Don't let me stop you."

Brent excused himself and, on his own, returned to the great room, ignoring his ill ease at being in a roomful of mostly strangers.

"Help yourself to some cider," Ansel said and pointed to a side table holding trays of appetizers, a Crock-pot of cider and stacks of ceramic mugs. "You won't be disappointed."

Brent did as Ansel suggested, ladling a portion of the steaming beverage into a mug. He'd skipped lunch, not wanting to spoil his appetite for today, and considered filling a plate with stuffed mushrooms and deviled eggs. Before he could, he felt a heavy weight knock into him and almost spilled his cider.

Brent looked down to see TJ on his knees and clutching Brent's boot with his chubby arms.

"Hey, buddy. What's going on?" Brent set down his cider on the table.

TJ tugged harder on the boot, the same one

he'd pushed around the bunkhouse floor the previous evening. "Want."

Brent understood that word well enough. "Maybe later. Not sure your grandma fancies me walking around her house in my socks."

TJ plunked down onto his behind, wrapped his legs around Brent and pulled with all his might, his small face turning nearly the same shade of red as his sweatshirt. "Want!"

Brent chuckled. "We're going to have to reach a compromise."

"TJ!" Maia hurried over. "I'm so sorry." She bent and retrieved her son. "He's been a little stinker since we got here. It's all the people and commotion and his older cousins roughhousing."

Cousins? Some of the kids playing must belong to Darla.

TJ squirmed and grunted in an attempt to break free of Maia's grasp. When she held fast, he started to cry. She put him down but kept hold of his hand.

"What am I going to do with you?" she complained with mock sternness, her expression filled with tenderness.

She wore a red sweatshirt identical to her son's. It was then Brent saw MacKenzie Family Thanksgiving printed on the front over a cartoon turkey. He glanced at Ansel and Darla.

They wore the same sweatshirt, as did Lois and two of TJ's cousins.

Corny. Also kind of nice. Brent's family hadn't done those kinds of things, and until today he'd have cringed at the idea. Funny how one's perspective could change.

"Here." Brent slipped out of his denim jacket and extended it to TJ, who grabbed the jacket with the same joyous abandon he had Brent's boot.

Struggling with the cumbersome jacket, TJ managed to insert an arm into the sleeve. Before Maia could stop him, he scooted off, dragging half the jacket on the floor behind him.

"Come back." She went after him.

Brent waylaid her with a hand on her wrist. "It's all right."

"What if he—"

"He won't."

"He could."

"Then he does."

She shook her head and grumbled, "You're as bad as he is."

Only then did he notice his hand remained on Maia's wrist. Reluctantly, he let go. He'd been here less than ten minutes and already experienced human contact twice after an incredibly long dry spell.

Lois's hug had been nice, but touching Maia was far nicer. He wouldn't lie.

Darla appeared beside them. "Come on, you two. Dinner's ready. Didn't you hear Mom calling?" She gave them a curious look.

Brent motioned for the ladies to precede him and grabbed his cider off the table. He needed to be less obvious around Maia. Her sister, their mutual employer, had become suspicious and not without reason.

The dining room table wasn't large enough to accommodate all the guests. A second folding table had been set up adjacent to it, and everyone crowded together, elbow to elbow, their spirits high.

Like the few family functions Brent had attended while growing up, the youngsters sat at a table in the kitchen. They were supervised by Darla's mother-in-law, who had insisted, so that the remaining adults could enjoy their meal. She'd flown in from out of town and claimed to relish every moment spent with her darling granddaughters.

Brent found himself sandwiched between a friend of the MacKenzies and Ansel's nephew. Maia sat four seats away from him, too far to engage in conversation. It seemed to Brent that Darla rarely took her eyes off him from her catty-corner vantage point.

Conversation flowed as platters, bowls and trays were passed from one person to the next. Brent needed little encouragement and took one of everything. He contributed little, preferring to listen. Especially when the conversation turned to the subject of Maia.

"I'm so proud of her," Lois declared to the group. "She works her tail off. Hardly a day goes by she isn't training."

"How many titles did you win before you quit?" someone asked.

"She didn't quit." Lois huffed. "She simply took a little break."

"It's okay, Mom." Maia smiled. "Most everyone here knows my story. I had a hard time bouncing back when my engagement ended and again after TJ was born. It happens. Life kicks us down, and we can't always get right back up."

"You needed some time to heal. That's all."

"Which I did, thanks to you, Dad and Darla."

Lois sent Maia a fond maternal look.

Brent tried to recall an exchange between him and either of his parents that came even remotely close to this one. There weren't any.

Memories hovered at the edges of his mind. He wasn't the only one his dad had high, sometimes unreasonable, expectations for. He'd demanded a lot from his mom, too. She'd once told Brent his dad was hard to love and had gotten that from his mom, Brent's grandmother. She hadn't been a warm person and believed sparing the rod spoiled the child.

Hearing Maia's voice returned Brent to the present.

"And to answer your question." She addressed the person across from her. "I've placed in a dozen other competitions. But none as prestigious or challenging as the Diamond Cup."

"Doesn't that start in Globe?" a man two seats over asked.

"North of Globe, yes. And ends in Monument Park here in Payson."

"That's what? Sixty miles?"

"Closer to seventy."

"And you complete the entire distance in one day?"

Maia laughed. "One long day."

"Over mountains, I might add, and across some mighty rugged terrain," Lois said.

The man helped himself to more mashed potatoes. "That must require a lot of conditioning."

"For me and the horse," Maia said. "Luckily, there are plenty of trails around Bear Creek Ranch and up by Christopher Creek. Dad usually drops me off at one of the trailheads and I ride back to the ranch. Sometimes he picks me up at another location." She sent Ansel an appreciative wink.

"I fret with her out in those mountains by herself." The look he returned held pride and admiration rather than worry.

"I'd take you along if you and Tugboat could keep up with me."

"If he went with you, I'd fret more about that poor old horse than I would Ansel," Lois said.

A round of laughter accompanied her remark, and the dinner continued. Brent was still considering what Maia had said about having a hard time bouncing back. Why couldn't he do the same? He reminded himself that she had her family, who were obviously close-knit and loving. Brent couldn't say the same, and the fault didn't lie entirely with his parents. He'd seldom visited after leaving home and made no effort to mend their differences. How could he expect their help and support? Unless he moved back to Wichita…

He rejected the notion the instant it occurred to him. Besides his work commitments here, he hated returning to his hometown a loser when he'd once been a rising young rodeo star.

"Brent?"

Realizing the woman sitting next to him had been speaking, he roused himself from his mental wanderings. "I'm sorry. What did you say?"

"Ansel tells us you're a bull and bronc rider."

"Former."

"How long did you compete?"

"Professionally, about eight years."

"Why'd you stop?"

"The time came to move on," he said instead of admitting he just hadn't been talented enough.

"Ever win any titles?"

"Some. State and divisional championships." *Less and less as the years went on.*

"That's exciting."

"I had a good run." But not quite good enough to retire a champion.

What if he'd stuck with it a little longer? Would that have made the difference? He'd never know.

"And now you're working for Ansel." The woman said with polite enthusiasm.

"Yes, ma'am."

Brent knew she meant well and was just making conversation. The fact he felt like a failure and didn't want to have this conversation wasn't her fault.

Maia abruptly stood. "I'll clear the table. Come on, Darla, you can help. It'll give us a chance to see what trouble our precious offspring have gotten into."

She smiled sweetly at Brent as she carried a load of plates to the kitchen.

He wasn't sure if she'd sensed his discomfort

and interrupted to spare him or was merely assisting with cleanup. Either way, he was grateful to her and relieved when Ansel drew him and several others into a conversation about the latest food drives for Payson Rescue Mission.

"WHAT ARE YOU DOING?" Darla whispered in Maia's ear.

"Um…breaking up a squabble?"

With dinner over, the kids had resumed playing—this time at the table in the kitchen. TJ had gotten into a tug-of-war with the neighbor's grandson over a plastic turkey centerpiece. Maia had been doing her best to intervene before the battle escalated to full-on warfare when her sister interrupted.

"Not them." Darla straightened, her hands propped on her hips. "With Brent."

Maia managed to extricate the plastic turkey from TJ and the little boy, who immediately lost interest. Scrambling off his chair, he disappeared into the next room, presumably to join his family. TJ began wailing, and Maia groaned. Honestly, he'd been a handful today.

"I don't know what you're talking about," she insisted.

"You were practically giddy when you introduced Brent to everyone," Darla whispered.

"Then, you were cozying up together over appetizers."

"I was not giddy, and we weren't *cozying up*." She'd been happy to see Brent. Nothing more. She'd also been happy to see her aunt Cecily and uncle Bennie. "We were just talking, and TJ started pestering Brent about his boots."

"His boots?"

"It's a long story." Maia resettled TJ at the table, giving him a stack of plastic holiday cups to keep him busy.

"I haven't seen you act like that since you and Luke were first dating."

Luke. Why did her sister have to mention her former fiancé? Maia couldn't imagine herself once giddy over him, but she supposed it was true. He'd been a charmer. He'd probably also charmed the two women he'd been seeing on the side while they were engaged.

"Brent's a nice guy," Maia said. "He doesn't know many people here, and I was putting him at ease."

"Did you forget this is me you're talking to?"

At a high-pitched squeal, Darla turned her attention to her youngest daughter who was tugging on her older sister's braid. Once peace was restored, she and Maia moved to the counter where they began transferring leftovers into food-storage containers. Maia was glad the lively chatter between their mom and the other two helpers drowned out her conversation with Darla. Just like Maia's dad, her mom was eager for Maia to dip her toe into the dating pool. If she thought for one second Maia fancied Brent, she'd needle Maia nonstop.

"Okay, fine," Maia said. "I confess. Brent's an interesting guy."

"And gorgeous."

"If you prefer the rugged outdoor type." Which Maia did.

"Look, I hate to be the romance police and ruin your fun, but he's your coworker. You shouldn't be seeing him socially. You can't see him. You signed a contract."

"I'm not seeing him. He offered to help me with Snapple's skittishness is all." At her sister's pointed stare, Maia added, "He used to work for the BLM, rehabilitating wild mustangs."

"I'm aware of that. It was on his employment application."

"I promise you," she said, sealing a cover on the remaining green beans and stacking the container atop the one containing sweet potatoes. "There's nothing between us."

"Other than you find him interesting. Which, last I checked, was potentially the start of a romance."

"I'm too busy for a boyfriend. And I'm not

sure I'm ready for one, to be honest. But even if I am, I have to be careful. I'm not the only one who would get hurt this time. There's TJ to consider."

"Aw, sis. No one wants you to be happy and find a great guy more than me." Darla and Maia carried the many containers to the refrigerator and found places for them. "I'm just not sure Brent's right for you."

"Not that I care, but why?"

"He's…" Darla hesitated as if afraid of revealing too much. "At loose ends."

"You say *loose ends* like he's harboring a deep, dark secret."

"I have my suspicions."

"Of what?" Maia asked. "Did he commit a crime?"

"No, no. I wouldn't have hired him unless he passed a background check. Plus, Channing vouched for him."

"What then?"

"His… Oh, I shouldn't say." Darla turned away.

Maia groaned. "You can't drop a hint and then clam up."

"There are some gaps in his employment history. And that's all you're going to get out of me."

"Gaps?"

"Not enough to concern me or Dad as far as hiring Brent."

"But they concern you as far as potential boyfriend material."

"Can't help myself. I'm your big sister." Darla dropped the remaining rolls into a plastic bag and sealed the top.

"Like I said, I have no intention of dating Brent."

But if she did date him, that would be her business, not Darla's. As long as Maia wasn't employed by Your Perfect Plus One.

Her parents might also have an opinion on the subject, though they be less vocal than Darla. Like Darla, they'd become overly protective of Maia after she discovered Luke's infidelity and wanted to look out for her.

But one lapse in judgment didn't mean she'd make a second one. She'd learned her lesson, and her family knew that.

"I love you and worry about you is all," Darla said.

"I love you, too." Maia bumped shoulders with her sister.

With the kitchen cleaned, she took TJ with her to the living room. She wasn't searching for Brent. Nope, not at all.

She found him near the front door, glancing

around and wearing an I'm-ready-to-leave expression. She hurried over with TJ in tow.

"There you are." She cleared her throat, attempting to mask her rising panic. "You're not leaving already?"

"Apparently not. I can't locate my jacket."

Whew! She'd caught him in the nick of time.

She lowered herself to TJ's level. "Sweetie, what did you do with the jacket?" Her son was at an age where he understood much of what was said to him even if he couldn't verbalize in return. Or, refused to.

"The jacket, sweetie. Where is it? Mommy's friend needs to leave."

TJ remained stubbornly mute.

"Hey, buddy." Brent winked at TJ. "Want to go outside with me?"

TJ whirled and stared up at him, his face bright with anticipation. He then hurled himself at the door and yanked on the knob with both fists. "Ya, ya, ya!"

"Okay. But you have to wear a jacket. It's cold outside."

TJ scurried off to the living room where he ducked behind a recliner in the corner. A moment later, he reappeared, dragging Brent's jacket by the sleeve.

Maia winced. "I'll pay to have it laundered."

Brent chuckled. "You worry too much."

When TJ reached them, Brent picked up the jacket and slung it over the boy's shoulders. The hem dragged on the floor.

"Let's go, buddy." He put a hand on TJ's shoulder.

Maia's heart melted a little. Luke wanted nothing to do with TJ, and here was a near stranger treating her son with kindness, patience and affection. What was wrong with Luke?

Worse, how could she have been so blind? She'd believed he loved her and that he wanted a family as much as she did. They'd often discussed the future during their engagement, sharing their goals and dreams—goals and dreams Maia had believed were mutual. And all that time, he'd been seeing two different women on the side. Her stomach still twisted at the memory.

He'd asked her forgiveness, claiming he was sowing his wild oats before settling down to a life of monogamy, and swore it wouldn't happen again. Maia thought she'd never heard such a load of hogwash. She almost hadn't told him about the positive pregnancy test. After several weeks of soul-searching, she had, resigned to allowing Luke a role in TJ's life, though not in hers. To her shock, he'd accused her of trying to trap him into marriage.

Trap him! As if she'd want him after what

he did to her. She'd told the jerk exactly what he could do with his accusation in no uncertain terms.

A few weeks later, once she'd cooled off and had a long talk with her sister, she again contacted Luke. She'd kept him in the loop during her pregnancy and left the door open after TJ was born. If Luke chose not to see their son or have anything to do with him, that was his decision and his alone. The monthly child-support payments were appreciated, but no substitute for an involved and caring father.

She hoped Luke was losing significant amounts of sleep over abandoning their son. And if not, thank goodness TJ didn't have to deal with someone so incredibly selfish and heartless. Though, it pained her to think her darling baby boy would grow up knowing his father didn't want him.

Outside, Maia and Brent watched as TJ half walked, half crawled down the steps to the front yard.

"Your jacket's leaving without you," she said.

"Give him a few minutes to blow off some steam."

"He is overly excited today." Maia considered Brent's observation an astute one for a single man with no children. His lack of concern for his jacket showed an appealing good-naturedness. "Did you have a nice time? You seemed kind of quiet at dinner."

"I had a real nice time. I thanked your dad before leaving, but please give your mom my regards. She's an excellent cook."

"I will."

They were quiet for another minute while TJ leaped from one spot to the next on the front lawn. Maia was about to make some banal remark about the holidays and small children when Brent spoke.

"I don't talk much about my rodeo career."

"O…kay."

"People always ask me why I quit."

Ah. The conversation at dinner when he'd become visibly uncomfortable.

"I suppose they do. People are curious."

"Given the choice, I'd rather not say."

"All right." She wasn't sure how else to respond.

"But I want you to know."

"You say that as if you're warning me."

"I guess I am." Brent drew in a breath. "I quit because I wasn't good enough. And rather than continue to publicly embarrass myself, I walked away."

"Not good enough or did you burn out? I've seen that happen in competitive trail riding."

"I wish I had. Sounds better than admitting I lacked the talent."

"I doubt you lacked the talent. You qualified for nationals. Multiple times."

"And then, one year, I didn't. Or the next year. Or the one after that. My rankings fell. Even a nongenius like me could see the writing on the wall."

She heard the disappointment in his tone, saw it in his eyes and felt it in her own heart. "You're being too hard on yourself, Brent."

"I'm being a realist."

"What you are is going through a rough patch. And there's no reason you can't come back from it. Lots of athletes do."

He paused, and she waited for him to continue. From what she'd learned about him, he was slow to open up.

Finally, he said, "Apparently, I'm not the best at handling setbacks and, because of that, I… have some problems."

Was that what Darla had been alluding to?

"Can I ask, what kind of problems?"

"I had a plan, and when that plan failed to materialize, I fell into a funk. Truthfully, I'm still in it."

Maia considered before responding, thinking of her own circumstances. "Losses come in all forms. Relationships ending, which I can speak to from personal experience. Death of a loved one. Grown children leaving home, so my mom tells me. Being laid off work. A health crisis. The list goes on. And losses, regardless of their nature, require a certain amount of grieving in order for a person to recover."

"Five stages," he said with false mirth. "I've read about it."

She had, too, and instantly regretted playing armchair psychiatrist. "Sorry. Sometimes I talk too much."

"Hey, I'm the one who brought it up."

"No excuse for lecturing."

"You weren't. And I'm curious, how'd you bounce back when things got hard?"

"I had help. My family, for one."

"Yeah. That's not an option for me."

Maia might have inquired about his family, but his stony expression stopped her. "I found a purpose. First and foremost, being the best mom possible to my son."

"Also not an option. The purpose, that is. I haven't found one."

"I joined a support group after TJ was born for women dealing with the pressures of single motherhood. I got a lot out of it. I realize you're not a single mom, but there are several support groups at the Payson Rescue Mission. Flyers are in the lobby."

"I'm not ready for a support group."

"Okay."

He avoided talking about himself, and she doubted he'd do well in a group setting. In fact, she was surprised he'd admitted everything he had to her. He must do better one-on-one.

"Have you spoken with your doctor? I did with mine, and she prescribed—"

"I don't need medication." His features abruptly darkened. "I'm not that bad off."

"No, no. Of course not. I wasn't implying you were. My doctor was the one who suggested the new mothers group. It was there I learned I wasn't alone. I guarantee, you aren't alone, either."

He nodded but said nothing.

"We all get into temporary funks. It's normal and part of life. We just have to find the right remedy."

"I'm hoping working for your dad and sister does the trick."

Well, that explained why he'd taken a wrangler job far beneath his qualifications. "Work is good for the mind and body. Even if I could afford to be a stay-at-home mom, I'm not sure I would. I need new experiences and to engage with people. It's another reason I like working for Darla, but don't tell her I said that."

Brent didn't smile as she'd hoped.

"It's getting late," he said. "I should go."

"You need your jacket." Maia caught up with TJ. As expected, he pitched a fit at losing his prize and quieted only when she swung him high in the air.

"Thanks again for the invitation," Brent said, accepting his jacket.

"Remember, you're partnering with Rowdy tomorrow. I probably won't see you. I'm training most of the day."

"Good luck."

She watched him amble down the driveway, her lower lip caught between her teeth. She couldn't help thinking she'd made a mistake offering advice instead of simply listening. Depression, even in its mildest forms, often carried a negative stigma. There were people who looked down on those suffering from mental illness, and, as a result, those suffering refused to get the help they needed for fear of being judged. It was a terrible cycle.

Heading back inside, Maia ruffled TJ's hair. "Mommy owes our new friend an apology."

Except, how did she give one without making Brent feel worse than he already did?

CHAPTER FIVE

BRENT CHECKED THE LEVEL in the horses' water trough while Rowdy pushed the wheelbarrow to the Dumpster behind the stables where he'd dispose of the manure. The last ride for the day had ended almost an hour ago, after which Brent and Rowdy had cleaned the pen. Not the most pleasant daily chore but a necessary one with this many head. Any cowboy worth his lick had cleaned his share of pens over the years, including Brent.

He'd started as a kid under his dad's supervision. Everett Hayes had been a three-time world champion. Yet another reason Brent's failure to make a name for himself in rodeo had sent him sailing over the edge into an abyss. He'd been compared to his dad his entire career, and not favorably in the end.

Rowdy returned just as Brent was shutting off the water spigot. The young cowboy drove into the pen on the ATV hauling a small utility trailer loaded with hay. The horses mobbed the trailer as if they hadn't eaten in a week, squealing and nipping at each other and reaching in to grab mouthfuls.

Brent sauntered over to the metal feeder and waited for Rowdy. He'd met his coworker and bunk mate two days ago on Thanksgiving evening when Rowdy returned late from spending the holiday with his girlfriend. Brent had immediately liked the affable twenty-two-year-old whose slow drawl and bowlegged swagger belied an impressive intelligence. Rowdy planned to resign from Mountainside Stables next May when he obtained his degree and, if all went as planned, hired on with the forest service. Appearances could be deceiving.

What, Brent wondered, did people think when they looked at him? Did he give the impression of having his life together or were the deep cracks he tried to hide obvious to all?

Maia could see them; Brent had no doubt. That was one of the reasons he'd approached her outside her parents' house on Thanksgiving. He thought she might be more understanding than most. But the second she'd suggested he seek medical help, he'd shut down and distanced himself.

He *wasn't* crazy or a weakling, and he certainly *didn't* have a mental illness. He just struggled with periodic dark moments. And who wouldn't in his shoes?

The quiet voice inside his head tried speaking up. Brent silenced it, refusing to listen.

Rowdy hopped off the ATV, leaving the engine idling, and helped Brent transfer thick flakes of hay into the nearest feeder. The horses vied for position, with the smaller and less aggressive ones forced to wait on the second feed trough.

"You think we should put some salve on Shorty's leg?" Brent asked.

The small black had scraped his knee on a jagged branch during the afternoon ride. And while not serious, Brent thought the scrape would benefit from a dab of antibiotic ointment.

"Probably," Rowdy said. "There's some in the tack room."

"I'll get it when we're done here."

The two of them had gone out together on the three short trail rides yesterday and two longer ones today, each ride traveling a different route. This morning Brent had returned the binder Maia lent him, having memorized most of the material. He'd continued to bring up the rear on the rides like with Maia, and was content to do so because it required less work and gave him the opportunity to watch and learn.

Also, to study the horses. From his vantage point, he'd observed them responding to the rid-

ers and noted any particular behavior that would
aid in matching riders to mounts on future rides.

Another benefit of caring for Mountainside's
livestock, he'd gotten to know Maia's big Appaloosa. Snapple insisted on being in charge,
which was typical for a horse of his size and
strength and with his competitive nature. He
was naturally curious and liked people, Ansel
in particular. He wanted to be part of whatever
anyone was doing, be that trimming manes or
examining a loose shoe. He adored Maia above
all others and had practically jumped into her
arms when she'd fetched him from the pen yesterday.

That had been one of the few times Brent and
Maia had crossed paths since their talk on her
parents' porch. He'd begun to wonder if she'd
canceled their scheduled training session with
Snapple without telling him. Then, she'd arrived bright and early this morning while he
and Rowdy were saddling horses for a group of
waiting customers. With a "Meet you at three"
from her, his question had been answered.

Snapple had been safely tucked in the horse
pen when Brent and Rowdy returned a short
while ago from their second trail ride. Maia
was home. Rowdy had mentioned in passing
that Ansel had driven her and Snapple to one
of the trailheads south of Bear Creek Ranch to-

ward Payson, making the majority of her practice ride uphill.

"You free for dinner?" Rowdy asked as he and Brent moved to the second feeder, the remaining horses plodding along after them. "Feel like heading to town for a burger and a beer? I'm buying."

"Sorry, man. Another time? Maia and I are getting together at three."

"That's right. You're helping her with Snapple."

"We'll see. I'm going to show her some of the techniques we used on wild mustangs when I worked for the BLM."

"No joke! You worked for the Bureau of Land Management? I need to hear about that."

"It's a long story. I'll tell you about it when you buy me that beer."

"I can wait until you and Maia are done."

Brent gave a casual shrug. "I have plans tonight."

"Ah…" Rowdy flashed a sly smile. "Do tell."

"She's just a friend."

A friend who happened to be a complete stranger. She and Brent would meet for the first time at a coffee shop near the wedding venue. Brent had already received her bio and an outline of the role he would play tonight—they'd been recently introduced by a mutual friend.

That would explain both their limited familiarity with each other and the reason she'd give for their relationship "fizzling out."

Unlike Thanksgiving eve, this wedding was a small affair. Following the ceremony at a local church, they'd attend a catered dinner in the home of the groom's grandparents. Brent doubted he'd run into anyone he knew. Definitely not Maia.

"Another time, then," Rowdy said.

"Count on it." Brent pointed toward the stables. "I'd better get that salve for Shorty."

Ten minutes later, they were done with their chores and coming out of the stables when Rowdy suddenly stopped in his tracks.

"Looks likes your date's here."

Alarmed, Brent followed the younger man's gaze. Had his wedding date showed up here rather than the coffee shop?

But instead of—what was her name? Brent would have to reread the email—Maia jogged toward them, pushing TJ in one of those exercise strollers. Brent's alarm vanished, and a different kind of anticipation rushed in to fill the space. Maia slowed as she neared. From the looks of her flushed face and disheveled ponytail, she'd had a long run.

"Lucky you," Rowdy said to Brent, his drawl infused with innuendo. "Getting to work with her."

"Strictly business."

"Whatever you say."

Maia reached them, cutting off Brent's response.

"Hi, guys." She stopped near the hitching post, blew out a long breath and propped her hands on her slim hips. TJ squealed and waved his arms in the air from his seat.

"Hey, Maia." Rowdy flashed a big ole smile. "Had yourself a run."

"Yeah. Seven miles."

"Wow." Brent didn't think he could run more than two miles without collapsing. All right, three. And a half. "That's some serious distance."

Even more impressive considering she'd already ridden Snapple for several hours through the mountains.

"Competitive trail riding takes a toll on the rider, too," she said. "Not just the horse. I need to build my stamina, or I'll lose steam halfway through the day."

Brent had worked and trained hard at rodeo and spent entire days in the saddle more than once while working for the BLM. Not, however, while charging up and down rugged mountain trails. He liked to think he was stronger than a slip of a gal like Maia, but realized he wasn't.

"You ready to start?" she asked him.

It was Rowdy who answered. "I'm just taking off. Catch you later, Brent." He ambled past Maia and TJ. "Take 'er easy, Maia. You, too, little man." He held out his hand, palm up, for TJ to high-five.

"I'll get Snapple," Brent offered and went into the stables for a halter.

When he returned two minutes later, Maia was unbuckling a now-wailing TJ from the stroller. "He's going to keep crying unless I let him out."

"Should we wait? Snapple's mighty big and TJ's mighty little."

"Don't worry." She hoisted him into her arms. "I'll be diligent. And if he escapes, back into the stroller he goes."

Brent continued to the pen, not entirely comfortable with a small child on the loose during training. Snapple came willingly once Brent put on the halter. Outside the pen, he tied the horse to the hitching post.

"Don't come too close," he cautioned Maia and then proceeded to thoroughly examine Snapple, running his hand along the horse's flank.

As Maia had reported, Snapple shuffled nervously when Brent got near the gnarly looking scar.

"Must have been some bite."

"Yeah," Maia agreed, disengaging her ponytail from TJ's grip. "I'd be sensitive, too."

"Tell me about what happens during a typical judging interval."

"They're usually every hour. A horse is scored on their rate of recovery. A vet listens to their heart and lungs, taking specific readings. The faster a horse recovers, the higher the score and the sooner a rider can resume the competition. During the examination, the horse is expected to exhibit good manners and a calm disposition."

"If not, you're disqualified," Brent finished.

"Like I said, Snapple used to bolt. I've been working with him since I bought him, and now he just gets antsy and sidesteps. But if the vet can't obtain his readings, he can't determine Snapple's rate of recovery. There is no getting around it."

Brent flicked his hand near Snapple's ear, and the horse instantly jerked his head back. "Well, he can see fine. His reaction to the scar has nothing to do with vision loss."

"I figured as much. He's just never gotten over that bite. Equine PTSD."

"Look at it from his perspective," Brent said. "In the wild, horses are prey. Snapple has a hundred thousand years of survival instincts encoded into his DNA. Being domesticated makes no difference. Horses with impaired senses, like vision loss, become overly fearful and run at the slightest hint of trouble."

"Self-preservation."

"Exactly. Since loss of vision isn't the case with Snapple, we have to assume the memory of being attacked from behind is imbedded so deep, he shies first and evaluates the threat later." Brent demonstrated by coming at Snapple from the front. "Notice he has zero reaction when he sees me coming."

"I can't ask a judge to come at Snapple from a different direction." Maia made a face. "There's no special treatment. Not for bad manners."

Brent went around to Snapple's other side. When he repeated his inspection and ran his hand along the horse's flank, a disinterested Snapple merely lowered his head to the ground and sniffed the dirt. Brent returned to Snapple's afflicted side and stepped back to study him.

"We saw this same behavior a lot in the wild mustangs. Self-preservation. It'll be hard to re-train Snapple, though not impossible. What we need to do is desensitize him. Teach him that what happened once won't happen again."

"How did you desensitize the wild mustangs?"

"Different ways, depending on the horse and

the problem. I'm partial to the fishing-pole-and-sock method."

"The what?"

TJ yapped loudly as if asking the same question as his mom.

"Tie a plain old white sock to the end of a fishing pole. I'll show you next time." Brent moved closer to Snapple. "You do have a fishing pole and sock?"

"Dad does."

Brent continued studying Snapple. "You've tried positive reinforcement? Rewarding him for good behavior."

"I have. That's how we progressed from running off to just sidestepping. Took some doing. A lot of trust building."

Brent started whistling. When he had Snapple's full attention, he moved his hand close to the scar. He got a whole inch closer than the last time before the horse began snorting and prancing in place.

"Okay. Easy does it, boy."

"That was a little progress."

Brent patted Snapple's neck. "We might try some other distraction techniques. But first, the fishing pole and sock. He has to learn not to be afraid, and that's a process. Often a long one."

"Thank you."

The soft quality of her voice compelled him

to meet her gaze for the first time since he'd begun working with Snapple. Light radiated from her smile, like sunshine in a bottle, and he wanted one for himself.

"I haven't done anything yet," he said, breaking eye contact. "Let's wait."

"I have a good feeling."

He wanted very much to live up to her expectations. He'd do anything if she'd just keep smiling at him like that.

"I'll put Snapple away," he murmured. "You have your hands full." He indicated TJ, who was doing his level best to twist free.

She gave TJ's ear a playful tug. "Then I can finally put this little wiggle worm down."

Inside the pen, Brent slipped the halter off Snapple and then once again tried distracting the horse with whistling. He was able to get his hand an inch closer before Snapple snorted and retreated several feet.

"Whoa, boy. Easy does it." He held out his palm.

After a moment's hesitation, Snapple approached and nuzzled Brent's fingers.

"There you go. Was that so hard?"

Snapple shook his head, spun and trotted off, his way of having the last word. Brent understood. There'd been a time he'd always wanted the last word, too.

"I'm impressed. You have a real knack with horses," Maia said when Brent returned. She'd put TJ down, and the boy played contentedly at her feet, stacking pebbles into a pile. "You could have your own YouTube channel or start a podcast."

"Funny."

"I'm serious."

His mood, previously good, took an abrupt dip. How did he respond to her? That besides having no postrodeo career plans, he had little motivation to do more than take vacationing Bear Creek Ranch guests on trail rides?

"Sorry. I need to get going," he said, desperate to safeguard what remained of his good mood for tonight. "I have a wedding to attend."

With a nod, he left, rounding the stables to where he'd parked his truck.

Another bullet dodged. Another question evaded. Another potential judgment averted.

MAIA LEANED BACK and centered her weight as Snapple carefully picked his way down the steep, rugged trail. She squeezed with her knees and grabbed the saddle horn to anchor herself when he hopped over a fallen branch. His metal shoes clanged on the sharp rocks, their slick surface causing him to briefly lose his footing.

Maia gasped but didn't panic. Snapple knew his stuff, and she trusted him completely.

He continued his descent, moving faster than was safe. Faster than anyone would normally travel on such challenging terrain. One misstep, and they'd both tumble hard, sustaining serious injuries when they hit the ground. Or worse. Eleven hundred pounds of horse could easily crush a hundred-and-twenty-pound human. Maia and Snapple were taking their lives in their hands—and hooves.

Her heart thundered inside her chest, from excitement and danger. She loved competitive trail riding. Snapple did, too. He attacked each new challenge like an invincible warrior. She didn't have to ask more from him; he willingly gave it.

She hoped Brent was doing all right. She heard him behind her on Lone Star. At least, she had heard him. She'd been too preoccupied during this very arduous descent to pay attention to anything other than her and Snapple.

If Brent and Lone Star fell, they might roll forward and crash into Maia and Snapple, causing a serious calamity. Lone Star, while a competent trail horse, was unused to rides at this demanding level. If he fared well, it would be entirely due to Brent's ability. So far, so good.

She straightened little by little as they reached the bottom of the mountain. Snapple leaped over the small creek, a tributary of nearby Bear Creek, and landed solidly on the opposite side. Only when they came to a stop did Maia look behind her.

Brent and Lone Star were about fifty yards up the mountain and doing all right from what she could tell. If they'd managed to keep pace with her and Snapple, she'd have been shocked.

"I slowed him down," Brent said after he and Lone Star had crossed the creek. Unlike Snapple, the lanky buckskin trudged through the water. "He was getting tired."

"What about you?"

"I could go another round." Brent grinned. "Not another fifteen miles. I'm not sure how you do it."

"Lots of practice." She patted Snapple's neck. Neither of them was breathing hard.

To be fair, neither was Brent. The same couldn't be said for poor Lone Star. His sides heaved from the unaccustomed exertion, and his head hung low.

"Can we take a short break?" Brent asked. "This guy did all the hard work and deserves one."

"You mind if we start walking back toward the ranch? I have a wedding this afternoon. We can go slow."

Brent nudged Lone Star forward. "Speaking strictly for my horse, we'd appreciate it."

She laughed at that, and he joined in.

They'd worked together almost every day this past week and had developed an easygoing friendship. Their mutual attraction had been set aside, though not forgotten. Maia still found Brent attractive, but she'd learned to temper her responses. Him, too, apparently.

The result? Things were much better now. Best of all, Darla hadn't mentioned Brent again.

Maia had also noticed he seemed to be in a better mood. There had been fewer sudden mood shifts and no withdrawing behind invisible walls. According to her dad, Brent was always on time, worked hard, complained little, learned fast and was good with the customers. Though quiet and private, he got along well with his bunk mates. Rowdy had reported that Brent created no problems and broke no rules. A model employee by all accounts.

"Did you learn anything about Snapple on our ride?" Maia asked. This was the first day they'd been able to go on a ride together so that Brent could gauge Snapple's responses.

"Well, you saw how he reacted at the start of the ride when I rode up behind you."

"I did."

Snapple had nearly unseated Maia when Lone

Star nosed his tail. He'd kicked out and then bucked furiously. Maia was better prepared the second time.

"He didn't notice us at all when we were going down that last stretch of mountain," Brent said.

"He was too busy concentrating on what was ahead rather than behind. Heck, I didn't notice you until you called out to me."

"We have to figure out a way to combine distraction techniques with reprogramming his fear responses."

They discussed various training approaches for the next fifteen minutes, with Brent telling her about a particularly stubborn mustang he'd rehabilitated for the Bureau of Land Management. Maia liked that he didn't once mention using force or punishment. She herself had never and would never inflict pain on a living creature, even if she lost her temper.

At the stables, they unsaddled and brushed the horses. While Maia returned Lone Star to the pen, Brent set up the fishing pole and sock that Maia had borrowed from her dad. He'd taken a group of riders out for a ride or he'd have been here, having expressed an interest in watching Brent. Maybe next time. Snapple would likely require several training sessions.

She returned to find Brent had already attached the lunge line to Snapple's halter and was walking Snapple in a slow circle at the end of the six-foot line. He held the fishing pole in his hand with the sock tied to the end, all the while talking to Snapple and encouraging him to relax.

"I'll just sit here," Maia said and plunked down on the bench beside the hitching rail.

Brent didn't appear to hear her. His focus remained riveted on Snapple. The horse's ears twitched, indicating he was alert and listening to Brent.

"That's right. Nothing to worry about." With his free hand, he lifted the fishing pole and slowly stretched the tip with the dangling sock toward Snapple. "It's just a sock, boy. Can't hurt you."

Snapple snorted and shook his head but kept walking.

Brent touched the sock to Snapple's hind end. The horse danced sideways for two steps before settling.

"Good job. See? Nothing there to hurt you."

Brent moved the sock along Snapple's spine toward his mane and then reversed direction, returning the sock to his rump. Snapple snorted again and abruptly stopped. Brent jiggled the lunge line and clucked to him. Snapple obediently resumed walking, turning his head and eyeing the sock with mild contempt.

This went on for five full minutes, until Snapple paid the sock no heed. Then, Brent changed the game and lowered the sock to Snapple's side, close to his scar. Instantly, the horse huffed and shied away.

"Settle down," Brent coaxed. "Just a sock, remember?"

He tried a dozen more times. Snapple's response would lessen by small degrees and then, suddenly, he'd blow up again, snorting and kicking out his back feet.

"I think we've had enough for one day," Brent announced after three circles with no reaction. He set down the fishing pole. "We should end on a positive."

"Yeah, I agree," Maia said. "He's making progress already. Each time he gets upset, he calms down quicker than the last."

"Hard to say for sure. The proof will be our next training session. Does he remember what we learned today or revert to his old ways?"

She pushed off the bench and stood. "I need to hit the road. I'd like to stop at the folks' and spend some time with TJ before the wedding. I hate leaving him so much with my mom."

Though her son appeared happy and healthy and well-adjusted, Maia didn't want him growing up with a part-time mother on top of an absent father. Plus, it wasn't fair to her own mother, putting so much of TJ's caretaking responsibility on her.

The extra money from Your Perfect Plus One was hard to resist, however. Especially during the holidays. TJ was older this Christmas. He'd get a thrill out of opening presents and attending the different holiday events with Maia and the family.

Presents cost money. As did her saddle. She'd pay off the balance in a few months, in time to break in the saddle before the Diamond Cup.

She was also determined that Santa leave plenty of gifts under the trees. She'd need a heathy checkbook balance for that to happen.

While she placed Snapple in the pen, Brent took the fishing pole and sock into the stables to store for the next time. When he didn't come right out, she followed him inside to see what had become of him.

"You lost in here?" she called.

He stood near the office door, staring down at his phone. "Sorry, I got a text from Darla. She had an employee cancel at the last minute and wants to know if I'm free to take his place." He began one-finger typing a response.

"You saying yes?"

"I am. If I don't pay down my credit card balances soon, they'll send someone after me."

Credit card balances? Maia digested that bit of information. Did Brent's joke hide a truth? Was he working a second job to pay off his bills?

"I hear you," she said. "That custom saddle of mine is costing me a small fortune." When he didn't respond, she asked, "Where's your wedding?"

He paused typing to reread the original text. "Um… Valley Fellowship Church. The reception's at some country club."

Maia thought she must have misheard. "Valley Fellowship Church? That's where my wedding is. Are you sure? Darla wouldn't schedule us at the same wedding. Not again." Not unless she had no choice.

"Yep." Brent shrugged. "That's what it says. Should I tell her no? Will it cause a problem?"

Before Maia could respond, her phone pinged. She pulled it from her jacket pocket.

"What do you bet this is her?" She quickly read the text. "She's telling me you'll be at the wedding and reminding me to pretend we don't know each other."

It was followed by a trio of stern-face emojis and then a heart. Maia sighed.

Brent's phone pinged.

"Let me guess. Darla sending you the same text."

He grinned. "You can't blame her for covering her bases. She has a business to run. And we were a little chatty at Thanksgiving."

"Humph. I think I'm insulted."

Brent tapped a reply.

"What are you saying?"

"I told her she has nothing to worry about."

"I suppose I should do the same."

Maia did. When she finished, she stuffed her phone back in her jacket pocket. "Looks like I'll see you later tonight."

"I'll see you, but not talk to you, *stranger.*"

Maia pretended to zipper her lips closed.

All kidding aside, she was serious about avoiding Brent and not disappointing her sister. Especially now that she knew he needed a second paycheck as much as she did.

CHAPTER SIX

EVERY ONE OF Brent's good intentions flew out the window the second he walked into Valley Fellowship Church. He immediately glanced around the foyer area for Maia. Had she arrived yet? Was she in the sanctuary or still outside?

"Thanks for filling in on such short notice," his date whispered.

"My pleasure—" he paused to think, relieved when his memory finally kicked in "—Lizzie."

She smiled.

"Hope I'll do. I know I wasn't your first choice."

"You're a guy, and you're here with me. That should be enough to stop my parents from nagging me about getting a social life."

Brent and Lizzie had met twenty minutes ago in the parking lot of the Mexican restaurant near her apartment building. He hadn't expected her to be so young—a grad student at Eastern Arizona College. Not that Brent was exactly old at twenty-nine, but he felt like he'd lived an entire lifetime longer than the elf-like woman beside him.

"They're convinced I'm too focused on school," she said.

"Getting an education is important."

Brent almost added he wished he'd gone to college, then remembered their cover story. They'd met at a robotics demonstration on campus. Lizzie was an engineering nerd who preferred designing prototypes to hitting the clubs or hanging out with friends. She cared nothing for fashion and had admitted needing to buy her outfit for the wedding—silver leggings and an oversize black sweater. Since a former professional rodeo cowboy was the last person on Earth she'd meet, much less date, Brent had left his cowboy hat and boots at home. But if her parents put him on the spot and expected him to talk knowledgeably about robotics, he'd be in trouble.

He and Lizzie sat in one of the pews on the groom's side. She'd explained her connection during the drive here. Brent had already forgotten. He'd been preoccupied thinking of Maia and looking forward to seeing her here tonight. In hindsight, he should have turned down Darla's request. Except she'd offered a nice bonus as incentive, and he could really use the extra money.

Lizzie wasn't inclined to chat much, which suited Brent fine. She introduced him to her parents when they appeared and sat down in the pew beside her. He made polite, nice-to-meet-you conversation. In the middle of her dad recounting a recent business trip to Seattle, Maia entered with her date. Everything Lizzie's father said after that became white noise to Brent.

Maia looked as perfectly matched to her date as he was ill matched to his. Tall and fit and oozing success, the man wore a tailored suit and sported a hundred-dollar haircut. He escorted Maia to a pew on the bride's side with an easy confidence Brent envied. Why he needed to retain Your Perfect Plus One, Brent couldn't guess. Guys like him didn't have trouble getting a date. Women asked them out.

When Maia smiled pleasantly at the guy, Brent's gut tightened. She was playing a role, he assured himself. Even so, she and the guy made an attractive couple, and Brent was jealous. He wanted to be the one sitting next to Maia and chatting amiably to the people sitting in front of them.

Except that guy was a far better choice for her than Brent and, from all appearances, had a lot more to offer. What did Brent bring to the table? Periodic dives into an emotional murk. Substantial debt. A job that put a roof over his head and food in his mouth but had no advancement potential. And he had no long-term career plans. Everything he owned could be carried in his truck.

His mood started to plummet. He tried to listen to Lizzie's dad. Wait, her mom was the one talking. About…her…social group. They… read books. No, made scrapbooks. Brent offered a generic comment when one appeared to be called for.

There'd been a time he dreamed of being the kind of guy with Maia—wearing tailored suits and striding into rooms with confidence. Having world champion tagged onto his name, the title opening all manner of doors.

What if he could still be that guy? Granted, he was down on his luck right now. But there was no reason he couldn't pick himself up and start over. People did it all the time.

There, he supposed, was the rub. Picking oneself up required a direction. A goal. Brent had only ever wanted to be a competitive bull and bronc rider. He'd seen himself making appearances postretirement and lending his name to gear or clothing or perhaps appearing in commercials. The fellow who'd won the world title two years ago had recently landed a bit part in a movie.

Brent continued to watch Maia, unable to tear his glance away. Maybe she was the motivation he lacked. A reason to spring out of bed every day with enthusiasm rather than trepidation. Pay off his bills. Get his life on track. Reinvent himself.

"Oh, look!" Lizzie's mom elbowed her. "There's Dillon. Whatever happened between you two? Remind me."

"Mom." Lizzie made a sour face. "I'm here with Brad."

Brad? Oh, yeah. Brent's fake name for this date.

"I always liked him," her mom continued, a wistfulness in her voice as she stared at the gangly young man awkwardly scooting past a seated couple.

Lizzie inched closer to Brent as if to make a statement. "I apologize for my mom."

"It's okay." In any other circumstances, Brent would have laughed. Dillon looked to be Lizzie's other half. The à la mode to her apple pie. The yin to her yang. "Let me guess. He's also majoring in engineering."

Lizzie rolled her eyes. "Biophysics."

Brent had no idea what that was and didn't ask.

Shortly after that, the wedding started. Thirty minutes later, they were filing out of the church. Apparently because of her distaste for socializing, Lizzie avoided engaging guests in conversation. She insisted she and Brent skip the receiving line, citing they wouldn't be missed. Weaving through the throng of people, they headed toward the church entrance to wait for her parents. Suddenly, Dillon materialized before them—possibly, on purpose.

"Hey." His goofy face broke into a wide grin.

Lizzie sniffed. "Hello."

"Figured I might run into you."

"Well now you have, and we have to go." She grabbed Brent's arm and spirited him away.

"You still like him," Brent observed with mild humor when they reached the entrance and Lizzie stopped to breathe.

"I do not."

"Why'd you break up?"

"I don't know." Her shoulders slumped. "School. We both had heavy class loads."

"And now? You still have a heavy class load?"

"Yes." She looked down. "At least, I do."

"Sometimes couples drift apart."

"Yes. We drifted apart."

Her parents found them, and the four went outside. After separating in the parking lot, they met up at the country club for the reception. Lizzie had grown even quieter during the ride. Brent assumed she was dwelling on their run-in with Dillon and didn't press her for conversation.

Though only the first weekend in December,

the country club was already decked out in holiday lights and decorations. A ten-foot Christmas tree occupied the main lobby, demanding attention. Imitation frost had been sprayed on the large glass windows. Christmas cacti with their cheery red blossoms had been placed on surfaces throughout.

The reception was held in a large banquet room where the holiday decor continued. In a corner of the room, a sprig of mistletoe dangled from a festive arch entwined with vines of green-and-red garland. Guests were already taking advantage of the photo op, snapping pictures with one-time-use cameras that instantly printed out a picture.

Lizzie and her parents found their seats. Brent fetched drinks from the bar, glad for something to do. On his return trip, he nearly collided with Maia and her date. The similarity to Lizzie and Dillon's meeting didn't go unnoticed by him.

"Oh, sorry," Maia said. "My fault. I wasn't looking where I was going."

He should excuse himself and continue on. He'd promised Darla he'd keep his distance from Maia.

Only he remained rooted in place. "The fault was mine."

She smiled. He did, too.

Her date didn't smile and, touching Maia's

shoulder, pointed to a table on the other side of the room. "We're over there."

"Have a good evening," Brent said to their retreating backs.

Idiot, he thought as he made his way back to where Lizzie and her parents waited. Him, not the guy.

"Did you know them?" Lizzie asked when he set down the drinks.

"What? No. Never saw them before today."

"Oh. You looked like you recognized them."

"I was apologizing for nearly running them over."

The reception progressed much like the one last weekend. Toasts were made before and after the buffet dinner. Tears of joy were spilled and humorous anecdotes shared, much to the bride's or groom's embarrassment. Guests mingled. Conversation and laughter filled the room with a noisy, happy din. Cake followed dinner, and dancing followed the cake. Once the bride had taken the floor with her dad, followed by her new husband, a group of eight guests donned Santa caps and broke into a choreographed routine that had everyone laughing.

"Would you like to dance?" Brent asked Lizzie when couples began drifting from their tables to the floor.

"Me?" She shook her head vigorously. "I don't dance."

"All right."

"Oh, Lizzie." Her mom let out a long, exasperated sigh. "You've got to let loose and have some fun."

"I am having fun."

Brent supposed she was, if staring at Dillon busting a move with not one but two women constituted having fun.

She suddenly sprang to her feet. "I've changed my mind. Come on."

Halfway through the lively number, Dillon approached, wearing the same goofy grin from the church and the Santa hat from the choreographed routine.

"Hey, dude," he said, addressing Brent. "Mind if I cut in?"

"That's up to the lady."

Lizzie huffed. "Seriously, Dillon?"

That was the extent of her objection. She said nothing else when he slipped his hand into hers and whisked her to another part of the dance floor. Chuckling to himself, Brent strolled back to his chair, feeling not the least bit insulted.

"She abandoned you?" Lizzie's mom asked.

"I think maybe the two of them have some unfinished business."

"You're taking this pretty well."

"Lizzie and I haven't been seeing each other very long."

"I figured as much. No offense, but there's a glaring lack of chemistry."

"No offense taken."

While she and Lizzie's dad chatted with the other guests at their table, Brent observed the dancers. He spotted Maia's date, surprised to see Maia wasn't with him. Scanning the room, he found her sitting alone at a table. Funny, once again their situations were similar. Both abandoned by their dates. Was hers dancing with an old girlfriend? He thought of texting Maia, then wisely reconsidered. Breaking their employment rules might jeopardize her job, not just his. He couldn't do that.

"Good grief. Is Lizzie *still* with Dillon?" her mom complained, peering at them huddled in a corner. "You should ask someone else to dance, Brad."

Brent grinned at her. "What about you?"

"Oh, for heaven's sake. There are plenty of much younger women sitting by themselves. What about her?"

She gestured to a woman who promptly sprang out of her seat and darted off as if she'd heard them.

"You don't have to worry about me. Honestly."

"Nonsense. You must be bored to tears.

There. What about her in the green dress? She's been sitting alone for the last fifteen minutes and staring at the dancers."

Maia. Of all the wedding guests, Lizzie's mom would have to suggest her. Brent scanned the dance floor, locating Maia's date. He was with a different woman now, prompting Brent to wonder why he'd brought Maia only to leave her stranded at the table.

"I'm fine." Brent wanted to dance with Maia. But he didn't dare. "Really, I am."

Lizzie's mom got out of her chair and marched over to where her daughter stood with Dillon, their heads bent together. Her dad offered a resigned shrug. Brent shifted his attention away from the family drama and settled into watching the antics at the arch with the mistletoe. Everyone wanted pictures of themselves getting or giving a kiss. Most involved shenanigans.

In hindsight, he should have paid closer attention.

"Brad."

He turned when Lizzie's mom tapped him on the shoulder, his gaze locking with Maia's startled one.

Brent faltered momentarily, trying to make sense of the situation. Lizzie's mom stood in front of him, though he had eyes only for Maia.

"I found you a dance partner," the older woman said, flashing a smile outlined by heavy red lipstick.

"I'm…here with your daughter."

"Could've fooled me. She and Dillon mentioned leaving together." Lizzie's mom gripped Maia's arm, preventing escape. "Until they do, or don't, you should enjoy yourself with this lovely lady."

"I don't think that would be right, ma'am."

"My daughter abandoned you. What's the harm?"

If she only knew.

Maia appeared as uncomfortable as Brent felt. "This nice lady said she had someone she wanted me to meet. I had no idea it was you."

Brent pushed back in his chair and stood. Remaining seated seemed impolite. Big mistake. Lizzie's mom took that as him agreeing to her crazy scheme. She nudged Maia toward Brent.

"You two have fun."

Neither Brent nor Maia moved.

"Come on," the other woman implored. "One little dance."

"Her daughter's old boyfriend is here," Brent explained to Maia. "She wants them to get back together." And keeping him out of sight might assist with her cause.

"I see." Maia's features gentled. She was clearly a sucker for a happy ending.

"Enough chitchat." Lizzie's mom put a hand on Brent's and Maia's shoulders and pushed them toward the dance floor. "Go on, you two, get your groove on."

Groove on? Did people still stay that?

Deciding they either danced together or made a scene, Brent took hold of Maia's hand and escorted her to the dance floor. Her slender fingers were soft and warm. He liked how they fit in his.

"What happened to *your* date?" he asked as they navigated the crowd.

"We danced once. He hasn't been back to the table since."

Reaching the edge of the floor, Maia slid into Brent's arms like they'd done this a hundred times before. His hand settled on her back, hers on his shoulder. She was the perfect height, her high heels putting her eyes only a few inches lower than his. They glided and twirled to a pop rendition of "All I Want for Christmas Is You" with Maia easily following his lead.

"Your date doesn't know what he's missing," Brent said, resisting the urge to fold her tight against him.

Maia met his gaze. "Neither does yours."

Oh, brother. He was in big trouble. Maia in

his arms felt like a wish being unexpectedly granted. On top of that, he enjoyed her company way too much.

"One dance," he said. "Only to appease my date's mom."

"One dance," Maia agreed, and they circled the floor. When one song merged into the next, they barely noticed. "Are you going to the Christmas tree lighting tomorrow evening?" she asked.

Brent had heard about the annual event at Bear Creek Ranch and seen workers erecting the massive tree in front of the main lodge. Javier and his girlfriend Syndee were planning on being there and had invited Brent to tag along.

"I haven't decided."

"You should come," Maia said. "It's really a lot of fun. The dining hall serves hot chocolate and desserts. There's roasting marshmallows in the outdoor fireplace and a raffle with the proceeds going to the shelter. I'm taking TJ. He's still young, but I think he'll get a kick out of seeing the tree. Fair warning, Dad makes a big deal out of it. He insists the entire family be there. Darla's bringing her husband Garret and the girls."

"I'm not much into celebrating the holidays," Brent hedged.

"Don't be a stick-in-the-mud."

A stick-in-the-mud was all he'd been the last two years. Might be nice to try something different. "I'll consider it."

That appeared to satisfy Maia.

Two dances later, Brent saw that Lizzie and Dillon had disappeared from the corner where they'd been huddling. Maia's date was with yet another new partner "getting his groove on."

"I should go back to my table," she said without much enthusiasm.

"I'll walk you."

Best they quit now before one of their dates complained to Darla, not that they appeared to have a reason. Even so, Brent and Maia were treading on thin ice.

"Hey, you two, come on over." The young woman in charge of the mistletoe photo station hailed to them as they passed. "You have to get your picture taken."

"Ah, no. We shouldn't." Brent looked to Maia for confirmation.

"Yes, you should," the young woman countered and corralled them toward the arch.

Were she and Lizzie's mom in cahoots? Was everybody? Between Lizzie, her mom, Dillon, Maia's date and now this woman, Brent and Maia were being thrown together as if by design.

"One picture," Maia said, relenting.

"Don't just stand there, kiss her." The woman made a hugging gesture once Brent and Maia were standing awkwardly beneath the mistletoe.

Brent doubted one kiss would be enough. He'd want more. Like a dozen.

"You sure about this?" he asked, giving Maia one last chance to decline.

She laughed. "You worry too much."

Hesitating only briefly, he leaned in and pressed his lips to her cheek. If he'd thought her fingers were soft and warm, they were nothing compared to her cheek.

He lingered. She sighed. Her breath tickled his ear, and he resisted the urge to seek her mouth with his.

Dimly, he heard the click of a camera.

"Wooo-hooo!" The woman clapped. "That's going to make a fantastic Christmas card."

Maia was slow leaving the circle of his embrace. When she finally did, the woman passed her the instant photo. She and Brent both stared, watching it gradually develop.

"Thanks," Brent murmured to the woman, and escorted Maia to her chair.

She sat, and he placed the photo in front of her. He couldn't help himself and glanced quickly at the now fully developed picture. The woman had caught them at the exact moment his lips connected with her cheek, the exact moment he'd been contemplating more than a chaste peck.

"You want this?" Maia asked, suddenly shy. Had she also experienced the same incredible connection?

"No. You keep it." How would she react if he asked for a copy?

"Okay." She slipped the photo into her purse.

"About what happened just now."

She gazed up at him, her eyes glittering with expectation.

Brent wavered, unsure what to say. They needed to talk about the kiss. Or should he keep his trap shut? Making a big deal out of it might be worse than pretending nothing had happened.

"We… What happened back there. I don't want you to get the wrong idea."

"I didn't."

He would have liked to say more, only he didn't get the chance. Maia's date chose that moment to return.

"Thanks for keeping her company," the man said, a hint of irritation in his voice. "I ran into some friends."

Brent produced a wan smile. "The pleasure was mine." He nodded at Maia. "Good night."

"Happy holidays," she answered as if they really had only just met.

With that, he returned to his table. Lizzie, he was gleefully informed by her mother, had left with Dillon. Good. Brent hadn't been ready to face her after kissing Maia.

He looked back over to see her once again sitting by herself. Anger at her date gnawed at him. The guy was a first-class jerk. Nonetheless, Brent wouldn't return. He would, however, run into her tomorrow at the Christmas tree lighting.

He'd made up his mind. He was through being a stick-in-the-mud.

CHAPTER SEVEN

MAIA TOOK SUNDAY off work. Wait. Who was she kidding? Day off? Very funny.

Rather than lounging about, she spent the entire morning catching up on housework. While she cleaned, TJ made messes. After lunch, she went grocery shopping. On the way home, she drove through the ATM, the pharmacy pickup window and filled up on gas while TJ napped in his car seat. Lastly, she and TJ ate and then dressed in warm clothes for the Christmas tree lighting at Bear Creek Ranch.

By the time she parked and unloaded the stroller, she was exhausted. TJ, normally growing tired by now, was firing on all six cylinders. They seldom ventured out past dinnertime. The change in routine, coupled with the crowd and activity, had him shouting, "Hi, hi, hi" and banging the stroller bar as Maia pushed him along the dirt path.

She scanned the courtyard in front of the main lodge as they neared, searching for her parents and sister. Right. Another joke. She sought Brent, hoping to spy his cowboy hat and denim jacket among the many dozens gathering on the wraparound porch or at the fieldstone fireplace. To her great disappointment, he wasn't there.

Had he decided not to come after their close encounter yesterday beneath the mistletoe? He'd seemed worried he'd overstepped or affected their friendship. In truth, she'd liked the kiss on her cheek and hadn't read more into it than there was. He had no reason for concern. But before she could assure him, her date had appeared at the table, interrupting them.

Should the opportunity present itself tonight, Maia would talk to Brent. If not, she'd find a moment alone tomorrow at work. Or the next day during Snapple's next training session.

"There you are!" Darla hollered to Maia from the porch. She and her husband, Garret, sat on a wooden bench while their girls played nearby with a trio of other children who most likely belonged to guests at the ranch.

Maia gave a holler in return and wheeled the stroller along the winding brick walkway. At the center of the courtyard, opposite the fireplace, stood an enormous Christmas tree, at least twelve feet tall.

As he did every holiday season, Jake Tucker, head of the family that owned Bear Creek

Ranch, had obtained a special permit. He and one of the maintenance staff had driven into the woods bright and early yesterday and cut down the tree. They'd hauled it home on a flatbed trailer and then strung endless yards of colored lights. The owner's wife had decorated the tree with unbreakable ornaments resembling crystals that wouldn't shatter if blown off by a strong wind or dislodged by a curious bird.

At seven thirty sharp, Jake Tucker would flip the switch and light the tree. Maia knew from previous years that spectators would be captivated, young and old alike.

"It's chilly tonight." Maia first hugged her sister and then her brother-in-law.

"We're supposed to have record lows this coming week," Garret commented. "And there's a chance of snow tomorrow."

A huge change from last week when the weather had been unseasonably warm. At the wedding where Maia had met Brent, she'd only needed a shawl. Tomorrow, when they were out on the trails, she'd be wearing her all-weather poncho.

Since when had she started contemplating her outerwear choices in relation to Brent?

Since their moment under the mistletoe. No. That was ridiculous. Absurd.

Though, she mused wistfully, the kiss had

been nice. Chaste, yes. Even so, she'd experienced an undeniable tingle of awareness. And she'd stared at the photo of them no less than thirty times, always recalling the thrilling sensation of his lips on her cheek.

"Hel-lo! Where'd you go, sis?"

"Hmm? Oh, nowhere." Maia bent to unfasten TJ from his stroller. "I was just thinking about Snapple's next training session."

"Thinking about Snapple or the cowboy helping you with his training?"

Was she that obvious? "Why do you even say that? Brent and I are just friends. We have a strictly platonic relationship."

The instant she set TJ down, he darted off in the direction of his cousins. Maia didn't usually grant him this much freedom, especially outdoors and with so many people. But he was nearby and in close visual range. That, and her oldest niece, while only five, was diligent about watching TJ.

"Okay, okay." Darla held up her hands in surrender. "No reason to bite my head off."

"Did one of our dates complain?"

"No. Why?" Darla's gaze narrowed. "Did you and Brent break any rules?"

"Seriously? You have to ask?" Maia swallowed, mentally crossing her fingers that Darla didn't notice her defensive tone and that she'd deflected rather than answer the question.

"All right." Darla smiled. "Just checking. I trust you."

Maia swallowed again, aware her throat had gone dry. Maybe she wasn't trustworthy. "Where are Mom and Dad?" she asked, attempting to redirect this time.

"They should be here any second." Darla peered over the heads of the crowd.

Maia followed her sister's gaze. Children had gathered in front of the fireplace to roast marshmallows while their parents supervised. Kitchen staff were busily setting up a refreshment table near the front entrance to the lodge. Maia spotted urns for coffee and hot chocolate as well as covered platters holding desserts.

"There they are." Darla raised her hand and waved. "And look who's with them."

Maia's head snapped up. Too late, she realized her mistake. Eagle-eyed Darla noticed.

"Strictly platonic?" Darla narrowed her gaze. "You sticking with that story?"

"What's going on?" Garret asked, not paying attention until now.

"Hello," Maia's mom called to them and waved.

Maia couldn't be more grateful for the disruption. "Hiya, Mom. Dad." She waited a beat. "Brent."

Maia's mom made straight for where her three grandchildren played and proceeded to spoil them rotten with treats and trinkets she produced from her coat pockets.

"Mom," Darla complained. "No candy. Between you and the hot chocolate, the girls will be up all night on a sugar high."

"You should know by now," Maia's dad said, joining her and Maia, "there's no stopping your mom."

"Her or you?" Darla gave him an affectionate hug. "Love you, Pops."

"How are my little girls tonight?"

At twenty-seven and thirty-one respectively, Maia and Darla were hardly little. Still, their dad adored them and they adored him in return.

"Evening," Brent said.

Maia started to say, "You came," only to snap her mouth shut when Darla answered first.

"Hi, Brent."

Maia's face went hot. He'd been addressing Darla. Not her. She'd almost given her sister another reason to complain about her.

"Sorry to impose on your family outing." He cleared his throat. "Again."

"Nonsense," Maia's dad said. "I invited you. And you're always welcome."

Darla raised her brows, her way of asking what was with the chumminess between their dad and Brent.

Maia shook her head. She had no clue.

All right. She suspected her dad of match-making. Not that she'd admit as much to Darla. No way.

"Who wants hot chocolate?" her mom asked.

Since everyone did, they all made their way to the refreshment table with Maia's mom running herd on her grandchildren. When TJ spotted Brent, he galloped over to him and grabbed his hand, taking Maia aback. The only man her son had ever voluntarily approached was his grandfather.

TJ's father hadn't seen TJ since he was an infant, and his paternal grandparents were out of the picture. Maia's attempts to include them hadn't been well received, and she'd let the matter drop. If they ever changed their minds, she'd allow them to visit TJ. She wasn't holding her breath, however.

While waiting in line for their hot chocolates, TJ lifted his arms to Brent and cried, "Up, up."

"Hi, buddy." When TJ repeated his demand, Brent turned to Maia, a look of uncertainty on his face.

"He wants you to pick him up."

"Okay."

Brent did, lifting TJ awkwardly into his arms, struggling with how to best hold a wiggly toddler.

TJ immediately grabbed the lapels of Brent's jacket with both his fists and tugged. "Mine."

Maia smiled. "He wants your jacket. See what you've started."

Brent boosted TJ so that they were eye level with each other. "It's a bit cold outside. Maybe later by the fire."

TJ promptly collapsed onto Brent's shoulder, his face nestled in the crook of Brent's neck.

Maia stared, openmouthed. She wasn't alone.

Brent and TJ were adorable together, and she felt a surge of tenderness. It increased when Brent lifted his hand and patted TJ's back.

With their hot chocolates in hand, they found a good spot to wait for the tree lighting. Maia tried to take TJ away from Brent, but her son would have none of it.

"He's getting kind of cozy with the family," Darla whispered in Maia's ear while Jake Tucker made his annual speech. "Don't you think?"

"By family, I'm assuming you mean me."

"You, Dad and apparently TJ."

Jake Tucker finished his speech and, after a round of applause, he flipped the switch—which was actually a plug he inserted into a heavy-duty extension cord. The lights illuminated in a burst of bright colors and to a chorus of oohs and ahhs. Another round of applause erupted, this one louder.

Darla, it seemed, wasn't finished speaking her piece. "Sis, I'm worried you're wading into dangerous waters."

"I told you—there's nothing between us."

"Yet."

"TJ's taking a shine to him. That's all," Maia insisted.

"Only TJ? I've seen how you look at him. And he's looking back."

"All right. You win. I find him attractive. There. Satisfied?"

"He has…" Darla compressed her lips into a thin line. "He's dealing with some stuff."

"He told me."

"He did? What did he say?"

"It's personal. And may be different than what he told you."

Darla harrumphed.

"Not that it matters, as he and I have no intention of becoming involved. We each really need our second jobs and won't jeopardize them."

"As long as we're clear."

At TJ's high-pitched squeal, they both spun to see Brent setting TJ down onto the ground not three feet from them. Shock rippled through Maia. How much of her conversation with Darla had Brent heard? Probably enough, given his next words.

"I have to go. Have a nice evening." He turned on his heel.

"Watch TJ," Maia told Darla and went after him. "Wait, Brent."

He stopped once they were away from the crowd.

"I don't know what you heard—"

He cut her off midsentence. "Your sister's right, Maia. I am dealing with some stuff. And as much as I like TJ, like your whole family, like you, I can't get involved while my life's a mess."

With that, he walked away, retreating behind those emotional barriers of his.

Maia wanted to but didn't go after him. Luke had left her, if not scarred, wary. She wasn't ready to risk her heart, and neither was Brent, as he'd made clear. Better that they give each other a little space before someone wound up hurt.

BRENT WALKED THE ENTIRE mile and a quarter to the bunkhouse in the dark, the chilly night air sneaking into the collar of his jacket and sending shivers down his arms.

He'd ridden to the tree-lighting event with Javier and hadn't wanted to bother his friend for a lift back. Javier had met up with Syndee, and the last Brent had seen, the two of them were cuddled together on a bench. He'd had no intention of cutting short their time together simply because he chose to leave early.

The quiet stroll gave him plenty of opportunity to reflect on the conversation he'd overhead between Maia and her sister and to talk himself out of disappearing into the dreaded murky place.

Darla wasn't happy about Brent getting close to her family. Maia especially. And while he understood Darla's position, hearing her say as much in plain terms had hit him like a cannonball between the shoulder blades.

Brent could easily explain away Thanksgiving and arriving tonight with Ansel. The older man had invited Brent on both occasions, and Brent had accepted in an attempt to remain on his employer's good side.

Finding moments alone with Maia, dancing together, kissing her, weren't part of the job and had been a mistake. A big one that wouldn't end well for either of them.

A gust of frigid air pelted him in the face, and he embraced the sting. He shouldn't have given in to temptation yesterday at the wedding. Even though it had seemed as if he and Maia had been pushed together by forces beyond their control, he could have—and should have—stopped before they got carried away.

Instead, he encouraged something that could never be and caused a problem for Maia and her sister.

What if Darla fired him? Brent had just sent a small payment off to his friend who'd lent him money and included a promise of more to come. He wouldn't be able to keep his promise if Darla let him go.

He needed to be more careful, starting immediately. He'd continue helping Maia train Snapple. Brent was a man of his word, and he'd given his to Maia. But as she'd told Darla, there wasn't anything romantic between them and neither would he encourage it.

A bird suddenly took flight from a branch in one of the tall pines and soared away from Brent, giving him a start. From the size of the bird and *whoop-whoop* of flapping wings, he guessed it to be an owl. He'd seen one the other night roosting atop the bunkhouse roof. In the distance, behind the stand of trees, the creek ran, the splash of water tumbling over rocks mingling with the rustle of mule deer moving through the brush and a coyote howling in the distance.

Brent listened, enjoying the sights and sounds of Bear Creek Ranch. He liked a lot about this place, including his job and the people. He hadn't felt like part of a community since leaving the rodeo world. There, he'd had friends and a respected profession and an ambition that gave him purpose. While he lacked some of those things here at Bear Creek Ranch, he was working steadily, making friends like Rowdy and Javier and, yes, Maia, and had an ambition of sorts—that of paying off his debts. Once he'd accomplished that, maybe he'd find a new purpose.

Too many positives to risk losing them. Tomorrow, he'd reestablish boundaries with Maia—starting with forgetting how much he'd enjoyed dancing with her and the softness of her cheek when he'd kissed her.

Yeah. Not gonna happen. Maia was unforgettable. But he'd try. For both their sakes.

Darla, he was sure, wouldn't fire her. The sisters were too close. Too devoted to each other.

Brent didn't envy Maia's relationship with her family. That would be a waste of energy. But if he ever repaired his broken life and met someone special, he'd be a better husband and father than his own. He'd lacked a good example while growing up and might not know what to do, but he certainly knew what *not* to do.

Around the next bend, the bunkhouse came into view. One lone light shone, indicating the place was empty and that everyone had gone to the main lodge. Brent would have an hour, possibly two, to himself. He could go to bed and bury himself under the covers. After hearing Darla and Maia's conversation, the urge to succumb to the ever-present gloom definitely appealed.

But he'd resisted all week and hated breaking his record. Actually, more than a week. Not since Thanksgiving at the MacKenzies' had he traveled to the dark place. A new record for him.

Once inside the bunkhouse, he made himself a cup of coffee to ward off the chill. He'd been looking forward to hot chocolate with Maia, but that hadn't happened.

"Quit feeling sorry for yourself," he murmured and started the coffee maker. Dwelling on what-ifs and if-onlys served no purpose other than to beckon the gloom.

Sitting at the small dining table with his coffee, the walls started to close in on him. Being alone did that to him. Instead of throwing a personal pity party, he took out his phone and began scrolling through the contacts. His finger stopped on the name and number he'd been thinking about a lot lately: his mom.

After mentally calculating the time difference, he clicked on her number and pressed Connect. She might be startled by a call this time of night, but she'd be glad to hear from him. And she was, given her cheerful greeting.

"Hi, honey." Her tone instantly changed. "Is everything okay?"

"More than okay. I just called to say hi. Been thinking of you lately."

"What's new? How's the job going?"

The smile in her voice caused his own mouth to turn up at the corners. He really should visit more often. At least phone regularly. "All right."

"Just all right?"

She'd wanted him to come home when his rodeo buddy in Tucson suggested Brent had stayed too long on his couch. Brent had declined his mom's plea. She'd pushed, only to back off when he landed the job at Bear Creek Ranch. As much as she wanted to see him, she wanted him gainfully employed even more.

"I'm staying busy," he said, "which I like. The work's not hard but it's honest labor for an honest wage. I get to spend most days in the saddle, live in the middle of the most beautiful mountains in Arizona and meet some interesting people. Could be worse."

He also got to see Maia on a regular basis. Though after that long discussion with himself on the walk home tonight, he didn't include that as a plus.

"What kind of people? Tell me."

His mom listened as he recounted several stories of trail rides, laughing when he imparted a particularly amusing incident. She was full of questions, and when he paused, asked about his side gig with Your Perfect Plus One. Brent told her, omitting the parts that included Maia. His mom would jump to a wrong conclusion.

She hadn't been subtle about her desire for Brent to meet a nice gal and settle down. Like many people, she thought being in a relationship was the answer to his problems, if not everyone's problems. Brent could argue differently. Having a girlfriend at the time hadn't helped him deal with the despair he'd experienced after accepting that a world title was beyond his reach. Then again, they hadn't been serious, and she'd eventually ghosted him.

It hadn't helped his mom, either, in the wake of her divorce from Brent's dad. She'd dated through the years. Once seriously, though they'd split after a couple years. But from what Brent had seen, no man was going to make his mom happy. Not until she learned how to be happy with herself and the person she was.

Discovering that pearl of wisdom differed from accomplishing it. Deep down, Brent wasn't happy and continued to struggle with the hard knocks fate had handed him. Only when he found a dream to replace the one he'd let go of would he also find contentment. The feeling of helplessness, of losing control, was what sent him on those frequent downward trajectories.

He did like his job at Bear Creek Ranch, but he wanted more than to be a wrangler. Not that there was anything wrong with it or it was anything to be embarrassed of. Like he'd told his mom, he was performing an honest job for an honest wage. It could also be a stepping-stone to something more rewarding. Ansel was a business owner. His own boss. Maia had talked once about expanding Mountainside Stables when she took over one day.

If Brent had ambition and an opportunity like those, he'd be happy, too. But he still loved rodeo and competing. He rose each morning wishing he could climb onto the back of a bull or bronc. He always imagined himself standing on the platform in the center of the arena at the National Finals Rodeo and accepting his championship belt buckle. He doubted that would ever stop.

A black cloud entered his peripheral vision. Though entirely in his mind, it was real nonetheless. If he didn't redirect his thoughts and change the subject, that cloud would surround him and then smother him.

"You sound good, honey," his mom said. "Upbeat."

He must be a very accomplished liar. "What are you doing for Christmas?"

"Millie invited me over for dinner. As usual."

Her neighbor. That would be nice. And much better than sitting at home alone, which was likely what Brent would be doing. He didn't expect an invitation from Ansel. And if he got one, he'd graciously decline rather than give Darla another reason to scold Maia.

Maybe he'd volunteer for a wedding date. Darla had mentioned the possibility when she'd hired him. She'd said Christmas weddings were very popular. He'd also heard Cash, the owner of Wishing Well Springs, was getting married on Christmas day.

"Give Millie my best when you see her."

"I will." His mom drew in an audible breath and then paused. "I… There's…"

Brent clenched his jaw. "What's wrong? Did something happen?"

"Oh, I've been wondering if I should tell you or not."

"Tell me."

She released the breath she'd been holding. "Your dad was hurt a few weeks ago. He's fine," she hurriedly added. "Broke his leg. Pretty badly, apparently. He had to have surgery and is still laid up."

"Hurt how?"

"He fell off a ladder. They were painting the house. Elaine Lester happened to mention it the other day. That's really all I know."

The Lesters were old friends of his parents. His mom and Elaine still kept in touch.

Brent began to relax. The news wasn't terrible. "Should I call him?"

"That's your decision. He might appreciate hearing from you."

His mom maintained a neutral role when it came to Brent's relationship with his dad. These days, unlike when he was young. She neither encouraged nor discouraged Brent. Mentioning his dad's fall wasn't expressing an opinion. Rather she was providing information, and Brent could choose for himself how to respond.

"I'll think about it."

With that, the topic was officially closed. They chatted another twenty minutes before winding down the call.

"I've kept you up late," Brent said.

"It's okay. I miss you."

"I miss you, too."

"If you won't come home for a visit, maybe I can come there." She sounded hopeful.

"Maybe." The more he thought about it, the more he warmed to the idea. "Yeah, why not? What about the spring?" That would give him time to get more out of debt and to arrange with

Ansel for a couple days off. "I'll call you again on Christmas."

"I love you, honey."

"Love you, too, Mom."

Brent continued sitting at the table, finishing his now lukewarm coffee, long after disconnecting. None of his bunk mates were home yet. He could crawl into bed if he wanted. Except he no longer felt the pull. Talking with his mom tended to boost his spirits.

Would talking with his dad boost them even more? They hadn't spoken for at least seven, no eight, months. No surprise Brent hadn't gotten a call after his dad's fall and surgery.

He checked the time. Was it too late? On impulse, he sent his dad a text saying hi and that he was sorry to hear about his broken leg. He nearly jumped when his phone rang a minute later, a photo of his dad filling the screen.

Brent hesitated a few seconds before answering. "Hey, Dad. Sorry if I woke you."

"You didn't. This darn cast keeps me up. I can't get comfortable."

"Must have been some fall. How are you doing?"

"All right. I assume your mother told you."

Wasn't it just like his dad to be more concerned about how Brent learned of his accident than the fact he'd called to check on him?

"No fun being laid up over the holidays," he said, refusing to rise to the bait.

"No fun at all. I'm driving Raelene and the kids nuts."

The kids. Brent's half siblings. Near strangers to him. Did his dad attempt to control them and Raelene as much as he had Brent and his mom?

After clearing his throat, he asked, "How long until the cast comes off?"

"Another three weeks. If my X-rays go well. Can't come soon enough for me. I hate sitting around the house all day."

"I get that."

"Yeah? I figured you liked loafing around, considering your lifestyle the last couple of years."

Not a very subtle dig. His dad hadn't reacted well to Brent's "retirement" from rodeo. Not an unexpected reaction from someone who'd won three national championships.

"I'm working now, Dad. I got a new job a few weeks ago."

"Doing what?"

"I'm a wrangler for Mountainside Stables at Bear Creek Ranch. It's north of Payson."

"Sounds all right. They raise cattle?"

For a second, Brent considered saying yes. "Bear Creek is a resort. I lead guests on trail rides."

His dad let loose with a barking laugh. "Can't say that's the kind of job I picture for you. But you're gainfully employed, and that's something."

Brent wasn't sure he'd heard correctly. Was it possible his dad's second family had mellowed him? Then next second, his old dad was back.

"Even if a girl could do the job."

A girl, a woman, did. Maia. And she could run circles around his dad on a mountain trail even without his leg in a cast. The image of her besting his dad brought a smile to Brent's lips.

"I like what I'm doing. And I like the people I work with."

"Any chance you're going to get serious and return to rodeo?"

"Not likely."

"Doesn't your old friend Channing Pearce own a rodeo arena in Payson?"

"His family does. Rim Country."

"I'm sure they have some bulls you can practice on."

"I'm not getting back into rodeo, Dad."

"You plan on staying a quitter, then?"

Brent heard the disappointment in his dad's voice. It crawled along his skin, leaving a stain.

He had quit; it was true. And then walked away. At the time, he'd thought it better than publicly humiliating himself with his mounting disqualifications and losses.

The black cloud hovering in Brent's peripheral vision moved closer. He felt its weight bearing down on him as it stole every molecule of oxygen in the air.

Why had he called his dad? Why had he thought this time would be different? Why did he keep trying to bridge a rift that was impossibly wide?

"It's getting late, Dad. I have an early morning."

"Look son." His dad paused. Inhaled deeply. "I know you think I'm too hard on you. Too demanding. Your grandma was the same with me. The Hayes aren't easy to live with, as your mom can attest to." He inhaled again. "I know what you're capable of, and I was only trying to encourage you."

His dad had a heck of a way of showing it. Impatience. Belittling. Bullying. Punishment. Apparently, he'd never heard of positive reinforcement.

"If you say so, Dad."

"You gave up too soon."

"Gotta go. Good night."

Brent disconnected, the invisible heavy weight bearing down on him.

Had his dad been encouraging him all that

time? Brent had always assumed his dad was attempting to turn Brent into a younger clone of himself.

Then again, he'd succeeded. With all his problems, Brent wasn't easy to live with, either.

The rumble of an approaching vehicle reached his ears. Someone was home. Thank goodness they hadn't arrived earlier to hear his conversation with his dad. Brent's hidden shame would remain that: hidden.

He avoided surrendering to his gloom long enough to greet Javier and get the lowdown on the Christmas-tree lighting. After that, he made his excuses, crawled into bed, closed his eyes and dove headfirst into the darkness.

CHAPTER EIGHT

"Where you off to?"

Hearing Ansel call to him, Brent stopped on the way to his truck and pivoted. "To the bunkhouse for a while. Then, I might be heading into Payson."

Rim Country Rodeo Arena had recently purchased a dozen new bucking broncs. Channing had twisted Brent's arm, insisting he come look at the stock and assess them like they had in the old days. He'd also invited Brent to stay on and watch the Friday night bull-riding practice.

Brent had yet to accept. Returning to the all-too-familiar rodeo arena would be hard on him, a glaring reminder of his failed career. He'd needed two full days to crawl out of the murky darkness after his phone call with his dad. To account for his glumness, he'd claimed a pulled hamstring. By the next day his mood had improved and only continued to get better as the week progressed.

This morning, Ansel had at last put Brent in charge of the trail ride. He wasn't keen on backsliding, which facing his past at Rim Country could result in. On the other hand, Brent hadn't seen Channing since arriving in Payson. He owed his friend a visit. And, who knew? Seeing familiar sights might have the opposite effect—heal rather than wound.

"Well, that's fine and dandy," Ansel proclaimed, a mischievous glint in his eyes. "You have time."

"For what?"

"To come with me. I need an extra pair of hands. Got a delivery for the shelter. And seeing as you might be heading to town… You can meet me there," Ansel continued. "Won't take long and then you can be on your way." The shelter—he must mean Payson Rescue Mission.

"Dad recruiting you?" Maia said, coming out of the stables.

Brent hadn't realized she was in there and forced himself to act natural. He'd done well since Sunday's tree lighting at the main lodge, maintaining his distance from her and limiting their conversations. As a result, he had another gig with Your Perfect Plus One tomorrow night. Darla seemed satisfied with him and no longer concerned he was getting too comfortable with her family. Maia especially.

"He is," Brent agreed. "But I don't mind. It's for a good cause."

To his surprise, he truly didn't mind. Not because he'd be winning points with his boss. Brent liked the idea of contributing to worthy causes. That had been a perk of working for the BLM rehabilitating wild mustangs. At times, he regretted his abrupt departure. Then again, that road had led to his job here at Bear Creek Ranch which he liked equally well.

Other than having to avoid the boss's daughter. There was the one drawback.

"Right you are." Ansel beamed. "And this is the season of giving."

Maia had accompanied Brent this morning on the four-hour trail ride. While two shorter rides were scheduled for the afternoon, Rowdy would be taking Brent's place. He'd originally had the entire day off but had switched with Rowdy. The young man was making a secret trip to the jewelry store. Unbeknownst to his girlfriend, she'd be getting a designer watch for Christmas. Brent was happy to contribute to the surprise.

"You still free tomorrow morning for a training session with Snapple?" Maia asked.

"Between rides I am."

They'd been making progress with the big Appaloosa. He was no longer bothered by the sock at the end of a fishing line. Tomorrow, Brent would play the role of a veterinarian, and they'd mimic the pulse and respiration stop Maia would have during a real competition— including listening to Snapple's heart rate with an old stethoscope she'd borrowed.

"Great!" Maia started for the horse pen, a half-dozen halters slung over her arm. "Have fun, you two."

He watched her go, an emptiness in his chest. She hadn't sent Brent a flirty farewell smile like she might have prior to the Christmas tree lighting. They were both on their best behavior. As much as he missed their former exchanges, this was for the best. And he'd just keep telling himself that over and over until it sank in.

A half hour later, he pulled in behind the shelter and parked beside Ansel's pickup. Brent had guessed the multitude of boxes stacked in the pickup's bed contained food, and, it turned out, he was correct.

"These are contributions from the ranch," Ansel explained to Brent while lowering the tailgate. "The owners have been collecting canned goods and nonperishables for the last few months. You probably noticed the donation box at the Christmas tree lighting."

Brent hadn't. His attention had been elsewhere.

"This morning," Ansel continued, "the kitchen added bread and baked goods, a box of potatoes and another of carrots and onions. Gonna really help with Christmas dinner. The shelter will feed upwards of two hundred folks."

"That many?"

"Hunger and cold know no bounds. Valley Fellowship Church put on a sock-and-glove drive. They delivered almost five hundred pairs this week. The elementary schools sold candy canes and raised nearly a thousand dollars."

Brent and Ansel stacked boxes on a hand-cart which they brought in through the delivery entrance. A pair of cheerful staff members directed them to a large pantry area. Delicious aromas wafted from the kitchen. A crew, Brent suspected, staffed mostly by volunteers like Ansel, worked at the counter or in front of the large stove, prepping and cooking food.

"You mind fetching the rest?" Ansel asked Brent. "I gotta review the food supply for Christmas dinner with Gunther over there." He motioned to a portly man around Ansel's age who, from his authoritative bearing, was clearly in charge.

"No problem." Brent returned to the truck.

On his second trip to the pantry area, he was approached by a rumpled-looking guy in a tattered camo coat and scuffed athletic shoes.

"You need help?" he asked Brent.

"Sure. Thanks."

Together, they brought in and stored the remaining two loads, some in the pantry and the rest in the walk-in cooler. Ansel was still conferring with Gunther, their heads bent over a clipboard. Brent glanced around for a place to sit and cool his heels.

"You want a coffee?" the guy asked. "There's a pot on the counter in the dining room. Free for the taking. Or we got bottled water."

"Coffee would hit the spot."

He accompanied the guy to the coffee station and helped himself to a paper cup of the dark brew. The first sip delivered a serious kick to the belly.

"You a new volunteer?" the guy asked. He appeared to be in no hurry to leave.

"Just giving Ansel a hand."

The guy nodded and fixed a coffee for himself. "I've been staying here the last few days. Name's Pete."

"Pleasure to meet you. I'm Brent."

"Lucky for me they had a bed available," Pete said. "Not sure what I'd have done otherwise. Mighty cold at night on the streets this time of year."

"I bet it is."

Upon closer inspection, Brent realized Pete was younger than he'd first thought. Not much older than him.

"I work for Ansel at Bear Creek Ranch." Brent chose an empty dining table and sat down.

Pete joined him, cradling his coffee as if his hands were chilled, though the inside temperature was comfortable. "I haven't been there. Heard of the place, of course. Everyone in town has, even those of us passing through."

"You leaving soon?"

"Not sure. It depends." He looked down. "Money's a little tight at the moment."

"I understand." Probably better than a lot of people, Brent thought.

"I was a project manager for a tech company until last year," Pete said. "We developed software applications for the manufacturing industry. I was laid off when the economy tanked."

"Sorry to hear that."

"My house went next. And then my wife." His voice cracked, and he sipped his coffee, swallowing with obvious relief. "Not sure where she is now. Then again, she doesn't know where I am, either."

The statement, made without apology, gave Brent pause. If not for friends like Channing, he could well be this guy. Living on the streets and grateful for a cot in a homeless shelter that came with a once-a-day hot meal. He had a lot to be grateful for.

"Some days are worse than others." Pete offered a wan smile.

"True story."

Ansel emerged from the kitchen. "You still here, Brent? I figured you for long gone."

He stood. "Wasn't sure you still needed me."

"We're all set." He smiled at Pete. "Howdy, partner."

"Sir." Pete also stood.

"He helped me carry in the boxes," Brent told Ansel.

"Did you? Appreciate it."

"I like to stay busy," Pete said. "Earn my keep."

"Always plenty of work needing doing around here." Ansel turned to Brent. "You ready to hit the road?"

Brent looked around. "I might be back."

"You're welcome anytime."

Was that Ansel's reason for recruiting Brent today? He hadn't really needed a hand.

"Hope to see you again." Brent reached out his hand to Pete, who hesitated and then shook it, his grip gradually growing stronger.

"Same here."

Ansel walked with Brent to where they'd parked. "Kind of you to indulge Pete. The men here get lonely and like to talk. Particularly with new people."

"He's an interesting fellow. I enjoyed myself."

"They're troubled. You know, emotionally and, well, mentally. Half are addicts or former addicts."

"And some have had a rough go and just need a break. Hopefully, they can get one here."

Ansel studied Brent as if seeing him for the first time. "Not everyone would be that understanding. You're all right, Brent."

"I've been down on my luck. I have you to thank for giving me a break. And Darla."

"Hey, I'm the one who got a skilled wrangler out of the deal. And a pretty accomplished trainer who can help Maia realize her dream of winning the Diamond Cup. I should be thanking you."

Ansel dug in his jacket for his truck keys, which spared Brent from having to answer in what would surely be a gravelly voice.

They went their separate ways after that, with Ansel returning to Bear Creek Ranch and Brent driving to Rim Country Rodeo Arena. He traveled the main road through town, noting the decorated storefronts, garland-wrapped signposts, plastic snowmen and Santas in front yards and a miniature Christmas village outside the antique store. Signs pointed the way to Christmas tree lots or holiday blowout sales.

On a whim, he tuned the radio to a station

playing holiday songs. For the first time in a long while, he felt a twinge of…not joy exactly, but optimism. He could pull himself out of this reoccurring funk. Change the course of his life. He still had a long way to go, but he was moving forward. That had to count for something. And who knew? Possibly, in time, he'd have something worthwhile to offer Maia.

Since he had nowhere to be on Christmas Day, he decided he'd volunteer at the shelter. Ansel would be helping with the midday holiday dinner. Brent could hitch a ride with him.

The twinge of optimism grew until it became a bona fide ray of hope.

WREATHS HUNG FROM the gateposts at the entrance to Rim Country Rodeo Arena. A sandwich-board sign announcing next week's Cowboy Christmas Jamboree sat just inside the gate. Another larger one appeared at the turnoff to the parking area, advertising a visit from Santa and rides in a pony cart for the kiddies.

Brent wondered if Maia was planning on attending and bringing TJ. She hadn't mentioned it. Then again, they were limiting their conversations to work and Snapple's training.

He refused to let the status of their relationship or reminders of his former rodeo life affect his improved mood. He was about to see an old friend, and the hopeful feeling from earlier continued.

Easing his truck into a free space, Brent stepped out and texted Channing. A moment later Channing replied saying Brent should meet him at the horse pastures. Having been to Rim Country often during his career, Brent required no directions. He strode briskly past the rodeo office, concession stand, the arena with its thirty-five hundred seating capacity, and the livestock pens where several dozen bulls milled about and pawed the ground.

Soon, the animals would be herded through the connecting aisle to the chutes for tonight's bull-riding practice. The participants would gather to assess the bull they'd drawn, along with their competitors' experience level. Their significant others, family and friends would be watching from the bleachers. Some of the competitors would be women. Their participation in the sport of bull riding was constantly growing. Rim Country had begun hosting women's calf roping—both breakaway and tie-down—in addition to barrel racing.

Brent continued walking. The arena had two pastures for their bucking horses. The smaller one housed older, retired stock who lived out the remainder of their days in leisure and comfort. Brent had heard from Channing how he and his fiancée were rehabilitating a few of the more complacent ones.

Brent found the idea intriguing, and he intended to talk to Channing about his techniques. He might learn something useful for Snapple. Taking a bronc bred to buck and training him to be a calm, reliable ranch horse was no easy task. Channing had mentioned that Cash's fiancée even used one of the former broncs in her halftime trick-riding act. Brent was eager to see that.

The larger pasture held the active bucking stock. In addition to supplying bulls and broncs for their own rodeos, Rim Country leased their stock to other arenas. The new horses Channing had purchased were an investment that, if all went well, would eventually pay off. Brent figured his friend was on the right track.

As he neared, he spotted a tall cowboy standing beside Channing at the pasture fence. When Brent got close enough, he recognized Cash Montgomery.

Brent knew Cash, though not as well as Channing did. The rodeo world was a small one, and Brent had regularly crossed paths with Cash during the years he'd competed. Cash had been one of the few who didn't judge or criticize Brent when he quit competing. In fact, rumor was, he'd defended Brent at last year's nationals, saying it took more courage to leave than to stay.

Cash was also co-owner of Wishing Well Springs, the wedding barn where Brent had met Maia his first night in town. What was the saying about six degrees of separation?

It suddenly occurred to Brent that Cash might have had something to do with Darla hiring him. It was possible. Your Perfect Plus One did a lot of business with Wishing Well Springs. He'd ask Cash if the subject came up.

"There you are!" Channing beckoned to Brent.

"Now the gang's all here," Cash added.

The gang? Brent's initial reaction had been to consider himself an outsider. But the sunny smiles as he approached put him as ease and, yes, gave him a sense of inclusion.

Another first-time-in-a-long-time feeling. He'd been having them regularly since coming to Payson and working at Bear Creek Ranch.

A round of handshakes ensued. Channing hooked an arm around Brent's neck.

"'Bout time you showed up, stranger."

"Sorry I didn't get by sooner," Brent said. "Been busy settling into the new jobs."

"Jobs?" Cash asked. "You doing something else besides wrangling for Mountainside Stables?"

Brent chuckled. "I hired on with Your Perfect Plus One. Thought you might have heard from Darla."

"I might have." Cash grinned, confirming Brent's suspicion. "How's that going?"

"Okay. I've met some nice folks, and I can use the extra money. I ran into Maia my first night in town. We were both at your wedding barn. Separately. With different people."

"Small world."

Brent shook his head. "I'm still trying to wrap my brain around how a former bull rider wound up owning a wedding barn."

"Co-owning," Cash clarified. "My sister and I are business partners. It was her idea to turn our grandparents' old place into Wishing Well Springs."

"He's marrying their wedding coordinator," Channing added. "How's that for keeping the business in the family?"

"I'm a lucky son of a gun. Phoebe's something else." Cash's expression went soft and goofy like a man besotted. "We're getting hitched in a couple of weeks. On Christmas Day."

"I heard," Brent said. "Congrats."

"You should come to the wedding."

"I don't want to impose."

"Are you kidding? We'd love to have you. Unless you've got other plans."

"I might be volunteering with Ansel at the shelter. What time's the wedding?"

"Early afternoon. One thirty. I'll send you the invitation. What's your email address?" They plugged each other's contact info into their phones. "You can come with Channing and his girl."

"Good idea," Channing chimed in.

"You and Kenna don't need a third wheel."

The way things were going with Channing and his fiancée, they were likely the next to walk down the aisle.

"She won't mind," Channing insisted. "She's a people person. The more the merrier is her motto. Besides, a bunch of the guys will be there."

More people who'd borne witness to Brent's downfall. Then again, he couldn't hide forever. He may be down, but he wasn't out.

"Thanks, Cash. I'll let you know."

"What do you say we get to looking at these horses?" Channing said. "Bull-riding practice starts in an hour. Hey, you should stick around, Brent. Take a spin if you've a hankering. Show 'em how a real bull rider does it."

"I'm retired. Haven't been in the arena for over two years now. What I'd show them is how to eat dirt."

"Ain't that the truth," Cash concurred. "I think

Channing is the only one of us who still climbs onto a bull or bronc."

"Just for fun. I haven't competed in... I couldn't tell you. Kenna's always lecturing me about being more careful now that I've taken over management of the arena from Dad. Doesn't want me hurt," he said with an air of someone who only pretended to be annoyed. He enjoyed Kenna worrying about him, and it showed.

Love. His two friends were up to their ears in it and couldn't be happier. Brent was glad for them and also a bit envious. His friends weren't competing anymore, and they'd both found new paths to travel that were equally, if not more, fulfilling than rodeo.

Why couldn't he? The new-path part, at least. That had to come before he could consider falling in love. Though, as Maia's face appeared before him, he realized he might not have any say in that matter. The heart didn't always listen to the head.

His emotions tumbled downward and beckoned the black cloud hovering nearby. Before it inched any closer, he forced his attention to the arena and the horses.

"That big sorrel on the left," he said and pointed. "The one with three white socks. He's got a lot of buck in him. Going to be one of your better performers."

"Not that I disagree," Channing said, "but what makes you say that?"

"The look in his eyes. He means business. Have you seen him perform?"

"I've seen all of them perform. Wouldn't have bought them unless they had a lot of buck. But Darth Vader there was one of the best. Any others you'd pick as ones to watch?"

Brent evaluated the herd, paying close attention to the horses' stance, their alertness, demeanor and interaction with their pasture mates. Did they keep to themselves or buddy up? He particularly studied how they held their ears and where they directed their gazes. When they walked, did they move with confidence or wariness?

"The buckskin," he finally announced. "He'll start out slow, lulling his rider into a false sense of security. But then five seconds into the ride, you'd better pay attention. He's going to explode."

Channing looked at Brent with an expression he hadn't seen aimed at him in a while. One of admiration. "You're right. That's exactly how he performs. Anyone ever tell you that you have a sharp eye when it comes to horses?"

"No better than the two of you, I'd bet."

"You have plans the rest of the day?" Channing asked.

"Not really."

"Stick around. I'm serious. Kenna's bringing some sub sandwiches for dinner before the practice. I'll tell her to throw an extra one in for you. You can watch the practice with me in the booth. Give me some more of your opinions on the new stock."

Brent faced Cash. "You staying?"

"I have to get home. Promised Phoebe we'd go Christmas shopping. We won't have any time after this weekend, what with the wedding and out-of-town guests arriving in droves." He shook Brent's hand. "If I don't see you before, I'll see you at the wedding. Remember to RSVP when you get that email invitation. My wedding coordinator is a little OCD about head counts."

Cash left after that. Brent and Channing meandered toward the arena, passing the holding pens where the livestock hands were readying the bulls for transfer to the chutes. At the arena, riders had begun arriving for the practice. Kenna would be here shortly with their sandwiches and, according to Channing, was eager to meet Brent.

At the steps leading to the announcer's booth, Channing's phone went off.

"I've got to take this," he said and lifted the

phone to his ear. As he listened to his caller, his brows drew closer and closer together. "Nope. I understand. No need to apologize." He paused. "I'll figure something out. You just take care of yourself. See you later."

He disconnected, exhaling forlornly.

"Problem?" Brent asked.

"That was Grumpy Joe. Our announcer during events."

"I remember him."

"He also fills in as a judge during bull and bronc practices and was supposed to be here tonight. Seems he caught a heck of a cold. Doesn't want to infect anybody before the holidays, which I understand. Except now I'm short-handed tonight." Channing rubbed a knuckle along his jaw. "It's only practice. Not like we need a real certified judge. Just someone who can spot penalties."

"What about your dad?"

"He and Mom are going to a party tonight for board members of the rescue mission."

Ansel had mentioned something to Brent about it.

Channing's gaze zeroed in on Brent. "What about you?"

"Me judge? No."

"Why not?"

Brent chuckled. "I've never done anything like that."

"It's practice. Not a rodeo. And besides having a sharp eye, you've got the experience. Enough to give the rider a reasonably accurate score."

Brent opened his mouth, fully intending to object. Instead, he said, "Okay. Why not?"

"All right!" Channing grinned.

Brent did, too. He'd been convinced returning to his old stomping grounds would be difficult. Instead, he was staying and judging the bull-riding practice.

The black cloud fell far behind when Brent followed Channing up the stairs to the booth, a jaunty spring to his step.

CHAPTER NINE

ALMOST SIX O'CLOCK, and TJ showed no signs of slowing down. He'd awoken this morning raring to go, typical for him. And according to Maia's mom, he'd been bouncing off walls all day. Also typical. By this time of the evening, however, Maia would have expected her son's eyelids to begin drooping or for him to nod off in his car seat.

Not happening. This was one of those rare days when TJ operated on some kind of endless energy supply. Swell. There went Maia's plans for a quick supper and hitting the hay early.

Her phone rang, and Darla's name appeared on the SUV's info display. In the back seat, TJ squawked. He'd been doing that lately whenever Maia's phone rang.

"Hey, sis," she said. "Good timing. I'm just on my way home from picking up TJ."

"Well, why don't you turn around and meet me instead?"

"Meet you where?"

"Rim Country. They're having bull-riding practice tonight. Garret signed up."

"Oh. Really."

Darla's husband had never rodeoed in his life. But he'd tried bull riding on a whim a few years ago and *discovered a new passion*—his words. *Middle-aged crazy*—Darla's words. He took lessons and went to practices whenever his schedule allowed. Darla fretted, convinced he'd break his neck. She fretted worse when she stayed home and, as a result, went with him to the lessons and practices. Just in case she needed to ride along in the ambulance.

Maia suspected her sister wanted a hand to hold when Garret blasted out of the chute on some big, angry beast. Any other night, she'd decline. Seven was TJ's regular bath time, and bed followed at seven thirty. But attempting to settle TJ when he was like this would end in a power struggle. Might as well go sit with Darla. Besides, she could always leave when Garret was done.

"Okay," she told Darla. "Meet you there."

"I have snacks and juice boxes if you're hungry."

"Awesome! More sugar." TJ would be impossible. "See you in fifteen."

Pulling straight ahead instead of turning right at the next intersection, Maia tooled through town, mentally reviewing the holiday-related tasks on her list. Shopping was her number-one priority. And mailing those cute photo cards of TJ she'd had printed. She might get a tree this year—TJ would love it. He'd been too young last year to notice and, truthfully, she'd been too exhausted between working and caring for a little baby to bother.

She'd also been down in the dumps, which was most likely a mild bout of postpartum depression piled on top of Luke refusing to acknowledge their child. That was why Maia had related to Brent and his problems. Also why she understood his reluctance to consult a doctor or join a support group. It was hard admitting you suffered from an illness, especially such a misunderstood one as depression.

It made people perceive themselves as weak. Sadly, it often made others see them as lazy. Slovenly. Selfish. Even stupid. They thought those with depression should just be able to pick themselves up and brush themselves off and get back to the business of living.

It wasn't like that. Not in the least. Those with depression hated the way they felt and would give anything to change if only they could. Some, like Brent, became good at hiding their condition. Some struggled and ended up in places like the Payson Rescue Mission.

Some lost the battle altogether and, unfortunately, took their lives.

Maia shivered. Brent was strong, she told herself. He would win his battle.

Arriving at the rodeo arena, Maia spotted the sign for the Cowboy Christmas Jamboree next weekend and then a second one at the parking area.

She'd go, of course. Her dad was in charge of the pony-cart rides. In fact, the entire family would be there.

Her thoughts circled back to Luke, where they remained. TJ was young and didn't notice his father's absence. Yet. Before long, he would start wondering why his dad didn't come for visits or live with them like his uncle Garret lived with his cousins.

Maia parked in an empty space. TJ squawked again and swiveled his head from side to side, sensing this wasn't their regular routine. She grabbed her phone off the passenger seat and was about to drop it in her purse when she hesitated.

Should she? What would be the response? A chummy hello? Cool disinterest? A voice mail greeting?

Uncertain, but doing it anyway, she pressed the speed dial number for Luke. Perhaps his heart had softened with Christmas right around the corner.

When the ringing sounded through her vehicle speaker, she quickly transferred the call from Bluetooth to her phone. TJ might not understand what the adults were saying, but he could discern tones and inflections and emotions. If Luke got short with her and lashed out, she'd hate for TJ to hear.

Luke answered on the fourth ring. Had he waited, debating?

"Maia?"

"Yeah. It's, um, me."

"Everything okay?"

Aware of the wobble in her voice, she swallowed and slowed her breathing. "Everything's fine."

"What's up?"

Not one mention of TJ. No *How's he doing?* Or *He's probably walking and talking by now.*

"Is this a bad time?" Maia asked. *Please say yes.* Then she could hang up and not call back unless it was an emergency, her conscience appeased.

"No. I just got home from work. Cheryl has dinner ready but that can wait a minute. This *is* only going to take a minute, yes?"

Cheryl? Maia didn't recognize the name. Must be Luke's latest. There was always a latest.

She swallowed again, grimacing at a bitter taste.

"I was thinking about Christmas," Maia said, mustering her determination. "Wasn't sure if you had any interest in seeing TJ. We could meet you halfway." She wouldn't invite Luke to her house. "Or at Bear Creek Ranch." Neutral territory.

"We're kinda busy." He drew out the response. "I don't know when I could squeeze it in."

Seeing his son was squeezing it in? Maia bit back a retort. Calling had been a stupid idea.

Maintaining a level voice, she said, "Well, if you change your mind, call me." She'd leave the door open as she always did. It was the right thing to do. "Good night, then."

"Maia, wait."

"What?"

"How are you?"

"Don't you want to know how *TJ* is?"

Several seconds of silence passed, a sure sign of Luke's annoyance. "How is he?"

"Fine. Fantastic, in fact. You're missing out on knowing a truly wonderful little boy."

"I told you—I wasn't ready for a family."

"You weren't ready for marriage, either." Before he could speak, she cut him off. "No reason to rehash this. Sorry I interrupted your dinner. Goodbye."

"Maia—"

She disconnected rather than fan the flames burning inside her and tossed her phone aside.

Looking at TJ in the rearview mirror, she said, "You ready, sweetums?"

She'd take him to watch his uncle Garret ride a bull, let him play with his cousins and forget all about the last ten minutes. Luke wasn't going to ruin her evening. And he sure as heck wasn't going to ruin her and TJ's Christmas.

Once she had TJ in the stroller and the diaper bag shoved in the compartment beneath the seat, she called Darla.

"We're here. Where are you?"

"On the west side. Front row. Section…102."

She imagined her sister glancing around to get her bearings. In the background, she heard her nieces' lively chatter.

"Be there in a sec."

They were easy to spot. Darla wore a bright red jacket and matching knit scarf. The girls were in holiday sweatshirts and stocking caps. They darted to and fro in front of Darla, exhibiting the same boundless energy as TJ. He went nuts the second he spotted them, what Maia called his yapping and clapping.

"Sit." Darla scooted over on the bleachers. "Take a load off."

Maia plopped down on the end seat and parked the stroller next to her.

"What's wrong?" Darla asked, always too astute for her own good.

"I stupidly called Luke to see if he wanted to spend time with TJ over Christmas." Maia leaned over and unbuckled TJ, who made the task almost impossible by flailing his arms and legs in excitement. "He wasn't interested."

"I'm sorry, hon. That must have hurt."

"What it did was make me furious." She set TJ on the ground.

"Chill. Seriously. He's not worth it."

"No. He's not." Maia squeezed her eyes shut and inhaled deeply. She opened her eyes a moment later when TJ collided into her legs while evading his cousins in a game of tag. "Hey, there, little man." She patted his head before he ran off. "Be careful."

"In the mood to talk?" Darla asked.

"No." Maia glanced around the arena. "I most definitely am not in the mood to talk." She paused and squinted, her heartrate involuntarily accelerating. "Is that Brent in the announcer's booth?"

"Took you a whole ten seconds to notice. Bet

you'd have seen him in five if you weren't so mad at your ex."

Maia ignored her sister's teasing. "What's he doing in the booth? I had no idea he'd be here tonight. Not that he has to report his whereabouts to me," she added at Darla's sideways glance.

"Garret said he's filling in as judge tonight. Grumpy Joe called in sick or something."

"Brent's judging?"

"Well, he has the experience. And it's only practice."

She sounded like she was repeating back what Garret had told her.

"I suppose."

Maia actually thought Brent judging the bull-riding practice would be good for him. He'd avoided anything to do with rodeo since he'd quit. This, on the other hand, was embracing his past and showed progress or, at least, a willingness to progress. Good for him.

From where she sat, the riders appeared satisfied with Brent's scoring. None of them complained, and Brent frequently came down from the booth to chat with a few of the riders, offering his opinion and advice—or so Garret told them when he came over to chat in between his two rides.

While Maia tried not to stare at Brent, she

couldn't stop herself. From the grin on his face and his relaxed manner, he was having fun.

A great time, actually. Maia imagined this was the carefree, confident and happy Brent from days gone by. The current version of him was more serious and more complex and, as a result, intriguing. But a lighthearted Brent also held a lot of appeal.

Despite TJ's energy fading and her brother-in-law finishing his two runs, she stayed. Yes, to watch Brent in his element. Eventually, Garret wandered over, saying he was ready to leave. Maia had no excuse to linger. Too bad. The second she loaded TJ into the stroller, he fell asleep, and they all started toward the parking area.

"My phone!" Maia halted abruptly and rifled through her purse. "It's not here. I must have dropped it back at our seats."

"Want us to watch TJ while you get it?" Darla asked.

"That's okay. You go on ahead. The girls are tired. Garret, too. I'll be right behind you."

"You sure?" Darla stared at Maia, suspicion shining in her eyes. "We can wait."

Her oldest daughter chose that moment to shove her youngest to the ground, which resulted in a firestorm of tears.

"Come on, you troublemakers," Garret said and rounded up the girls.

Darla reluctantly followed, glancing repeatedly over her shoulder.

Maia hurried toward the arena, her heart pounding and the stroller wheels bumping. She'd fibbed to her sister. Her phone was tucked securely in her purse. She wanted to talk to Brent and experience this different version of him up close.

Darla had surmised as much, and Maia would doubtless face the consequences later.

"WELL?" CHANNING SIDLED UP beside Brent and rested his forearms on the arena fence. "What'd you think?"

"The better question is, how did I do?"

"You're hired."

Brent laughed. A real laugh. Not forced. "Very funny."

All but a few of the three-dozen participants had left. A trio of cowboys hung out by the gate, engaged in a heated debate on which of them had the best ride. The lone woman participant slung her canvas equipment bags over her shoulder and joined her boyfriend. She'd scored higher than him, impressing Brent along with everyone else there tonight.

"I'm serious," Channing said. "We can use an extra judge on call. This isn't the first time we've had a last-minute cancellation."

"I'm pretty sure judges have to undergo some kind of training and testing to become certified."

"They do. But certified judges aren't required for practices or non-PRCA and non-PBR events."

Brent glanced toward the holding pens where the livestock hands herded the last of the bulls to the waiting trailer. Once loaded, they'd be returned to their regular pasture on the other side of the arena grounds, across from the horse pastures.

Tired after a night of hard work, the bulls were complacent and ready for a well-deserved rest—in stark contrast to the energy and unruly temperament they'd shown earlier.

"You know your stuff," Channing continued. "And you're fair. In the meantime, while you work on your certification, you can help us out here. It's a win-win."

Brent shook his head, unconvinced. "I had a great time tonight. I did. But I already work two jobs." Not to mention, he spent a portion of his days off with Maia, training Snapple.

"I'd pay you. Not a lot, mind you. Enough to cover your time and trouble." Channing named an amount.

"That's too much."

"It's the going rate."

As much as Brent could use the extra money, he hesitated taking on another commitment. Still, he asked, "How often are we talking about?"

"Once a month. Maybe twice."

He supposed he could manage once or twice a month. And rather than send him hurtling into the dark place, judging the bull-riding practice had left him…heartened, he supposed was an apt description. And who knew? Judging on a regular basis might prove therapeutic.

"Can I think about it?" he asked.

"Take as long as you need. We're not going anywhere. And I hope neither are you."

Brent liked the idea of returning the favor Channing had done him. Maybe he would research the requirements for becoming a professional judge. Just for kicks.

"Lookie there." Channing peered past Brent's shoulder, a grin spreading across his face. "One of us has company, and it's not me."

Brent cranked his head around. At the sight of an approaching figure, his pulse instantly quickened. Maia came toward them, pushing a sleeping TJ in the stroller.

"Evening, Maia." Channing tipped his cowboy hat. "Good to see you. Been a while."

"How've you been, Channing?" She flashed

him a small smile, which brightened considerably when she greeted Brent. "Hi."

"I thought you left already."

He'd noticed her from his vantage point in the announcer's booth. And seen her leaving.

"I, ah, dropped my phone and had to come back for it. Then I…spotted you and came over."

"Speaking for the both of us," Channing said, "we're glad you did. Aren't we?" He elbowed Brent.

"Yeah." Very glad.

He and Maia had maintained their strictly platonic relationship this past week. So why was she here?

Channing must have decided three was a crowd for he suddenly made an excuse to leave. "Sorry to run out on you, but I'm needed at the livestock pens. Merry Christmas, Maia. Give your family my best."

"We'll probably see you next weekend at the Cowboy Christmas Jamboree."

"Tell your dad we appreciate him giving the pony-cart rides. They're a big draw."

"He appreciates Rim Country's sponsorship."

Brent had heard from Ansel that proceeds from the pony-cart rides were going to the rescue shelter. Perhaps he should offer to lend Ansel a hand.

"Later, pal." Channing clapped Brent on the

back. "Let me know what you find out about the judging."

"Judging?" Maia asked when she and Brent were alone.

He rubbed the side of his neck, still absorbing his conversation with Channing. "Bull and bronc riding. Channing thinks I did okay and should research what's required to become certified."

"That's a fantastic idea! You absolutely should. Garret was impressed with your advice, and from where I sat, you looked like you were enjoying yourself."

"I was." Her enthusiasm and praise filled some of the empty places inside Brent. "A lot."

"Then do it. What do you have to lose?"

"I might." He would. First thing tomorrow.

Funny, when he'd arrived at the arena this afternoon, his only intention had been to visit a friend and check out the new bucking horses. Now Brent had not one but two people urging him to consider becoming a certified rodeo judge.

Life never ceased to amaze him. It was full of twists, good and bad. Opportunities around unexpected corners. He'd decided in a single moment to walk away from his rodeo career. After a phone call from Channing, Brent had abruptly moved to Payson. Was he due for another big change?

"If I pursue this, and that's a big if," he said, "I promise it won't interfere with Mountainside or your sister's company."

"I'm not worried about that." Maia dismissed his concerns with a wave. "Nobody remains at Mountainside or Your Perfect Plus One for very long. Both are short-term jobs that will hopefully lead to something better."

"Your dad and your sister have been good to me. I won't leave them in a bind."

"You're just researching, not making any decisions."

"True."

They started walking slowly from the booth to the other side of the arena, Maia pushing the stroller.

"What's involved in judging bull and bronc riding, anyway?" she asked. "I know part of the scoring is based on how well the bull bucks. Other than that, I'm clueless. Oh, except that the ride has to last eight seconds."

She was making polite conversation. She couldn't possibly be interested in the nitty-gritty details of rodeo judging. Yet, Brent told her all the same, his excitement growing.

"There are two judges at professional events. We only had one tonight because it was practice, and the scoring is purely a learning tool. And you're right, bulls and broncs, as well as the rider, are scored on their performance. Up to fifty points each for a combined total of one hundred, though anything in the eighties is decent. Like you said, if the rider is thrown before the buzzer goes off, they're disqualified."

"Not too complicated. Buck hard. Stay on."

Brent chuckled. "There's a little more to it—that's why a judge is necessary. If a rider touches either the bull, the rope or himself with his free arm, they're disqualified. That's why you see the rider holding their free arm high over their head."

The arena had completely emptied by now. Still, Brent and Maia stayed and continued talking. He'd been avoiding the subject of rodeo as much as possible these past two years, the reminders of his failures difficult to bear. Talking with Maia was different. He'd forgotten how much he loved the sport even if he'd never compete again or be a world champion.

"You've been a good sport listening to me," he told Maia when their conversation wound down. "You must be bored to tears."

"On the contrary. I was riveted."

Her eyes twinkled with the same merriment he'd noticed during candid moments. When she gazed at her son or bickered with her sister.

After Snapple conquered a difficult challenge on the trail. At the wedding reception where she and Brent had danced, and he'd kissed her cheek beneath the mistletoe.

Emotions stirred inside him. Were it not a terrible idea, he'd lean in and claim another kiss from Maia, this time on the lips.

But it *was* a terrible idea, and one that could only get them in trouble. Again. Something neither of them could afford.

CHAPTER TEN

"I'LL WALK YOU to your car," Brent said, needing something—anything—to distract him from thoughts of kissing Maia.

She beamed at him. "Thank you, kind sir."

"You're welcome." He grinned in return, his attempts not to flirt entirely unsuccessful.

They headed in the direction of the parking area where their two vehicles sat a short distance apart. TJ continued to sleep, a plush rabbit clutched tight to his chest.

"Sorry if I talked your ear off," Brent said in the least flirty tone he could muster. But saying the word *ear* caused him to think about nuzzling hers.

"No apologies necessary. You took my mind off my woes, and I needed that."

"Something happen?"

She groaned. "I made the mistake of calling TJ's dad on the way here. I stupidly thought he might want to see TJ over Christmas. But no. He still wants nothing to do with his son."

"That must have hurt."

"It did." She sniffed and blinked her suddenly damp eyes. "A lot."

"TJ's a great kid. I can't understand not wanting to see him."

"He is a great kid. And I shouldn't let his jerk of a father annoy me." She glanced away. "Sorry. I don't usually resort to name-calling."

"I think in this case it's warranted."

She shrugged. "That's my sad story, and now I feel much better because of you."

They reached her SUV and stood, neither of them seeming in a hurry to part ways. If anything, they moved closer together. Maia exuded an attraction impossible for Brent to resist. It didn't matter he had nothing to offer her, that she deserved better than him, and their employment contracts with Your Perfect Plus One prohibited fraternizing. The pull was too strong, fueled by a deep admiration.

Maia had battled the hard knocks dealt her and emerged a better, stronger person. She'd set goals for herself and was determined to achieve them. She was smart and hardworking and immensely talented.

That wasn't all. She had a way of bringing out the best in Brent. She made him want to try when, until meeting her, he'd been content to give up without a fight.

"I should go." If he remained with her any

longer, his will to resist would dissolve as it had at the wedding. "And it looks like your partner there is tuckered out."

She glanced tenderly at TJ. "He's had a full day. We both have."

After lifting him from the stroller, she laid him against her shoulder and opened the SUV's rear passenger door.

"Drive careful," Brent said, turning to go. "Lots of traffic from tourists in town for the holidays."

"Wait a second. There's something I forgot to ask you."

He halted, not trusting his waning willpower.

She finished loading TJ in the car seat. He did no more than sigh softly during the entire process. Next, she collapsed the stroller and, with Brent's help, placed it in the SUV's rear compartment. With the press of a button, she lowered the door.

"Okay if I'm a little late for Snapple's training session tomorrow? TJ and I have an appointment at the pediatrician's."

"Sure." Why did he feel like he was agreeing to something more than a training session?

Suddenly, they were at the driver's side door, but he didn't remember getting there.

"Good night, Maia."

"Tell me what you find out about becoming a certified judge."

She inched nearer. A half step more, and she'd be in his arms. Then what? Brent wanted to find out.

Before he surrendered to his impulses, sound judgement prevailed, and he retreated.

He didn't get far. Maia reached up and linked her fingers around his neck. With one tug, he was close enough to see moonlit shadows dance across her face. Or claim that kiss.

His pulse hammered. "Maia."

"Shh," she murmured. "I know what you're going to say. This is a mistake."

"A huge one."

"Right now, I don't care." She raised her face to his. "And I think you don't care, either."

"You're wrong."

"Then why haven't you left yet?"

Good question. Brent tried once more to retreat, but his legs wouldn't cooperate.

"That's what I thought," Maia said and brought her mouth to within a hair's breadth of his.

"Even if we were to… This can't go anywhere."

"Maybe not." She smiled, the twinkle reappearing in her gorgeous brown eyes. "At least we can satisfy our curiosity. You can't tell me you haven't been wondering what it might be like to kiss me. *Really* kiss me."

"I have." Why lie? Maia wasn't stupid and neither was she blind. She could see the truth as if it were stamped on Brent's forehead.

"What if you wake up tomorrow with regrets?" he asked.

"I might." Her voice lowered to a whisper. "But I'd have the memory, too. And that will be so worth it."

Maia's arms were around his neck, and she wanted to kiss him. He need only narrow the tiny distance between them to experience a glimpse of heaven.

Why did she have to make that remark about having the memory? He wanted to create one right now.

"I must be crazy," he murmured and wrapped an arm around her waist.

"Let's be crazy together." She unlinked her fingers and cradled his cheeks with her hands.

Her soft touch was a soothing balm to his wounded soul, and he craved more. "Yes."

One of them moved. He couldn't be sure who. But the next instant, Maia was nestled in his embrace, and her soft lips were pressed firmly against his. He willed time to stand still, for this moment to last an eternity. Too long had passed since he'd held a woman, felt her warmth mingle with his, and never a woman like Maia. Kissing her, there was nothing he couldn't accomplish and no distant star beyond his reach.

For a brief moment, Brent was his old self with a future full of promise and potential. Then, the kiss ended, and the real world with its many disappointments returned.

Maia eased out of his arms and met his gaze unabashedly. Something else he liked about her.

Smiling, she said, "That was worth any trouble we might get into."

He wasn't sure he agreed, but the kiss had been incredible and, perhaps, life altering. For him.

He brushed a stray strand of loose hair from her face. "You're something else."

"Please don't break my heart by telling me this can't happen again. I want to believe things will change one day for us, and we'll be kissing often."

He wouldn't tell her they shouldn't kiss again, but he'd be thinking it.

A tightness gripped his chest making it hard for him to speak. To breathe. He looked about but didn't sense the black cloud anywhere near.

"Good night, Maia."

"See you, Brent."

He'd be seeing her, all right. The way she'd

gazed at him, as if he meant the world to her, would stay with him always.

She opened the SUV door and slid in behind the steering wheel. Brent lifted his arm as if to stop her and then let it fall.

The next instant, she was driving away. He fully expected his mood to nose-dive during the drive home. With every soaring flight into the stratosphere came the inevitable plummet back to earth.

It didn't happen this time. When Brent walked into the bunkhouse twenty-five minutes later, he was welcomed by Javier and Rowdy and actually accepted their invitation to play poker.

MAIA SAT ASTRIDE SNAPPLE, fuming. Not at the horse but at Brent, who rode behind her on Lone Star. He'd been silent the entire ride. Same for the last however many days. He'd either avoided her or acted like nothing had happened.

Had he not felt the fireworks? Yes, he had. No one kissed like that unless they were into the other person. So why the walls again?

Needing an outlet for her frustration, she urged Snapple to go faster and climb harder. Let Brent keep up with them now. She dared him.

To her great annoyance, he did. How he managed to get speed and power out of an old plug like Lone Star mystified Maia.

Branches slapped Maia's arms and legs as she and Snapple climbed the steep, rocky incline. She leaned forward in the saddle, keeping her head low to avoid injury to her face and eyes. A helmet and sunglasses provided only so much protection. The redistribution of her weight also enabled Snapple to charge up the trail, his front legs churning like massive pistons.

At the top, the ground leveled out. Maia reined Snapple to a stop where the trail widened, then dismounted. Brent came up behind her, Lone Star breathing heavily as if he'd scaled a great height—which he just had. Snapple merely snorted once, his lungs functioning at an amazing capacity, not dissimilar to those of a racehorse.

Brent also dismounted. He left Lone Star to rest and joined Maia. As had become their routine during similar training rides, he assumed the role of a veterinarian at a competition trail ride. He approached Snapple from behind, withdrawing the stethoscope from his jacket pocket. Purposely letting the stethoscope dangle from his hands, he then inserted the ear tips.

When Snapple didn't react, Brent held the stethoscope drum between his thumb and forefinger and pressed it to Snapple's flank behind his left front leg. From his other pocket, Brent removed a stopwatch, which he clicked to start.

After a minute had passed, he announced Snapple's heart rate.

"One hundred and thirty."

Maia lifted her shoulders. "Not bad."

This was the first they'd talked since starting the ride an hour ago. Before that, conversation had been minimal. Okay, she got it. Brent's extra caution was hardly a surprise. He'd warned her, after all. But, really, he was taking this keep-things-between-them-professional thing a bit too far. He didn't have to behave like they were strangers.

Or did he? Hadn't they proven—not once but twice—that they had zero willpower? She'd been the one to practically throw herself at him. But, oh, she'd wanted that kiss. And he hadn't disappointed. Best ever. No exaggeration.

"Can he get back down to sixty-five beats per minute in the allotted time?" Brent asked.

"That's why we're doing this, isn't it?" At his raised brows, she cleared her throat and tried again in a nicer tone. "His stats generally return to normal quickly."

Brent busied himself inspecting Snapple's hooves. Maia ground her teeth together. This attitude of his was annoying to say the least.

Granted, kissing had been a mistake, she'd concede to that. But they wouldn't lose control a second time. Darla was depending on them, and they both needed the extra paycheck. Brent more than her. Besides his credit card bills, he had some upcoming expenses.

She'd overheard him talking to her dad about bringing his mom out for a visit. She'd have rather Brent told her himself, except that would have been a *personal* conversation, and those were off-limits.

"Last time he was slow recovering," Brent said, stepping back to evaluate Snapple.

She should be glad at how quickly Brent had picked up on the lingo. "Only by a few minutes. What matters most is that he's not reacting to you and the stethoscope and hasn't for the last three practice rides."

"He's getting used to me." Brent ran a hand along Snapple's scar. "We should try this with someone new. What if we arranged for Javier to meet us at the stables when we return?"

"Does he have any experience with horses?"

"A little. Enough he can hold a stethoscope and pretend to time Snapple's heart rate. Unless you have someone else in mind."

"No." The suggestion was an excellent one, and Maia's irritation waned. "Will he be willing?"

Maia listened while Brent made a call to his bunk mate, gathering from his side of the conversation that Javier was indeed willing and would meet them at the stables.

When Brent disconnected, her impatience won out, and she blurted, "Do you regret kissing me that much?"

He went quiet while pocketing his phone, finally admitting, "I don't regret it. Kissing you was nice."

Where did *nice* land on a scale of one to ten?

"Then why the invisible wall?" she asked.

"Less a wall than a safety zone. My way of resisting temptation."

Wait. Were those slight curves at the corners of his mouth? She squinted her eyes. They *were* slight curves.

"I really like you," she confessed.

"Maia."

"I'm in agreement. We table any romance for the present. But I still want to be friends and go back to the way things were before."

"That's not easy for me. Until I'm better, maintaining some distance between us is easier on me. Fewer ups and downs."

Maia released a long breath. She'd been so preoccupied with her own feelings, she hadn't given any consideration to Brent's. "How's your mood been lately? You don't have to answer if you'd rather not."

"Not bad. Steady. I...did some research last night online."

"Yeah?"

"I joined a support group."

"That's great, Brent." She didn't say more, not wanting to embarrass him.

"I'm just reading posts. I haven't participated yet."

"Reading posts is good. Take your time. You'll participate when you're ready."

"We'll see." The curves at the corners of his mouth deepened. "And, by the way, that was a *stellar* kiss. Off the charts. Knowing I'll never have another one is a definite mood killer."

She took his teasing as a sign of encouragement. "Never say never. Who knows what the future holds?"

Brent reinserted the ear tips. "Time to re-check this horse."

Ouch. His abrupt retreat stung a little.

He put the stethoscope's drum to Snapple's flank. The horse didn't twitch. Didn't move. Didn't blink. A remarkable difference from two weeks ago. From last week, even.

"You've done an amazing job with him," Maia commented. "A sock attached to a fishing pole. Who'd have guessed?"

"He may blow up with Javier." Brent clicked on the stopwatch and stepped away. "Eighty-seven beats per minute, by the way. His rate is coming down more quickly today."

"You're changing the subject."

"I'm not. We came on this ride to improve Snapple's conditioning for competition."

"Speaking of research, did you start looking into rodeo judging yet?"

"Now you're changing the subject," he accused.

"Am not. We were talking about things between us going back to the way they were and you getting better. Researching a new career falls into both categories."

He groaned. She thought he might refuse to answer her, but then he did.

"I went online but couldn't find a whole lot. I asked Channing yesterday for the names of the judges Rim Country uses and if he'd mind me contacting them."

"And?"

"He'll let me know. He didn't feel right giving me their phone numbers without first obtaining their consent. I also put in a call to the PRCA. The person I need to talk to is on vacation until after the first of the year. I left a message and will follow up if I don't hear back."

"I'm impressed. Even if you decide being a rodeo judge isn't for you, you've taken steps. Big ones."

"It feels good. Positive. I like waking up in the morning with something to look forward to even if it's just a phone call."

Such a small thing most people took for granted. Maia chided herself for being too hard on Brent. "I understand. Looking forward to something positive is what helped me through my own rough times."

He hesitated before responding. "I have a long road ahead of me, Maia."

"Yes. You do."

"No guarantee how long I'll take to reach the end. You shouldn't wait on me. Not when there are plenty of other guys out there whose lives aren't in shambles."

"Who says I'm waiting on you?"

At last, she got a full-blown smile out of him. With a resigned chuckle, he checked Snapple's heart rate again.

"Sixty-seven."

"Great." She reached for the reins and slung them over the saddle horn. "You and Lone Star are doing well. Want to take the lead the rest of the way?"

"No thanks. You and that army tank you call a horse will run us over." He handed her the stethoscope and returned to where he'd left Lone Star tethered. Halfway there he paused. "One good thing about you."

She climbed into the saddle, attempting to ignore the fluttering in her middle. "What's that?"

"I'm motivated again."

"Yeah. Me, too."

"To get my life together. Not…us."

"That's what I was talking about, too. Well, that and winning the Diamond Cup this spring."

Maia glanced away, avoiding Brent's sharp gaze. One look at her, and he'd read the fib in her eyes. She'd totally been talking about them.

Reining Snapple to the right, she trotted him toward the trail. Two miles from the ranch, she literally left Brent and Lone Star in her dust. The veteran trail horse had grown tired and fallen behind as Snapple, sensing they were nearing home, poured on the steam in a late burst of energy.

Brent must have called Javier in advance, for the prep cook was waiting by the hitching post when Maia arrived. She motioned for him to remain where he was and brought Snapple to a stop twenty feet away. She wasn't taking any chances lest the horse spook at the sight of a stranger. But he appeared unbothered by Javier's presence. Then again, he was used to customers milling about the stables.

His calm demeanor could change in a flash, and she debated waiting for Brent. On second thought, Brent would be nowhere near during an actual competition. Today could be a true test of how well Snapple responded to his training.

She hopped down from the horse. "Brent's fifteen or twenty minutes away. Maybe more. You willing to give this a try without him?"

"He told me not to wait on him."

"He did, huh?" Clearly, she and Brent were of like mind. "Okay. But get out of Snapple's way if he makes the slightest move. You hear me?"

"No need to tell me twice." Javier grinned. "I have no desire to be wearing his hoofprint on my forehead."

She led Snapple to the hitching post where she handed over the stethoscope to Javier, relieved the horse continued to pay the prep cook no heed. "Don't worry about actually monitoring his heart rate. Just go through the motions."

"Right." Javier hooked the stethoscope around his neck. Leaning forward, he cautiously placed the drum on Snapple's side.

Maia maintained a firm hold on the reins, watching Javier's every move almost as closely as she watched Snapple's. Other than a flick of his ears and a quick sideways glance at Javier, the horse stood quietly.

"How long you want me to do this?" Javier asked.

"I'll tell you when. We need a full minute."

Thirty seconds later, she gave him a nod. "Okay. That's enough."

"Whew." Javier straightened.

"You brave enough to run your hand along his back to his rump?"

"Um, I guess."

Snapple stomped a front hoof at the unfamiliar contact and gave Javier another look.

The prep cook startled and retreated a step. "Whoa there." After a few seconds, he relaxed. "Again?"

"Only if you're comfortable," Maia said.

Snapple resumed ignoring the humans in favor of sniffing the hitching post.

Javier sent Maia a sheepish grin. "Can't have Syndee learning I chickened out."

Ah. His girlfriend. "She won't hear it from me."

Laughing, he ran his hand along Snapple's back, visibly relaxing when the horse failed to react.

"Thanks, Javier. I owe you."

"Anything for Brent. He's a good guy." The prep cook moved away, out of kicking range, showing he was no dummy.

"If you and Syndee want to go on a trail ride one of these days, let me know. Free of charge."

"Seriously? She'd like that."

When Brent rode in on Lone Star a short

time later, both rider and horse were moving slowly. Maia had already unsaddled Snapple and walked him around the stables a few times to cool him down.

"Everything went well, I take it," he said, dismounting near the hitching post.

"Javier call you?"

"No. Your smile told me."

"Thanks, Brent. Your training techniques have really paid off."

"Happy to help."

They might have stood there gazing at each other and reconsidering that whole tabling-romance stuff if not for her dad and Rowdy coming down the road with a half-dozen riders. Timing, as the saying went, was everything.

CHAPTER ELEVEN

"EASY DOES IT, BOYS," Ansel called from the back of the horse trailer. "Quit your fussing."

At the side of the trailer, Brent untied Mr. Big Shot's lead rope and tossed it over the speckled gray's neck. He'd done the same a few minutes ago with Boss Man.

"One at a time," Ansel groused as he lowered the gate.

Inside the trailer, the nearly identical pair of ponies shuffled and stomped with their dainty hooves, eager to escape their confinement. Though they'd only been in the trailer for a short five-mile drive, they behaved as if they'd been confined for hours.

Ansel had borrowed Mr. Big Shot and Boss Man from a friend for tonight's Cowboy Christmas Jamboree. He'd then recruited Brent and Pete from the shelter to help. Neither of them minded. Brent was free—he'd attended a wedding last night for Your Perfect Plus One. Pete had told them on the drive from the shelter he was glad for the chance to be useful. And while inexperienced with horses, he'd demonstrated a willingness to perform any grunt work asked of him.

He was also good company. From what Brent had learned, Pete made himself useful at the shelter—something that hadn't gone unnoticed. Ansel had offered to speak to the head of maintenance at Bear Creek Ranch and see if there were any job openings.

Pete was grateful, even getting a little choked up. He didn't care that the job was a far cry from his former occupation of project manager.

Brent knew exactly how the man felt. He'd been similarly grateful when Ansel hired him. If there weren't any open positions in maintenance, he'd ask Javier about a kitchen job for Pete.

"Let's go, boys," Ansel said and stepped back from the rear of the trailer.

Mr. Big Shot and Boss Man twisted in half circles, battling for which of them would be first out. They created a racket as they scrambled down the metal ramp. Once on solid ground, the pair settled, content to stand there and look awesome with their long, silky tails and braided manes intertwined with red-and-gold ribbons.

"All that fuss for nothing," Ansel told the ponies and bent to pat their heads—which came no higher than his waist.

Mr. Big Shot and Boss Man would pull the cart filled with kids in a large circle around the arena grounds. Pete was in charge of selling tickets while Brent would load and unload passengers. The ponies' owner had decorated the cart with shiny garland and battery-operated Christmas lights. The rear seat would hold two to three kids, depending on their sizes.

In addition to pony rides and holiday-themed carnival games, Channing had hired a band to provide Christmas music. The musicians were currently setting up in front of the concession stand. A lighted tree rivaling the one at Bear Creek Ranch stood in the center of the open area. Hundreds of candy canes free for the taking hung from the branches. Inside the arena, a maze of straw bales, sawhorses and barrels had been constructed. Life-size mechanical reindeer trimmed with blinking lights showed the way.

At the end of the maze, Santa awaited on his makeshift throne. Photos with the jolly old elf cost five dollars each. Like with the pony rides, all proceeds would be donated to the Payson Rescue Mission's holiday food drive.

Brent hadn't noticed any mistletoe, but he remained on the lookout. He'd been serious when he told Maia he was avoiding temptation.

Together, he and Pete unloaded the cart and equipment. While Brent and Ansel harnessed the ponies, Pete parked the truck and trailer out of sight behind the horse barn. He returned on foot just as the sun inched toward the horizon. The jamboree would start promptly at five thirty and end at eight thirty. Between unharnessing the ponies, loading them and the cart into the trailer, returning them home, and, lastly, dropping off Pete at the shelter, it would be a late night for Brent and Ansel.

Again, Brent didn't mind. Though not a purpose exactly, contributing to a worthy cause put him in the Christmas spirit.

He still struggled periodically. There was no instant cure for what ailed him. Three or four times a day a memory had him teetering on the edge of the dark place. His conversation with his dad. A reminder that he and Maia had no future together. The monthly interest hitting his credit card balances. Learning from Rim Country's judges that becoming certified, while possible, required time and money Brent didn't have.

But he told himself, there were plenty of positives to balance out the negatives—something the online support group had been teaching him. He mentally ticked off the list. If all went as planned, his mom would come for a visit in February. Snapple continued to respond well to his training—Maia had entered a local competition next month as a test run for the prestigious

Diamond Cup. Brent had sent two payments to his old pal who'd lent him money, which was two more than he'd sent last month. And speaking of friends, he'd counted two new ones in his circle: Javier and Rowdy. Ansel, too, if a boss could be considered a friend.

Maia was also a good friend. She'd listened to him lament and offered good advice even if Brent refused to take it.

"Snap the clamp to the D ring," Ansel instructed Brent. "Pete, make sure the brake's engaged."

Both hurried to do their boss's bidding. They'd decided Ansel would drive the pony cart. Brent was more than able to handle Mr. Big Shot and Boss Man, but he had thirty pounds and four inches on Ansel. The boys, as Ansel called them, could only pull so much weight. Best to conserve their strength.

Ansel climbed onto the cart seat. "I'm going to take the boys for a short spin around the place. Get the kinks out before the first paying customers. You want to come along, Pete?"

The shelter resident's face lit up brighter than any five-year-old's. "You bet."

He climbed in beside Ansel, the two of them squished together in the small seat. Ansel clucked to the ponies, and they took off at a jaunty clip. Having a few minutes to spare,

Brent made his way to the concession stand for a bite of dinner. He'd just finished his hamburger and fries when Channing approached.

"Saw the pony cart on the way here," his friend said, sitting down at the picnic table with Brent. "They look great." He wore a Santa cap instead of his usual cowboy hat and had a red woolen scarf around his neck. When he caught Brent staring, he said, "Kenna and my mom's doing. They insisted me and the hands dress the part."

"Wait. I need a picture." Brent opened the camera app on his phone and aimed it at Channing. "To show at your bachelor party. Or better yet, your wedding."

"Ha, ha. Very funny."

Brent snapped a picture.

"Speaking of weddings," Channing said, "where's Maia?"

Brent almost dropped his phone. Had his friend learned about his and Maia's kiss? Kisses. Then he realized Channing was referring to Brent and Maia's shared employer, Your Perfect Plus One.

"She and the rest of the family will be here soon."

At least Darla would be in the vicinity to prevent Brent from repeating past mistakes. He didn't dare kiss Maia, beneath the mistletoe or anywhere, with her sister a few feet away.

"Hey, listen," Channing said. "Are you free January fifteenth? Also, possibly, the twenty-eighth?"

Brent checked his calendar on his phone. "I don't have any weddings scheduled. What's up?"

"We're having an extra bull-riding practice and adding a bronc-riding one to the calendar. Our first in a while. Gonna need a judge."

"Grumpy Joe's not available?"

"He's working the Lucky Eights Rodeo and the Cattle Country Livestock Show."

Brent narrowed his gaze. "For real? You're not just doing me a favor?"

Channing pointed to his cap. "Would Santa's helper lie? I'll shoot you a text with the details."

"I'd feel better if I were qualified. I think your participants would, too."

"You will be soon enough."

"I haven't decided to begin the certification process."

"Okay. Until then, you can judge a few practices."

Brent blew out a breath. "I could use the money."

"A good enough reason for me."

Brent had leveled with his friend about the full

extent of his financial predicament. Not, however, what had caused it and his continuing battle with depression. A true friend, Channing would respond with sympathy and compassion—and unintentionally leave what little pride Brent had left in shambles.

"Any chance you can eventually quit Your Perfect Plus One?" Channing asked.

"Not yet. Darla pays too well."

"But you could if you obtained your certification and we hired you as a permanent judge."

"There are just too many costs involved, and paying off my debts comes first."

"What if you had a sponsor?"

"For getting certified? Who would sponsor me and why?"

"Rim Country. And we'd sponsor you to guarantee having a reliable judge on the payroll."

Brent chuckled. "You're crazy, man."

"Think about it."

"What would you want in return? And don't tell me there are no strings attached."

"I haven't decided."

"Let me guess. You just came up with the idea two minutes ago."

"Mmm, more like five minutes ago," Channing admitted with a grin. "We could treat the sponsorship as an advance, if that makes you more comfortable. You'd sign a contract for, say, two years, and we'd take a little off the top of your monthly wages to repay the advance."

"I already have too many loans."

"Not a loan. There's no interest."

Brent crumpled a napkin and tossed it into his empty paper food tray. He needed time to think. He wasn't making any rash decisions that might come back to bite him. "We'll talk after I hear from the PRCA."

"All right. No rush." Channing's grin widened. "But here's something else for you to chew on while you're at it. If you didn't work for Darla, then you and Maia could date."

Brent sat back and studied his friend. "I never said I wanted to date her."

"You didn't have to. It's pretty obvious."

Brent grumbled. He thought he'd done a better job of masking his feelings for Maia. "What I want and what's possible are two different things. I'm in no position to get involved with her or anyone."

"She doesn't care that you aren't rich."

"But she does care that I'm down on my luck and wandering through life with no real direction. Trust me."

"You *were* down on your luck," Channing said. "You're on your way up now."

"I've taken a few steps. Up is still a long way

off. Call it ego or self-esteem…whatever…but I need to be in a better place before asking Maia out. She's going places, and I refuse to be an anchor holding her down."

"Okay." Channing nodded in agreement. "I respect that."

"Besides, Darla's counting on me. I made a commitment to her, and one thing I have that's still worth something is my word."

"You don't think she'd be okay with you leaving if it was for a better job with long-term potential and to date her sister, who happens to like you, too?"

"I'm not going to find out," Brent insisted. "And for all I know, Ansel isn't in favor of his employee dating his daughter."

Channing pushed his Santa cap back on his head and contemplated Brent. "When you fall for a gal, you sure don't make it easy on yourself."

"I made poor choices after I quit rodeoing. I won't make another one that drags Maia down with me, no matter how much I like her."

"She may be willing to wait for you. Ask her."

"No!"

"She's a catch. What if some other guy comes along?" Channing asked, his tone serious. "You'd lose your chance."

"Then I lose my chance. Better than her coming to resent me because I'm not the man she thought I was." Brent couldn't live with that.

"Well, speak of the devil." Channing stared at the concession stand entrance. "This is getting to be a habit."

Brent didn't have to turn around. His spidey senses were already tingling. Or should he say Maia senses?

He spun his head around, expecting to see her son and entire family with her. Nope. She'd come alone. Completely alone.

Brent was in trouble. At least Channing was here and able to act as a buffer.

"Whoops. I'm running late." Channing stood and swung a long leg over the picnic table bench. "Evening, Maia. Brent, I'll text you that info."

He sauntered off, leaving Brent and Maia in the very situation he'd hoped to avoid.

WEIRD. IF MAIA didn't know better, she'd swear Brent was nervous to see her. Those compelling hazel eyes of his had widened and then glanced away. When she'd offered a bright *Hi there*, he'd responded with a murmured *Hello*.

Not waiting for an invitation, she slipped into the seat across from him that Channing had vacated. "I ran into Dad on the way over. He said you might be here."

"Were you looking for me?"

"No. He just mentioned you were grabbing dinner."

Either her imagination was working overtime or worry tinged Brent's voice. Why? They'd seen little of each other this past week since the practice trail ride when Javier had played the role of vet.

Not because they were avoiding each other. At least, she hadn't been avoiding him. Their hectic schedules were at fault. Maia had been inundated with Christmas-related tasks: shopping, wrapping presents, house decorating, cookie baking and attending get-togethers with friends.

"Actually, I was elected to go on a beverage-and-snack run. Which, in hindsight, doesn't seem fair. I think my brother-in-law, Garret, is a better choice. He has longer arms and can carry more. My nieces call him the gorilla man."

Her efforts to get a laugh out of Brent were wasted.

"Are you mad at me?" she asked.

"No."

"Is something wrong?"

He shook his head.

All right. She could take a hint and stood.

But rather than leave, she tried again. "You mind giving me a hand? I doubt I can handle seven drinks, a large bag of kettle corn and three cinnamon rolls by myself."

"Um, sure." Brent climbed slowly out of the picnic table as if his boots were filled with cement.

This should be interesting. "Thanks."

Maia hadn't been entirely honest with Brent. She'd been dispatched to bring back four drinks and a bag of kettle corn. On impulse, she'd inflated the order. Something was bothering Brent, and she had the distinct impression she was at the root of it. He may not want to talk to her, but she wanted to talk to him.

They chose the shortest of the three lines in front of the concession stand.

"What's new with Channing?" she asked.

Perhaps Brent's worry was actually annoyance and had to do with his friend, not her. He and Channing had been engrossed in conversation right before she'd showed up. That could account for his startled reaction at seeing her.

Another possibility, he was in one of his funks, as he called them. But then, what had triggered it?

"Nothing much," he said.

"You two looked awfully serious."

"He asked me to judge a couple practices in January."

"No fooling! That's fantastic."

Brent didn't reply.

"Isn't it?"

"He's paying me too much money. I'm not worth it."

"You most certainly are. You showed your worth the other night."

"He's doing me a favor."

Maia snorted. "I don't believe that for a second. Channing's a smart businessman. He wouldn't overpay you out of friendship. The practices generate money for the arena, and he needs reliable, expert judges."

"He mentioned Rim Country sponsoring me."

"Wait! What? Are you competing again?"

Brent shook his head. "The sponsorship would cover the costs of me earning my judging certification."

Maia brightened and involuntarily touched his arm. She couldn't help herself. "No kidding!"

"I haven't said yes. There's a lot to consider."

"I suppose," she conceded. "But it's a wonderful opportunity. You won't get another one like it. A sponsor," she repeated with a bit of awe.

"I insisted on paying back the money. I won't take charity."

"I wouldn't call a sponsorship charity, but okay." From what she knew about Brent, he'd want to pay his own way. "I can understand your reasoning, especially if you make a full-time career of judging and work for other arenas."

"Hmm. I haven't thought that far ahead."

"You could be heading for a brand-new career. That's exciting."

"I guess," he hedged.

Was he afraid? Maia doubted it. Hesitant? Sure. Who wouldn't be? The idea of changing careers was intimidating. Risks were involved. Changes necessary. And Brent wasn't coming from a place of strength and security.

"You'd have to travel," she said. "Maybe move." *Please don't move.*

"I would have to travel. But I'd establish a home base."

"Where?" *Say Payson.*

"Around here, I suppose. Seeing as I'd work primarily for Rim Country." He rubbed his chin in thought, only to drop his hand. "I'm getting ahead of myself. I haven't even decided if I'll obtain my certification."

If he was ahead of himself, Maia was in the next county over. She'd already jumped to a future where she and Brent were seriously dating and considering marriage.

Would she be okay with him leaving every week? Maia had always assumed she'd meet a man who wanted to put down roots and stay in one place. TJ already had a father who never saw him, and he deserved more than a part-time stepdad. Not someone who spent a few days out of the week at his *home base*.

Something else occurred to her. Didn't professional cowboys have a reputation for being players? Maia'd had her fill of infidelity with Luke—enough to last a lifetime. She wouldn't tolerate being cheated on again. No way, no how.

Brent didn't impress her as the cheating kind, but, in all honesty, he might have been a different person during his years on the rodeo circuit. He'd never talked about any previous relationships with her. Because he'd been a big-time player? Maybe he still was. Her gut told her no, but she'd been fooled once before and paid the price.

Oh, good grief. What was the matter with her, wasting all this mental energy? Brent wasn't ready to date. He'd told her repeatedly. Indulging in silly fantasies served no purpose other than to make herself miserable.

"I could see myself living here permanently," Brent said as they moved ahead in line.

Swell. Just when she thought reality had returned, here came another silly fantasy.

"Who wouldn't?" she said, trying not to read anything into his statement. "Beautiful scenery.

Large town with a small-town feel. Mild winters. Gorgeous summers. Friendly people. The big city is far away but not too far to be inconvenient."

"The scenery is beautiful," he concurred. "Different from Tucson, where I was staying before coming there. Really different from Wichita."

"I bet."

"I spent some time in Colorado," he mused. "The mountains there are spectacular. It's like living on the edge of heaven, or what I imagine heaven to be."

Colorado? That was a twelve-hour drive. "You have any old friends there?" She gave herself credit for not adding *girl* in front of *friends*.

"One." He didn't elaborate further.

The couple ahead of them moved aside, putting an end to Maia's fishing expedition. She stepped up to the counter and placed her order, wincing slightly when she recited the bogus items. Someone would surely want to eat a piping-hot cinnamon roll that smelled like a dream come true.

Paying with her debit card, she handed the first drink caddy to Brent, along with straws and the bag of kettle corn. She carried the second drink caddy and the cinnamon rolls.

Her family waited by the arena fence, their

reactions varied at spotting Brent with Maia. Her mom's face lit up like a beacon, and she hollered, "Yooo-hooo! Over here," as if they were a hundred feet away instead of ten. Garret grinned and asked, "Are those cinnamon rolls?" before being distracted by his two daughters tugging on his arms. Darla produced a polite smile but not fast enough. Maia had glimpsed the initial scowl.

TJ ripped his hand free from his grandmother's grip and galloped toward Maia in that silly gait of toddlers. No, not toward her. Brent was his target.

He collided with Brent who, by some miracle, didn't drop his drink caddy.

"Hey, pal. Whatcha doing?"

TJ reached up and pulled on the hem of Brent's jacket with both fists.

"Sorry. You can't wear my jacket. Not tonight. It's cold out here."

Maia handed off her drink caddy and kettle corn to her mom, who gushed at how impossibly cute TJ and Brent were together.

Darla leaned in close to Maia and hissed, "Why is he here?"

"I needed help carrying everything."

"Right. You are so full of—"

"Maybe we should get in line for the pony-cart rides," Maia announced in a loud voice. "It's getting long."

"We're talking about this later."

"There's nothing to talk about. Brent happened to be at the concession stand when I got there."

"How convenient."

Dividing the food between everyone—Brent didn't want any—they headed en masse over to where a line formed for the pony-cart rides.

"I want a candy cane," Maia's older niece cried when they spotted the Christmas tree.

"Me, too!" chimed her younger sister.

Naturally, they stopped and collected candy canes. Darla had to remind her daughters repeatedly to take only one. The two girls prattled on in their high voices about seeing Santa and the list of toys they planned on requesting. Maia's mom attempted to explain Santa to TJ, who was much more interested in unwrapping his candy cane.

"Have you made any plans for Christmas?" Maia asked Brent while Darla was distracted by her girls.

"I'm volunteering at the shelter."

"Dad twist your arm?"

"I want to."

Not the answer she'd expected. "That's nice of you."

"Getting out of the house on a holiday is good for me. Better than sitting alone by myself."

"Yeah. I remember how hard it was for me that first Christmas after Luke and I split."

Even with her family there, Maia had struggled to stay in the moment and not be consumed by the past. Had he not cheated on her, she'd have been married and celebrating Christmas with her new husband.

Their breakup was for the best. Maia knew that deep in her heart. The knowledge hadn't stopped the memories from stinging or the doubts from surfacing. What might she have done differently? Why wasn't she enough for him? How could she have been so blind? Would she ever meet anyone new and fall in love again?

"I spent the better part of last Christmas holed up in a hotel room," Brent said. "Volunteering at the shelter will be a big improvement."

"You're a good person. Kind. Compassionate."

Luke wouldn't have been caught dead at the shelter, much less volunteering. She should remember that the next time she considered committing to a man. Did he regularly volunteer or donate to worthy causes?

"My reasons are selfish," Brent said. "I'm comfortable there. I relate to the residents."

Maia almost asked Brent if he'd checked out

any of the support groups at the shelter, but she decided against it. Last time she mentioned him seeking help and seeing his doctor, he'd become defensive. Plus, he'd joined the online support group. She wanted to ask about that, too, but, beside not being the right time or place, it was too personal of a question. He'd tell her if he wanted. She was just glad he'd taken a step to seek help.

Finally, they were first in line. A few minutes later, Maia's dad drove up with the gaily decorated cart and striking pair of ponies.

Darla appeared beside Maia. "One of us has to go with Dad and the kids."

Maia contemplated before answering. If she insisted Darla go, her sister might suspect Maia of wanting to be alone with Brent. While Darla had nothing to worry about, she might not see it that way. Maia didn't want to add tension to an otherwise lovely evening out with the family.

"I'd love nothing better!" she said.

CHAPTER TWELVE

MAIA HELPED LOAD TJ and his cousins into the back seat of the pony cart. Though the cart sat low to the ground, Maia's dad had installed a rope safety harness to prevent little passengers from falling or climbing out. Maia sat in the front seat with her dad, the top half of her body twisted sideways to maintain a watchful eye on the youngsters and, with luck, prevent mishaps.

"Behave." She leveled a finger at her son and nieces. "No fighting. Santa's watching you."

"Is he?" Her youngest niece's mouth dropped open.

"We'll behave," her older niece promised, serious as only a five-year-old could be.

"Gud, gud," TJ repeated. He was already attempting to squirm out of the rope harness.

Maia kept one hand within easy reach to grab a fistful of coat if necessary. "This is wonderful, Dad," she said when they started out, the ponies clip-clopping at a brisk pace. "What a stunning view."

Rim Country Rodeo Arena was situated in

the foothills a half mile above Payson. The lights of the town's many decorated houses and businesses glittered merrily in the distance, creating the type of charming scene common in sappy holiday movies. For the record, Maia loved sappy holiday movies.

Rather than comment on the view, her dad said, "Glad we have a moment alone to talk."

"About what?" Alarm coursed through her. "Is something wrong with Mom?"

"Whatever gave you that idea?"

"You sounded so serious."

"I am worried, but not about her." He turned the small team left, and they rounded the arena's far side. "You and Brent are getting awful cozy lately."

Darla had used that same word with Maia at Thanksgiving.

"We're friends, Dad. Nothing more."

"You sure about that? I've seen the way you look at him. The way he looks at you."

She and Brent really needed to work on being less obvious.

"We've talked, and you can quit worrying," she said. "We've agreed the timing's not right for us."

"I'm glad to hear that. He's going through a lot. Depression is no cakewalk."

Maia couldn't hide her surprise. "He told you?"

"Not exactly. He hinted, and I know the signs. I've seen a lot of residents at the shelter battling the same demons. Brent's not as bad as some. Or he's more adept at hiding it."

"Some of both, in my opinion. Plus, he's making progress." She glanced at the kids, glad to see they weren't shoving and pushing each other. "When he first told me what he's been going through, I suggested he join a support group at the shelter."

"And?"

"He wasn't receptive to the idea. Not coming from me. He might be more receptive if you were to suggest it."

She didn't mention Brent's online support group to her dad. That was Brent's news to share, not hers.

"Possibly," her dad said. "We'll see. I'd hate to offend him. A proud man like Brent doesn't like admitting he's dealing with mental illness."

"No one does," Maia agreed.

"He was under a lot of pressure to succeed, from his dad and from himself. That took a severe toll on him when he quit rodeo."

"I'm not going to pressure Brent," Maia said, picking up TJ's hand and placing it back inside the cart. "If that's what you're hinting at."

"You have to ask yourself what's best not just for you but Brent, too. If the two of you were to get serious, that is. When the timing's right," he added with a smile.

"I'd be supportive. Not demanding."

"You'd be the most supportive girlfriend ever. I have no doubt. You were to Luke, even when he didn't deserve it. The thing about depression is, while Brent needs support of those around him to get better, he also needs space. As much as you might want to help him, you could be doing him a disservice. He might shut down."

Maia hadn't thought about it like that before. She started to mention Channing's offer for Rim Country to sponsor Brent's judging certification, then changed her mind. That was his business to tell people when he was ready.

"You're right. And like I said, you don't have to worry about Brent and me. We're solidly in the friend zone."

Her dad continued as if not hearing her. "There's TJ to think about, too. Any man you make a part of your life will be a part of his. Brent isn't ready to take on the responsibility of a child, even if he wanted to."

"Got it."

"Sorry, kiddo. Didn't mean to lecture."

"You're not."

Actually, he was lecturing her. A little. But

she didn't want to fight. Not tonight. She took his advice in the loving spirit it was given.

They spent the remaining ten minutes until the ride was over talking about gift ideas for her dad to get her mom. As usual, he'd procrastinated until practically the last minute.

"No appliances," Maia warned when he suggested a new blender. "And no slippers. Give her a coupon book instead."

"A coupon book?"

"Make twelve coupons that she can redeem, one for every month of the year. You can include things like a romantic dinner at her favorite restaurant. A foot massage. A shopping trip to the candle store that you hate and she loves. A long afternoon or evening walk. A week when you cook dinner every night and clean the kitchen."

"Have you forgotten how bad my cooking tastes?"

"You can manage for a week, Dad. Order pizza. Pick up a deli chicken and sides at the grocery store."

"I suppose I could," he grumbled and then leaned over to kiss her cheek. "That's a swell idea, sweetie. Thanks."

"I can probably help you with the coupon book."

"I'm counting on it."

They reached the end of the ride. Her dad

reined the ponies to a stop at the makeshift depot near the Christmas tree. Even after several trips round the arena, "the boys" weren't the least bit winded. Maia admired their stamina. If bigger, they'd do well in a trail-ride competition.

Two-dozen-plus people waited for their turn in the cart. Brent, Maia observed, wasn't among them. He hadn't left the rodeo grounds, though. He was supposed to help her dad return the ponies to their owner later tonight.

TJ's piercing squawks had her climbing out of the seat. "Hang on a second. Mommy's coming." To her dad, she said, "Thanks. For everything."

"Love you, puddin' pie."

Darla appeared. She and Maia unloaded their children, who wanted to pet the ponies, please, please, please. Maia commended herself for not asking Darla if she'd noticed where Brent had gone off to.

"Hurry," Darla said, shooing the kids away from the ponies. "Time to explore the maze and to see Santa."

Her girls let out a loud cheer. TJ joined in, although he didn't understand what all the excitement was about.

Maia's mom and Garret came over as Maia's dad set off with the next group of passengers for another loop of the arena. When Maia attempted to put TJ in his stroller, he squealed and squirmed and kicked in protest. Eventually, she gave up and let him walk.

"Okay, fine. Have it your way." She feared she'd regret her decision.

They wandered past the concession stand where dancers two-stepped to lively holiday classics. Kids and adults alike carried prizes won at the carnival games. Candy canes were clutched in fists. Heads were adorned with reindeer antlers and elf ears. Bags containing fudge and treats purchased from the food vendors dangled from fingers.

"Enjoy yourself," a teenage girl in a Santa cap and with jingle bells on her boots said as she gestured them into the maze. "Don't get lost."

Darla's girls scurried ahead until she called them back. Maia clasped TJ's hand firmly in hers. If not, he'd have run after his cousins.

"Which way next?" Maia's mom called out, letting her granddaughters choose their path.

Despite the teenager's warning, the maze wasn't very complicated. Maia and the rest of them went along even when the girls chose incorrectly. Twice, TJ stopped and tried to climb one of the mechanical reindeer.

"You have plans Christmas Eve?" Darla asked

Maia during a break when the kids were debating whether to take the left or the right fork.

"Hitting the hay by nine. TJ will be up at the crack of dawn, and I figure on arriving early at the folks' to give Mom a hand with breakfast."

Every Christmas, the MacKenzies celebrated by opening gifts together and then having a huge breakfast. That allowed Maia's dad to spend the rest of the day at the shelter helping with the Christmas dinner. Also for Darla and Garret to take the girls to his parents' house for more celebrating.

Her mom usually went to the shelter to assist with cleanup. Maybe Maia and TJ would tag along. And, no, Brent had nothing to do with her decision.

"If I asked Mom to babysit," Darla said, "would you be interested in working an afternoon wedding for me? I have a special request. Just came in while you were on the pony-cart ride, actually."

Maia pursed her mouth with displeasure. "I wasn't planning on working."

"I know. And, believe me, I wouldn't ask if it weren't an emergency."

"Christmas Eve is six days away. You can't find someone else in that time?"

"Maybe. But that's not the problem. It's the client. Well, the bride is the client."

Maia frowned in puzzlement. "I don't understand."

"She needs a date for her brother. Her
younger, nerdy brother who's painfully shy and
can't get a date on his own. The bride specifi-
cally requested someone who'd be sweet and
patient with him. I have no one on staff better
suited for that than you."

"Flattery will get you nowhere," Maia scoffed.

"I'm serious. And in a bind."

"How old is he?"

"Twenty-one. A junior in college. Premed.
Very intelligent, I'm told."

"Yeesh. I'm too old for him."

"Seven years older. That's nothing these days.
Besides, you can pass for twenty-four."

"Again, quit with the flattery. It's not working."

"Please, Maia," Darla pleaded. "The wedding's at Wishing Well Springs. Cash and his
sister are very good to me. They've referred
dozens of clients. I owe them, and this is a big
wedding. A real moneymaker for them. Also,
Cash is getting married the next day. This would
be like a wedding gift to him and his fiancée."

"Your wedding gift to them, not mine."

"They're good to you, too. You've attended
lots of weddings at Wishing Well Springs."

Maia felt herself weakening and tried to remain strong. "I hate leaving TJ. It's Christmas Eve."

"I'll pay extra. Holiday compensation."

"Why does the guy need a date? Would anyone at the wedding really care?"

"It's kind of a sad story. The bride said he was bullied in high school. She claims the experience shaped him and damaged his confidence. She thinks if he attends the wedding with an attractive date, people will notice and that will boost his confidence."

"I see some problems with this plan," Maia argued. "First, it's shallow. People judging him based on the attractiveness of his date? That's terrible. And demeaning to both him and me. Second, I'm sure he needs a lot more than one date to repair years' worth of emotional trauma."

"I agree. But the bride dotes on him and is convinced she's helping. Who am I to argue?" Darla turned puppy-dog eyes on Maia. "She works for the *Payson Tribune*. Your Perfect Plus One could be featured. Imagine what that'll do for business."

"She's bribing you. That's worse."

"No, no. I'm just hoping for a mention in the paper."

"That's almost as bad."

"Maia. I'm in a bind," Darla repeated.

"How does the bride's brother feel about her hiring a wedding date for him? Talk about a blow to one's confidence. She's doing him more damage than good, if you ask me."

"He's going along with it."

Maia studied TJ, who was pestering his grandmother to lift him up onto the mechanical reindeer. He was young. Christmas Eve was just another night to him. Maia was the one attaching significance to it. The extra money would come in handy, too. After this, she could pay off the custom competition saddle. No more scrimping and saving.

"All right," she relented. "I just hope I don't regret this."

Darla smothered her in a tight hug. "Thank you, thank you."

Santa came into view at the maze's exit. The red-faced man hired to play the part wore the customary red suit, complete with matching cap and long white beard. Four-foot Christmas trees flanked each side of the throne, their lights twinkling in sync to tinny-sounding recorded music. Eager kids and their parents waited on a red carpet leading up to the throne. A man took pictures with a fancy camera while a woman collected money.

Maia was reminded of the wedding where Brent had kissed her cheek beneath the mistletoe, and her heart executed a series of hops and skips. What if he did stay in Payson? They might indeed have a potential future. She wouldn't mind if he traveled for work. She'd be supportive.

And then, suddenly, he was there. He and Channing approached from the other side of the arena, the two of them talking quietly. About the judging-certification sponsorship?

At that same moment, TJ spied Brent and took off stomping through the soft dirt of the arena.

"TJ! Come back." Maia went after him. Sometimes, she swore she spent half her life running after her son.

She wasn't fast enough, and he reached Brent well ahead of her. A string of gibberish followed as TJ hugged Brent's knee.

"What's up, pal? Here to see Santa?" Brent bent down and lifted TJ into his arms without a trace of the awkwardness from the night of the Christmas tree lighting at Bear Creek Ranch.

Maia came to a standstill and stared as TJ put his face nose to nose with Brent's and said, "Be doo doo."

"Be doo doo to you, too. Whatever that means."

TJ hugged Brent around the neck.

Maia's heart dissolved into a puddle. This was the kind of man she'd hope to find. One who delighted in seeing TJ, not considered him an irritating and unwanted responsibility.

She closed the distance between her and Brent. Channing seemed to disappear, for he was suddenly nowhere around.

"Let me take him," she said to Brent.

TJ was having none of it and gripped Brent tighter.

Brent smiled. "He's no trouble."

Why hadn't some woman nabbed this guy already? Had he been too focused on his career and then too down in the dumps after losing it?

She glanced over her shoulder at the line of people waiting to see Santa. Darla watched Maia and Brent intently from her place near the back. She wasn't the only one. Maia's mom watched her and Brent, too, her delighted expression in stark contrast to Darla's annoyance.

"I should…go." Maia hitched a thumb at the line.

"Yeah." Brent hefted a complaining TJ from his arms to Maia's. "We don't want to upset the boss."

Ah. He'd also spotted Darla.

"She can't get too mad at me. I just agreed to do her a big favor and work a wedding Christmas Eve at Wishing Well Springs."

Brent's brow furrowed. "You did? She asked me last week if I'd work the same wedding."

He and Maia stared at each other. Then, in unison, they turned to stare at Darla.

What had happened to her sister's insistence on Maia and Brent keeping their distance? What about their own similar commitment?

"We can do this," Brent said.

"Yeah. We can," Maia agreed.

One wedding. A large, crowded wedding. Surely they could manage to avoid each other for a few hours.

BRENT STARED AT HIMSELF in the bunkhouse bathroom mirror and adjusted his bolo tie. Freshly shaved and showered, in his recently dry-cleaned Western suit, he supposed he'd meet his wedding date's expectations.

Since the night of the Cowboy Christmas Jamboree, he and Maia had avoided discussing the Christmas Eve wedding they were both attending. An easy feat as they hadn't seen much of each other. From what Ansel had told Brent, she'd been busy. As a result, Brent had led almost every trail ride.

His hard work appeared to be paying off. Ansel had mentioned Brent was doing well and fitting in. Several clients had left positive feedback about Brent on the Bear Creek Ranch web page.

Did fitting in refer to Mountainside Stables,

Bear Creek Ranch or the community in general? Whichever, Brent had taken the praise to heart. As a result, he'd had a good week. The black cloud continued to follow him wherever he went, but it lagged well behind.

This past Sunday, he'd attended a holiday open house at Channing's parents' home. Brent had initially gone out of a sense of duty—a sense of duty he'd forgotten all about soon after arriving with a box of candy for his hosts. Channing's parents were warm and friendly and made everyone feel like a long-lost relative. Brent knew several other people there, either from the rodeo world or from having met them at the bull-riding practice the other night. For once, he hadn't felt like a stranger.

One plus of attending, he'd gotten to know Channing's dad, Burle Pearce, on a more personal level. Burle had mentioned the judging certification sponsorship when he and Brent had a moment alone and assured Brent that Rim Country would gain as much from the arrangement as Brent. His argument was convincing, and Brent was leaning toward accepting.

Javier and Rowdy had been doing their part adding to Brent's sense of inclusion. They'd dragged him on their outings whenever Brent was free and insisted he eat breakfast with them every morning at the kitchen. Brent was certainly less lonely than he had been the previous two Christmases—less lonely and more like his old self.

He'd even begun interacting with the members of his online support group. Not a lot. A response here and there to someone's post. He'd even asked a question about medication and which were the best. If he did wind up going to a doctor, he wanted to be prepared.

Could he be on the road to recovery or was this a temporary reprieve? Brent was a realist and knew his emotional state remained tenuous at best. He was, and might always be, an elephant walking a tightrope. One misstep, one distraction, one shift in balance, and he'd fall crashing to the ground. But if he concentrated, kept his eye trained on the platform at the end of the tightrope, he just might make it all the way across.

Where did he go from here? Remain at Mountainside Stables in a job with little advancement potential but was steady employment and a place he felt safe? Or did he pursue a judging certification? A move not without risks, but one that could lead to a whole new career.

He'd failed at his last one. Miserably. He could fail again. What if Brent wasn't good enough? Talented enough? Dedicated enough?

Lucky enough? He could hear his dad's voice berating him.

You don't have what it takes. No son of mine is a quitter.

Brent squared his shoulders and continued to study his reflection in the mirror. With sudden clarity, he realized he wanted to stay in Payson regardless of which path he chose. He'd been afraid to admit as much for fear of having his hopes dashed again. If that happened, his depression would return worse than before.

Or not. The last month had changed him, given him courage and motivation to, as the saying went, get back in the saddle. No reason he couldn't continue working at Mountainside Stables and judging practices at Rim Country while obtaining his certification. And, if he chose, go on the periodic gig for Your Perfect Plus One.

It was a lot. He'd be busy. But Brent wasn't afraid of hard work. In a few months, he'd be able to pay down a good chunk of his debts and have enough money to purchase his mom's plane ticket to Arizona.

His life could, might, *would* come together. He just needed to stay on the tightrope and not lose his balance. That included maintaining the status quo with Maia. For now. He wanted more, dreamed of more, but he'd have to wait. And if she found someone else in the meantime, then they clearly weren't meant to be.

He quickly shoved that last very unpleasant thought aside before it affected his mood. Stay in the moment, he told himself, repeating something he heard a lot in his online group.

Running a comb through his hair one last time, he collected his shaving bag and headed out of the bathroom to the bunkhouse's main room.

Whistles and catcalls greeted him from his four bunk mates.

"Aren't you pretty," Javier joked.

Brent glared at him, hiding his amusement. "Don't you have someplace to be?"

The dining hall had closed early today so that the employees could have Christmas Eve off. Guests at the ranch were either driving to town or eating in their cabins. The staff would return early tomorrow morning for breakfast and lunch services, then be released after cleanup to spend the rest of Christmas with family and friends.

Mountainside Stables was closed and wouldn't reopen until the twenty-sixth, giving Brent the entire day off and allowing him to attend Cash's wedding at Wishing Well Springs. He hadn't accepted the invitation until the open house at Channing's parents' where Cash and his lovely fiancée had refused to take no for an answer. Yet another feeling of inclusion.

"I'm heading to Syndee's in an hour," Javier said. "Her best friend from high school is in town for Christmas."

"Ah! Getting the best friend's approval." Brent slipped his heavy coat on over his suit jacket and plunked his cowboy hat onto his head.

Javier groaned. "I swear, the two of them are like this." He crossed his first and second fingers. "If I don't pass muster, Syndee will kick me to the curb."

"If that happens," Jimmy Roy, the bunk-house's oldest resident said, "give her my number, will you?"

"No way, amigo. She's too good for you."

They all laughed at that.

"Don't wait up for me, guys." Brent swung open the bunkhouse door and stepped out onto the stoop.

A blast of cold air hit him square in the face. Tilting his head back, he stared up at the late-afternoon sky, a dense blanket of gunmetal gray. Tiny snowflakes drifted downward to land on his face where they melted on contact. If the light dusting gained momentum and morphed into a snowstorm, it was possible they'd wake up tomorrow to a white Christmas.

He met his date at their prearranged place outside a bookstore in a small strip mall. They shook hands and introduced themselves. Olive was an attractive fortysomething HR director at the *Payson Gazette*.

"I work with the bride," she told Brent. "I'm her supervisor."

He smiled. "I read that in your bio."

She blushed. "Yes. I forgot. This is all new to me."

"You'll do fine." He gestured toward her car, marveling that he was the experienced one attempting to make a client comfortable. "Shall we?" They'd previously agreed she'd drive to Wishing Well Springs.

"I suppose you think it's silly, me requesting a younger man for a wedding date," Olive said once they were on the road.

"Not in the least." He'd learned during his employment at Your Perfect Plus One that clients had all sorts of reasons for their date choices.

He took her elbow on the walk from the parking area to the wedding barn. Strings of white lights climbed tree trunks to weave among the branches above, glittering like stars in the light snowfall. While creating a beautiful picture, there would be no outdoor receiving line or dining tonight. Even giant space heaters would be useless against the frigid air.

Inside the barn, they entered a Christmas wedding wonderland. A majestic tree stood to their left. Beside it sat a table decorated with curling ribbons and holding the guest book. Olive stopped to sign their names. More red ribbons adorned the pews and poinsettia plants had been placed throughout the room. Piped-in holiday music floated on the air along with a hint of pine.

Brent escorted Olive up the aisle. She chose a pew midway on the bride's side, and they excused themselves as they squeezed past an elderly couple on their way to the vacant seats in the middle.

"Is this all right?" Olive asked.

"Fine."

Brent immediately glanced about for Maia and saw no sign of her. Was she not coming? Then he remembered her date was the bride's younger brother. The family often entered last, shortly before the bride made her appearance. Maia was likely with the bride's brother and due any moment.

A set of parents and their young daughter entered Brent and Olive's pew from the far side, the adults smiling as they sat.

"We're friends of Shelby's," the woman said, referring to the bride.

"Olive and Brad." Olive pointed to herself and Brent.

"Nice to meet you," Brent said, responding to his fake name.

As Olive shared a story about working with the bride, Brent leafed through the paper program. Like before, the reception was being held at the Joshua Tree Inn next door. The same place as that first wedding where Brent had met Maia. The similarities between then and tonight were adding up.

Except back then he'd seen her merely as an attractive wedding guest. Now she was someone he knew, liked, admired and respected. Someone he could care for a lot if things were different.

Olive barely paused to breathe as she talked about her teenage son—she worried he spent too much time playing video games—and her sister, who'd apparently married a perfect ten. Brent sensed a slight trace of jealousy between Olive and her sister. Was that the reason she'd wanted to appear in the wedding photos with a younger man?

Inside his suit jacket pocket, his phone buzzed once, alerting him of a text message. He checked it only when Olive said, "Go on—I don't mind."

The message was from his mom, wishing him a merry Christmas and sending her love. He fired off a quick reply, returning the sentiment and saying he'd call tomorrow.

Should he text his dad, too? Brent returned his phone to his suit pocket. His dad would probably say something upsetting, and Brent was feeling too good to take any chances.

Several elegantly dressed individuals appeared and walked down the aisle, before sitting in the front pews on the groom's side.

"Looks like the family's arriving," Olive whispered in Brent's ear.

More people strolled past, their expressions ranging from serious to beaming. Brent forced himself to appear mildly interested and not waiting in eager anticipation for Maia.

"Here comes the bride's brother," Olive said. "Wow, his date is really pretty."

Brent couldn't help himself and turned to stare. Maia wore the same outfit she had to the wedding where they'd first met. Another similarity.

One big difference today was his heart raced. No, that was incorrect. His heart soared at the sight of her—a vison in shimmering gold, her silky brown hair tumbling past her shoulders to gather in soft, touchable waves.

She glided up the aisle alongside her date as

if in slow motion. When she passed Brent, their gazes locked and lingered until continuing to do so was impossible.

"Do you know her?" Olive asked.

"No." Brent shook his head.

The single word was all he could manage, his throat having gone completely dry upon seeing Maia.

He hadn't fallen for a woman in a very long time. But not so long that he'd forgotten the sensation. Rather than deny or resist, as he should, he closed his eyes and embraced the heady rush.

CHAPTER THIRTEEN

"DO YOU KNOW HIM?" Maia's date, Simon, asked once they were seated in the front pew on the bride's side.

"Um…" Should she lie? Hard to explain her prolonged staring session with Brent other than with the truth. "Yes. We've met before. At work. My day job. I wasn't sure at first it was him."

A version of the truth. Thankfully, Simon seemed satisfied and didn't question her further.

He really was a nice young man. Insecure and shy—Darla hadn't exaggerated. Every time he spoke to Maia, he swallowed first as if gathering his courage, his Adam's apple bobbing.

"Does that happen a lot?" He swallowed. "Running into people you know?"

"Not usually," Maia said. "I mostly attend weddings for out-of-town couples."

"We're not from out of town."

She didn't admit this date had been a bit of an emergency and instead offered a vague response. "It all depends."

Maia spoke low so as not to be overheard. As

it turned out, the people in their immediate vicinity weren't paying attention. They fidgeted in anticipation and chatted excitedly, waiting on the start of the wedding.

"Cool" was all Simon said, then he tugged at his tie.

Maia suspected he rarely wore a suit and felt uncomfortable. The complete opposite of Brent, who carried off formal wear with the same ease he did jeans, boots and a denim jacket.

He may have suffered from depression, but that hadn't affected other aspects of his personality. The confidence he'd gained from years of competing professionally had stayed with him on some level and was evident in how well he handled himself in new situations. Maia took that as a sign he possessed the strength and determination to conquer his problem, even if he didn't realize it himself. Yet.

Her and Simon's pew filled up with his family—his grandmother and grandfather, a cousin and the cousin's husband.

The parents came next. The groom's mother wore a flattering dress of deep Christmas green adorned with a red rose corsage. An usher escorted the bride's mother. Her dress was of a similar color but trimmed with gold. Once the parents were seated, the groom, his best man and two groomsmen emerged from behind a corner to stand at the altar.

The groom smiled nervously, as most grooms do, and exchanged words with the minister. His best man—a brother, given their strong resemblance—put an arm around his shoulders.

All at once, the piped-in music faded to silence, and the air filled with excited tension. A gray-haired guitarist sitting on a stool to the left of the altar began playing a short melody of traditional Christmas songs with flourishing strokes of his fingers, ending with "Here Comes the Bride."

Everyone stood, and then the bride materialized at the end of the aisle, a Christmas angel in a snow-white wedding dress adorned with matching fake-fur collar. A sheer veil like liquid ice hung from a crown of lilies on her head to well past her waist.

Gasps of delight filled the wedding barn, and Maia pressed a hand to her mouth, struck by the stunning vision strolling elegantly down the aisle on the arm of a middle-aged man. Maia and Luke had talked about a spring wedding. In hindsight, *she'd* talked about weddings. Luke had simply gone along. She should have realized something was amiss with them, but she'd believed herself in love and been blinded by her desire to marry and start a family. In Luke's defense—no, in her defense—he'd treated her well and been attentive. Until he didn't and wasn't.

She tamped down the twinge of sadness that surfaced at the memory of her former fiancé. It quickly vanished. Maia had learned the hard way not to dwell on the past.

Was this how Brent felt when he struggled with his moods? Only, he couldn't shake off his negative emotions as easily as Maia did hers. Even during her most difficult periods, she'd been able to keep moving forward.

She'd had TJ to focus on and worry about and care for. He'd been—he was—her reason for overcoming her struggles. Brent didn't have that same motivation, none that he'd told her about. There was no special woman in his life, he was estranged from his dad and half siblings and he lived halfway across the country from his mom. According to him, he'd burned bridges these past two years with all his friends save Channing. And while employed, he had no solid plans further ahead than tomorrow.

Despite his difficulties, he showed up every day for work—two jobs and soon to be three—plus helped her with Snapple's training. That spoke highly of him and his drive to get better.

Was it any wonder she admired him? More

than admired him, though she wasn't ready to put a name to the emotions growing inside her.

"Your sister is beautiful," she whispered to Simon. The bride had reached the altar and smiled radiantly at her soon-to-be husband.

"Yeah. I guess." After a moment, he said, "Mom wanted me in the wedding."

"I'm not surprised."

From Maia's experience, a lot of grooms asked their future brother-in-law to be a grooms-man or an usher. Then again, this groom could have several brothers and best friends. Or his parents had applied pressure.

"I didn't want to," Simon mumbled.

His shyness. Of course. That made sense.

Maia was quiet after that, watching the beautiful wedding unfold. She couldn't help imagining herself in the bride's place, gazing into the eyes of the man she loved and reciting her vows.

A soft, warm feeling filled her chest. Despite all she'd been through, the disappointment and betrayal that might have soured her on love forever, she still believed in happy endings and finding her soul mate.

The touching ceremony came to a close with the newlyweds sharing a happy kiss. Cheers and applause rose from the guests. Once the couple and the wedding party had walked back down the aisle, the first pews began to empty. The parents went first, followed by the rest of the family. Maia and Simon were among the last.

Near the entrance, he was swept up by his mother who, giving Maia a friendly but brief hello, guided him over to the wedding party. Maia had expected this—the newlyweds and their families were forming the receiving line. She wouldn't be part of that, naturally, having just met Simon.

Instead, she moved away to a secluded place along the wall where she could watch. After checking her phone, for no reason other than she was standing there doing nothing, she dropped it back into her clutch and looked up—to catch Brent's gaze across the large entryway. She went still, watching until he and his date entered the receiving line.

Maia shouldn't have cared; she *didn't* care, she told herself, but studied his date, nonetheless. The very attractive woman was probably fifteen years older than Brent. Funny, they were both on dates with people either much younger or older than them. Then again, Maia had noticed all manner of age combinations at the many weddings she'd attended.

He gestured for his date to precede him through the line. At the end, they blended in with the other guests, and Maia lost track of Brent.

Just as well, she assured herself. They'd promised Darla to be on their best behavior.

"Aren't you Simon's date?" a woman beside her queried.

"Yes." Maia produced a smile.

"I'm his neighbor. My husband and I have lived next door to his parents since Simon was just a tiny tyke."

"Oh. That's great." They shook hands. "A pleasure."

"Don't take this wrong, but you're a little older than the women he usually dates. Not that he dates a lot from what I hear, or ever has."

"Age is merely a number." Maia amplified her smile. She wasn't "going there" with this woman. "Personality matters more, and Simon is a sweet guy."

"Yes. He is." The woman appeared disappointed and cut her conversation with Maia short. "My husband is waiting for me. See you at the reception."

"Looking forward to it."

The woman had no sooner disappeared than Maia felt a presence behind her, one her senses instantly recognized. Brent.

She turned to find him not a foot from her. "You shouldn't be here," she said in a murmur.

"My date forgot her mittens." He held them up.

"Ah."

"You handled that well."

"The neighbor? Hmm." Maia rolled her eyes. "She was fishing for some juicy gossip. I didn't bite."

Brent nodded at the receiving line. "Looks like the last of the guests have gone through. You're back on the clock."

"This hasn't been my worst date by any means. I was telling the truth when I said he's a sweet guy."

"I'd better get these mittens to my date."

"You'd better."

Brent hesitated. For a moment, Maia thought he might reach for her cheek. But he didn't and melted away.

She sighed. They shouldn't have spoken; their dates might have noticed. And if they were caught, no good could come of it.

Eventually, Simon meandered over, his gait lanky and loose-jointed. He was joined by his sister Shelby.

"I just wanted to meet you," she gushed and took both of Maia's hands in hers. "Darla spoke so highly of you."

"Congratulations on your wedding," Maia said. "Your dress is stunning, and the ceremony was lovely."

"Thank you."

"Simon." The bride turned to her brother.

"Go ask Dad to bring the car around, would you?"

"Okay," he grumbled and shuffled off.

Maia pegged Shelby to be about ten years older than Simon. She was probably used to bossing him around, and he was used to doing her bidding.

Once Simon was out of earshot, Shelby leaned in close to Maia and said, "I appreciate you being so nice to him."

"I've enjoyed getting to know him."

Shelby glanced over at Simon talking with their dad. When she faced Maia again, her expression had become serious. "He has a tiny crush on you."

"Really? I had no idea. We only just met."

"Yes, but I can tell. Simon's easy to read. So, please be careful. He's very sensitive."

"I will. You have nothing to worry about." Seeing Simon return, she flashed him a smile. "Hi, there."

"Thanks." The bride winked at her, mussed her brother's hair, which elicited a groan, and then danced away in a swirl of white satin.

"Ready?" Maia took hold of his arm.

Simon's eyes went wide, and he grinned like he'd won first prize at the science fair.

Mission accomplished, thought Maia. She'd

be careful not to encourage Simon, but she was also glad she could help boost his confidence.

AT THE RECEPTION, Maia and Simon sat with both sets of his grandparents, his uncle and great-aunt. Normally, the date of the bride's brother would be someone well-known to the family, or at least not a complete stranger. As a result, Maia found herself the subject of much curiosity and was put on the spot more than once. Forced to improvise, she received little assistance from Simon.

"How do you feel about dating a younger man? What do your parents think of it?"

"You know Simon's premed at college. He won't be ready to have children for years."

"You say you met at a sci-fi convention? Were you wearing one of those costumes?"

Maia answered those questions she could and dodged the rest. She ignored the many raised eyebrows and whispers behind the shield of hands. No one had ill intentions, rather they cared about Simon. They probably worried she'd break his heart and were only looking out for him.

Maia wished she could offer reassurances. She'd be out of his life in a matter of hours and soon after that a distant memory. People would point at the few candid wedding pictures in which she appeared and ponder, "Who was that woman with Simon? Did they ever go out again?" Eventually, she'd become a random guest with no identity.

Following a delicious dinner, cake was served and toasts made. Simon reluctantly participated in a hilarious Christmas-themed skit—something he'd agreed to only to appease his sister and their parents.

As the guests laughed and played along, Maia allowed her gaze to roam the room. She wasn't searching for Brent. No. Absolutely not. And if you believed that, she had some ocean front property in Arizona for sale.

There he was! At a table near the far wall, chatting amiably with his date while they watched the skit. He abruptly stopped when he spotted Maia staring. Her face went hot, and she glanced away. Fortunately for her, the skit ended at that moment. None of the applauding and laughing guests paid her the slightest attention. Or so she'd thought.

"Are you all right, my dear?" Simon's great-aunt asked. "You look a little flushed."

"I'm fine." Hardly.

"A bit too much champagne?"

"Maybe." She'd had only one glass.

"Wasn't the wedding lovely? Christmas Eve. Who'd have guessed?"

"It was very lovely. And the best way I can think of to spend Christmas Eve."

A large group of merrymakers pulled Simon aside, so Maia continued engaging his delightful great-aunt in conversation.

"I had a June wedding." The elderly woman sighed wistfully. "We were married outdoors in my parents' garden. The roses were in full bloom. My mother made my bouquet."

"Sounds wonderful."

"We had a four-piece band and danced the night away." She sighed again. "I so miss dancing. My Joseph died three years ago. That man could trip the light fantastic."

"Tell me about him."

Maia listened, enjoying every moment of Simon's great-aunt's stories, until he returned and quenched his thirst—or perhaps hid his embarrassment—with a long drink of water.

While his great-aunt was chatting with another guest at the table, he leaned in and whispered to Maia, "Aunt Edna is a talker. I hope you don't mind."

"Are you kidding? She's a treasure." Maia suddenly missed her late grandmother.

"Yeah. She's cool in her way."

Maia smiled at him. He may be young and unworldly, but he clearly adored his great-aunt. That made him a-okay in her book.

"You're an all right guy, Simon."

He swallowed and blushed and looked away. When, after a moment, he returned his gaze to her, his expression was filled with childlike earnestness. "I don't suppose…"

"What?"

"That, um…" He grinned sheepishly. "That we could go out sometime? For real."

"Oh, Simon." She reached over and patted his hand. Thank goodness his sister had warned Maia of Simon's tiny crush. Otherwise, she'd have been flummoxed and ill prepared. "Under any other circumstances, I'd say yes. But it's against company policy."

Actually, she'd stretched the truth. Darla's employment contracts contained a clause prohibiting employees seeing clients, but only for the first ninety days post wedding date. This was Maia's way of letting Simon down gently.

His features crumpled. "Okay. I get it."

"You're going to meet an amazing girl one of these days," she said. "Trust me. She'll see the real you and fall head over heels."

He chuckled mirthlessly. "Right."

Maia patted his hand again. "You'll see."

At that moment, the DJ announced the father/bride dance. The sentimental pop song he played was a special request by the bride's father. Midway through the song, the bride's new husband cut in to claim her. Applause followed. Maia, along with several others nearby, wiped away a tear.

"Would you like to dance?" Simon asked Maia three songs later.

"I'd love to."

She rose from her seat. Simon's great-aunt Edna had turned her chair around in order to watch the dancers and tapped her toe in time to the music. Maybe he'd ask her to dance next when he and Maia returned. She hoped so.

On the dance floor, she slipped into Simon's arms. He wasn't the most skilled dancer, but he managed not to stomp on her feet. A far cry from when she and Brent had danced, and he'd guided her across the floor with a confidence that almost had her swooning.

Perhaps Simon would loosen up when the DJ played more lively party numbers.

"Excuse me," he said when he inadvertently propelled Maia into another dancer.

Maia spun. When Brent's face appeared inches from hers, she gasped.

"My fault," he said and smiled at her.

She took a wrong step, and her knee buckled. It was Brent who caught her by the arm, not Simon.

"You okay?"

"Y-yes. Thanks." Aware that people on the

dance floor were watching, Maia returned to Simon's arms and, assuming the lead, danced them away from Brent and his date to the opposite side of the dance floor.

"That's the guy you know," Simon said. "Isn't it?"

"Yes." She tilted her head to the side. "Sorry about that. The dance floor's crowded."

"My mom saw you talking to him earlier."

She had? Darn it. Maia and Brent should have been more careful. "Um, yes. We said hello."

When the song ended, Simon escorted Maia to their table. She was more than a little relieved when he didn't suggest a second dance. The close encounter with Brent had left her unsteady.

Ridiculous. Absurd. She wasn't a teenager pining over a heartthrob.

Yeah, tell that to the butterflies playing soccer in her stomach.

The bride appeared at their table. "Come on, Simon. The photographer wants some pictures of the family in the courtyard outside with all the Christmas lights. You don't mind, do you?" she asked Maia.

"Absolutely not. Go. Have fun."

Simon groaned but went along with his sister and their grandparents. Maia expected the bride to ask Great-Aunt Edna as well, but she didn't.

Maia suffered a pang of sympathy when the elderly woman stared after them, intense longing on her face. The next moment, she resumed watching the dancers, no doubt remembering her late husband.

A few minutes passed, and Maia spotted Brent striding purposely toward her. She gripped the edge of the table. What in heaven's name was he doing?

He stopped at the table, a gentle smile on his face that had her wishing they were alone and not in the middle of a crowded room.

"Would you care to dance?" He held out his hand.

Not to her. Rather, to Great-Aunt Edna. Maia blinked in surprise, then smiled when she realized that had been his intention the entire time.

"Me?" the elderly woman twittered.

"I saw you tapping your toe and thought *that lady needs a partner.*"

"Surely, a handsome fellow like yourself is here with someone. Your wife?"

"A date. But she doesn't mind. She said she wanted to sit this one out."

"Then I accept." Giggling, Simon's great-aunt took Brent's hand, and he helped her to her feet. "My name's Edna, by the way."

"Brad."

They started toward the dance floor, but not before Brent, a.k.a. Brad, sent Maia a wink.

She stared after them, her heart melting into a warm puddle. Out of everyone here, Brent had noticed Great-Aunt Edna longingly watching the dancers and tapping her toe. Out of everyone here, only he'd asked her to dance. Such a small gesture that required little effort. And, yet it meant a great deal.

He was kind and compassionate. He acted in ways that truly counted. He cared. He also owned his mistakes. Granted, he'd gotten himself in serious debt, but he was diligently eliminating that debt by working three jobs. He wasn't shirking his responsibilities or looking for a free ride.

He acknowledged he had a problem, and, she believed, he was on the verge of seeking professional help. He'd joined that online group, had finally sought information about the men's group at the shelter and reached out to residents like Pete—the last two according to her dad. Brent had also opened up to her and Channing, which was a big step for someone as private as Brent.

If Maia let herself, she'd fall head over heels for him.

Who was she kidding? She'd already fallen a little.

No, he wasn't perfect. Neither was she. Minor flaws aside, Brent had all the important qualities Maia wanted in the man she married. The qualities she'd once thought her former fiancé had until she'd learned different. Luke wouldn't have asked an elderly woman to dance, not unless Maia had nagged him. He'd cheated on her. Twice.

Don't let Brent get away.

The thought came from nowhere. Wait, not nowhere. It came from the place inside Maia where she hid her deepest secrets.

Tell him how you feel before it's too late.

She should. He'd say he wasn't right for her and not in a good place. Maia didn't care. She had everything that mattered in life. A happy, healthy son, her family, a small but comfortable home, a job she loved and the chance to follow her dreams.

He'd say their employment contracts prohibited them from dating. Maia would dismiss his concerns. She'd have her saddle paid off soon and could quit Your Perfect Plus One. They'd be free to explore what the future held for them.

They just needed to be patient a while longer and stay the course. Easy-peasy.

Tell him, the voice repeated.

Should she? Maia had no doubts Brent harbored similar feelings for her.

Tomorrow. She'd find the right moment to talk with him. Or tonight. After the wedding.

Seeing him and Great-Aunt Edna approaching, she broke into a wide, happy grin that must have conveyed the entire contents of her heart because Brent responded with a broad, happy grin of his own.

Why wait until tomorrow?

He helped Great-Aunt Edna into her seat.

"Thank you so much, young man. You made my evening."

"My pleasure. Merry Christmas, ma'am."

His glance met Maia's, and she saw in his eyes he wanted to ask her to dance. He wouldn't, though. He'd resist.

Not Maia. Unable to hold back the flood of emotions surging inside her, she popped out of her chair and snatched her clutch off the table.

"Brent, do you have a minute? There's something I need to tell you."

He hesitated. Rules were rules.

She was the rebel between the two of them. "It's important."

"Okay."

"Do you two know each other?" Great-Aunt Edna asked.

Maia didn't reply. Neither did she look behind her to confirm that Brent was following or to question her actions. Walking on air, she wove a path through the tables to the dining room exit, confident her and Brent's lives were about to change.

CHAPTER FOURTEEN

BRENT WAS CRAZY. He had no business following Maia out of the wedding reception. They'd agreed to avoid each other tonight, and he'd already broken that vow once by seeking her out earlier at Wishing Well Springs. Then again when he'd asked Edna to dance—something Olive had actually suggested when they'd seen the elderly lady tapping her foot.

But the second Maia's dark brown eyes lit up at the sight of him, his brain had short-circuited. He'd barely noticed returning Edna to her chair. He'd seen only Maia. When she'd said she had something to tell him, he'd followed, his misfiring brain sending go-go-go signals to his legs.

What did that say about the intensity of his feelings for her?

He taken the long way around the room so as not to draw attention to themselves and then met up with her outside in the hall.

She led him past the hostess podium outside the dining room entrance, and around a corner. Once hidden from view, she pivoted to face him, their faces close, their lips a millimeter away from kissing. Brent tried not to think about that.

"What's up?" he asked.

"I, um…" She faltered, a blush coloring her cheeks. "I thought I knew what I was going to say."

"Are you okay?" Perhaps he'd misunderstood. "Is it your date? Did he say or do something inappropriate?"

"What? No. He's sweet. This has nothing to do with him." She drew in a long breath. "You made Edna's night. Probably her entire week."

"This is about her?" Now Brent was confused.

"You're a nice person, Brent. You saw she wanted to dance and asked her when no one else did."

"Actually, Olive suggested it. But I could relate to Edna. I know what it's like to sit on the outside looking in. I've been doing a lot of that the past two years."

"Not so much lately." Maia placed a hand on his arm.

"No, not so much."

"Brent." She paused again. "Seeing you with Edna got me to thinking. I realize the time's not right for us, and the last thing I want to do is pressure you."

"Where is this leading, Maia?"

"You're…you're the kind of man I've been hoping to find. I realized that tonight. And I wanted you to know I'm willing to wait. For however long it takes."

"You are."

He took a moment to let what she'd said sink in. They'd discussed their mutual attraction and that the timing couldn't be worse. He'd told her she deserved someone with their life together, not in shambles.

Yet, she stood here with him, bearing her heart and saying she'd wait no matter how long.

"I'm still broken, Maia."

"You're making progress."

"I may not be that man you've been waiting for when I come out on the other side."

"I don't believe for one second you aren't the same man you were two years ago before you walked away from rodeo or the man you'll be two in two years' time. Plus or minus a couple of tweaks. People don't change that drastically."

He stared into her eyes. She was the kind of woman he'd been hoping to find, too. Regardless, he held back.

"Call it ego," he said, "or pride, but I need to have a good job before we get serious."

"You're working on that."

"I'd rather be further along in the process and not buried in credit card bills."

"Like I said, I'm willing to wait. I just needed to tell you before I lost my nerve."

His chest filled with a range of emotions he hadn't experienced in a long, long time. Joy. Gratitude. Optimism. Hope. Anticipation for the future.

"You have no idea what it means for me to hear you say that."

"You're wrong." She stood on tiptoes. "I do have an idea."

"I don't deserve you."

"You're wrong about that, too."

And then, her lips were on his, pliant and tender and giving. Brent abandoned resisting and wrapped his arms around her. This was the magic he'd been chasing his entire life. Not a world-championship title.

For the first time since quitting rodeo, Brent wasn't just wanting to change, he was ready. He had a reason to fight. A future to run toward rather than shy away from. Because of Maia.

The kiss came to an end, but they didn't break apart.

"I'm going to join a men's group at the shelter," he said, his lips finding and nuzzling her ear.

"You are?"

"I suddenly have good reason."

"Me?" Her eyes twinkled.

"You. And Rim Country Rodeo Arena."

"You accepted the judging sponsorship!"

"I planned on telling Channing Monday." He traced the curve of her cheek with his fingertips. "I may not wait now."

"Oh, Brent. I'm so happy for you."

"Yeah, well, I've got my work cut out for me. Professionally and personally."

"You can do this. I have complete faith in you." She kissed him hard.

Faith. He couldn't recall his father ever speaking the word. His mother, yes, during the early days of his career. Not recently. Only Maia.

"Sweetheart." He brushed his lips across hers. "There's something more I want to tell you."

Should he? Was it too soon? How would she react?

"What?" she breathed, her face aglow with expectation.

"I—"

"Mindy!" A squeaky male voice cut him off. Mindy?

Maia pulled away from Brent and looked past him, her eyes growing wide with horror and dismay. "Simon. I'm… Oh, God." She gasped.

Simon? Brent turned, momentarily confused at the figure staring at them accusingly. The confusion faded quickly. Clarity dawned with a vengeance, and he froze.

Maia's wedding date had rounded the corner and stood facing them, his expression a combination of shock and anguish. "Mindy," he repeated, this time on a whine.

"Simon, I am so, so sorry. I didn't mean..." She squeezed past Brent. "I can explain. Let's go back to the reception."

"You ditched me," he said in the same whiney voice. "I waited for you and waited for you and when you didn't show I came searching. I thought you'd left."

"Again," Maia pleaded. "I'm sorry." She reached out a hand to him. He glared at it as if she held a snake and retreated a step. "Please, Simon. I didn't ditch you. I..." She bit back a sob.

Brent wanted to kick himself. Or worse. What had they done? How could he have let this happen? Uncertain of what he'd say and consumed by guilt, he started forward. Maia shook her head and mouthed, "Don't."

"You're supposed to be my date," Simon accused, his demeanor visibly changing to anger.

"Hey, pal," Brent said, attempting a congenial tone. No way would he let Maia take the blame for what happened or the brunt of her date's wrath. "This was my fault. Don't be mad at her."

"Who are you?"

"My question exactly." Another voice entered

the fray. "And what the heck are you doing hiding behind the corner with my brother's date?"

Just when things couldn't get worse, the bride had joined them, a white whirlpool of indignation. Her keen gaze instantly assessed the scene, and she obviously reached a conclusion not far off the mark for she fired a full arsenal of invisible daggers at Brent and Maia.

Brent placed a palm on the small of Maia's back and propelled her out from behind the corner. Staying where they were made them look like a pair of petty criminals—which maybe they were no better than.

Darla would agree. She'd be furious and with good cause. Why hadn't Brent told Maia no when she asked to speak with him? Then none of this would have happened, and they'd all be in the reception, dancing and celebrating.

There was only one choice. One course of action. Brent had to fix this and fix it now. And, in the process, spare Maia from any repercussions.

"I'M BRENT." He stepped forward. "Brent Hayes. I work with Maia at Mountainside Stables. And Your Perfect Plus One," he added.

"Who's Maia?" the bride and her brother asked at the same time.

"Me," Maia said. "I… Mindy is the name I use for…weddings."

The bride clamped a hand to her forehead "This is completely unacceptable. You can bet I'm going to call the owner."

"I understand."

"Don't blame her," Brent said. "I'm the one responsible."

Maia faced him. "No, you aren't. It was me." She swung back to the bride. "I asked him out here to talk."

"You were doing a lot more than talking," Simon accused.

The bride fired a second round of invisible daggers at Brent and Maia. "Guess you aren't just coworkers."

Maia answered before Brent could. "I'll see that Darla issues you a full refund."

"Darn right I'll get a full refund." The bride put an arm around her brother's shoulders. "Poor Simon's mortified."

He stiffened with annoyance, whether from his sister's show of sympathy or at being the center of attention. Brent wasn't sure which and hated himself for the part he'd played.

"I'll speak to Darla," he said. "Make this right."

"Speak to Darla about what?" a voice asked.

Everyone whirled in unison to see the newest member of their gathering: Brent's date, Olive.

Swell. Could this fiasco get any worse?

"Brian?" Confusion clouded her eyes.

"Olive." He cleared his throat. "This is Maia. She's my coworker. And my friend."

"*Girl*friend," the bride answered sharply.

Olive blinked. "I thought she was your brother's date?"

"She is. His hired date. And I'm guessing Brian or Brent is yours."

"He is." Olive went quiet.

Brent couldn't feel more like a heel if he tried. "Olive, I'm sorry."

"*Is* she your girlfriend?"

Brent shared a glance with Maia. They hadn't gotten that far in their conversation. "We're involved."

"They were kissing," Simon said, still miffed.

A man appeared. The groom. "Honey? Is there a problem?"

Brent's spirits sank. Where was a hole in the floor when you needed one?

"Maybe we could all return to the dining room," Maia suggested, "and let you get back to your reception."

"You're kidding, of course." The bride glared at her. "I think what should happen is you and he leave. Now would be good."

"Wait a minute," Olive objected. She turned to the bride. "I know you're upset."

"Upset? I'm going to have them fired. And get my money back."

Olive reached up and straightened the bride's tiara like she was dressing a small child. "You just got married." She sent the groom an appreciative glance. "To an incredible guy, I might add, whom you're madly in love with." The smile turned sad. "Some of us aren't that lucky. We, and I'm talking about me, not just Simon, hire dates because we can't stand the idea of people thinking we're losers."

"No one thinks you're a loser, Olive."

"Brian is a great guy."

"His name is Brent."

"Whatever his name, he made me feel special. On Christmas Eve, a night I expected to be alone and miserable because that's how I spent last Christmas Eve. And I'm sure, until a few minutes ago, Simon felt special, too."

The young man stared at the floor, neither agreeing nor disagreeing with Olive.

"I forgot Brian…Brent…whoever…was my hired date," Olive continued. "I bet it was the same for Simon. What these two people do—" she indicated Brent and Maia "—is pretty incredible, if you ask me. They make people's lives better, just for a little while, and change our entire outlook. I looked forward to tonight when a few weeks ago I was dreading it.

I danced and toasted and laughed rather than sitting in a corner. Brent cared. He was attentive and considerate. I'm sure Maia treated Simon similarly." She visibly struggled for composure. "With so much love to give, is it any surprise they found each other?"

"Olive." The bride's features collapsed. "I had no idea you dreaded coming to my wedding."

"I would have come no matter what. Wild horses couldn't have kept me away. But with Brent as my date, I truly enjoyed myself."

"I wanted to come alone," Simon grumbled and kicked the carpet with the toe of his dress shoe.

The bride pulled him close. "I shouldn't have insisted. I love you, and I meant well. Please forgive me."

He extracted himself with aw-shucks awkwardness. "It's okay, sis. But I can take care of myself."

"I know you can." She brushed the hair away from his eyes. "I messed up. I'm sorry."

"Don't be hard on Brent and Maia," Olive said. "I agree they shouldn't have disappeared together. But they're in love. You of all people should understand."

"We're not. We—" Maia faltered.

Brent didn't correct her. He'd been seconds away from confessing his feelings for her before Simon appeared. This wasn't the time or place to complete that comfession.

"I suppose you're right." The bride stepped around Olive and addressed Brent and Maia. "I admit, I possibly overreacted."

"You didn't," Maia insisted. "We were wrong."

"Yes. But I won't get you fired. Olive has a point." She reached for her husband's hand. "Besides, it's my wedding day."

"Thank you," Maia answered humbly.

"I do want my money back."

"We'll see to it," Brent said. "We promise."

The bride lifted her chin with an air of satisfaction. "It's up to Simon and Olive if you're invited back to the reception. I'm leaving the decision to them."

"Whatever," Simon grumbled. He hadn't looked at either Maia or Brent since his sister showed.

"Tell you what," Olive said, linking arms with him. "Why don't we let Brent and Maia leave, and you be my date for the remainder of the reception?"

"Me!" He gulped and gawked at her. "You're joking."

"I've never been more serious." She tweaked his lapel. "A good-looking young man like you?

I'd be flattered. All the single women here are going to be sooooo jealous of me."

"Um, okay. Sure. Yeah." The beginnings of a goofy grin pulled at the corners of his mouth.

"Well, come on then." Olive tugged Simon along with her. Not before sending a mischievous smile at Brent that he interpreted as, *You're welcome.*

"Let's go," the bride said to her husband. "I'm ready for another glass of champagne."

"Your wish is my command."

"You say that now. What about twenty years from now?"

"Darling, I'll be saying that fifty years from now."

Grabbing the sides of her voluminous dress, the bride made a grand exit in the wake of Olive and her brother. The groom accompanied her, their murmured voices carrying across the widening distance. Brent and Maia had given them a lot to talk about.

"I suppose things could have gone worse," he said to Maia. There would be some explaining to do. The good news was Maia wouldn't lose her job.

She evidently didn't share his opinion.

Heading down the hall toward the inn's main entrance, she said, "We need to call Darla and implement damage control."

There was that. Brent's mood threatened to plummet with each step he took.

By some miracle, he remained steadfast. This wasn't the time for him to dive into the darkness. Maia was depending on him.

CHAPTER FIFTEEN

MAIA HADN'T PLANNED on standing outside at night in near-freezing temperatures. Thank goodness the snow, such as it was, had ceased falling an hour ago.

"Where's your truck?" she asked Brent, hugging herself to ward off the chill.

"Not here. My date drove."

"Mine, too." She groaned and rubbed her upper arms.

Stranded. No less than they deserved. She discarded the idea of returning to the dining room for her coat, preferring not to encounter Simon or his sister again.

"I'll get us a ride service." Brent reached into his pocket for his phone.

"Okay," Maia said, her teeth chattering.

Brent shrugged off his suit jacket. "Here. Take this."

"I'm f-fine."

"You're freezing."

She relented. Brent had worn a lined vest over

his cotton dress shirt. Warmer than the thin fabric of her outfit.

They could huddle. Conserve body heat.

Probably not wise under the circumstances. Huddling was what had gotten them in trouble.

"We screwed up tonight," she said.

"Yeah." He opened the app on his phone and began tapping on the screen.

She slid her arms into the jacket sleeves, anxiety sparking like a live electric wire. "Darla's going to mad, and it's all my fault."

"No, it's mine."

"I invited you to talk," Maia insisted.

"And I should have said no. I knew better."

"I *really* knew better. Darla and I've had multiple discussions about this." Maia let out a long groan. "I know you think my sister can be difficult and demanding. But the company rules are in place for good reason. To prevent disasters like tonight."

"I don't think she's difficult."

"She's poured her heart and soul into Your Perfect Plus One. Her family depends on the income."

"We'll get through this," Brent assured her and finished requesting their ride. "The driver will be here in eight minutes. I expected longer on Christmas Eve."

"Yeah. Christmas Eve." She grimaced at the

reminder. "I don't want to think about what it'll be like tomorrow at my folks'. Darla will tell them, of course. They'll be disappointed in me." Maia closed her eyes and saw her parents' faces. "I've ruined Christmas for the whole family."

"Do you want me to go with you? For moral support?"

"No! Absolutely not." At the injured look in his eyes, she added, "Thanks for the offer. But I think you being there would only make the situation worse. Darla may become defensive if it appears we're siding together against her."

He nodded. "I'll call her tomorrow. When's a good time? I don't want to interrupt her holiday."

"We need to call her right now." Maia removed her phone from her clutch. "The sooner the better. The only chance we have of salvaging things is to tell her what happened before the bride or Olive does. Otherwise, we're doomed."

"We're doomed anyway."

Maia prayed for strength and pressed the speed dial for her sister. Darla had likely put the girls to bed already. She and Garret were either wrapping last-minute gifts from Santa or spending a quiet evening together. They may have even fallen asleep from sheer exhaustion. In which case, Maia would wake up Darla. She didn't like being woken up.

Darla answered on the third ring with a very alert "What's wrong?"

Maia didn't call when she was on a date unless she had a problem. "I'm here with Brent at the inn. There's been a…a…complication."

"Tell me."

Maia could hear her sister's voice echoing as she walked from room to room through the house. She must be getting out of earshot from Garret and the girls if they were awake. One tiny positive, Maia had reached Darla before either the bride or Olive.

"Brent and I left the reception."

"Why?"

"We meant to leave for only a few minutes. To talk. Out in the hall."

"You went out in the hall to talk," Darla repeated, her voice level.

"Then…" Oh, gosh. This was so hard. Brent must have sensed Maia's anguish for he placed a hand on her shoulder. She steeled her resolve and continued. "We kind of kissed."

"Kind of?"

"We kissed. Then my date came out and found us. He was upset." That was putting it mildly. "After that, um…" Maia faltered. "The bride came out."

"The. Bride."

"She was upset, too."

"What about Brent's date? Where was she during all this? Please don't tell me she came out, too." When Maia didn't respond, Darla sucked in a breath. "Who else?"

"The groom."

Darla muttered a word she'd scold her daughters for saying.

"I'm sorry."

A lengthy silence followed during which Maia considered and then discarded a dozen different excuses and explanations.

Darla finally murmured, "Continue."

Relaying only the relevant details—Darla wouldn't be moved by Maia and Brent's conversation about their potential future together and their feelings for one another, not right now, anyway—Maia spilled the entire awful tale.

"Brent's date gave this nice speech about wedding dates," Maia said, "and the bride was fine with everything."

"I highly doubt that."

"She wants her money back, naturally. Which you can take out of my pay."

"My pay," Brent insisted.

"Brent's pay, too," Maia told Darla.

"I'm giving Brent's date a refund, too."

"That's more than fair."

"Is he with you?" Darla asked, her tone hard to read.

"Yes."

"Put me on speaker."

Maia did as her sister requested and held the phone out so that both she and Brent could hear and be heard. "Go ahead."

"Brent?" Darla asked.

"Yes?"

"You're fired. I understand you care for my sister, but my duty is to my clients. They have a right to expect their wedding date isn't going to leave with someone else."

"I understand." To his credit, he didn't miss a beat.

Unlike Maia, who squeaked out, "Darla, no."

"I love you, Maia. I want nothing more than to help you with your dream of winning the Diamond Cup. But you're fired, too. For the same reasons as Brent."

A pitiful sound escaped Maia's lips. She should have seen this coming and yet she hadn't, and the pain cut like a knife. She and Brent deserved reprimands, for sure. But fired? Without a chance to plead their case and make amends? Without Darla talking to the bride and Olive? They hadn't been angry. Yes, at first. The bride. Not Olive. They'd been understanding. Even appreciative, in a way.

Maia instantly realized her error. She and Brent hadn't just breached their employment contracts, she'd hurt Darla. Deeply. Perhaps irreparably.

"Okay," Maia managed, her voice fracturing. "Can we talk later?"

"We'll all three talk. On Monday. I'm not going to let this spoil Christmas. Plus, I need a day to process."

"Right. I'll see you tomorrow?"

"You'll see me. Good night."

Compared to the chill in Darla's voice, the winter night air now felt like a tropical breeze. The family gathering tomorrow would be far from jovial. Thank goodness the kids were young. The adults would put on a good show for them, and they'd be none the wiser.

Maia returned her phone to her clutch, her mind in a jumble. She didn't care about her job. She cared about Darla and Your Perfect Plus One's reputation and repairing the damage she'd caused.

"Where's our driver?" she asked.

Brent looked at his phone. "Two more minutes."

She slapped her arms again, as much to get her blood circulating as to ward off the cold. "I don't know what I was thinking."

"We weren't. That's the problem."

"I'm not like that. Impulsive. Thoughtless. Selfish."

"We were caught up in a moment," Brent said.

"That's no reason. My family's always been good to me. They've supported me unconditionally at every step—when Luke cheated on me, when he turned his back on me after I found out I was pregnant. Mom babysits TJ so I can work and train. Dad lets me set my own hours at the stables. Darla gave me a part-time job to earn extra money. And look how I repay them." Maia covered her face with her hands. "I'm a terrible daughter and sister."

"You're not."

"What if this damages Darla's business?"

"I doubt that will happen."

Brent's lack of concern suddenly irritated Maia. Did he really have no clue? Did he possibly not care?

"Our dates could post terrible reviews that discourage potential clients. They could tell their friends and family about their awful experience. Darla relies heavily on word-of-mouth advertising."

"Your sister's going to refund their money. They might be annoyed, but they can't say she refused to make things right. And you heard Olive. She won't post a bad review."

Maia stared. "You're missing the point."

"I'm not. We made a mistake, and it's going

to have serious ramifications. But us being fired, or your dad letting me go isn't the worst. It's that you lost Darla's trust and may not earn it back."

All right. He wasn't missing the point.

"I betrayed her."

"Not intentionally."

"That may not make a difference."

"Possibly," he agreed. "I'm not taking any bets."

She heard the despondency in his tone. The hints of hopelessness and despair. "Dad won't fire you," she said.

"He'd have good reason."

"He can't fire you because you screwed up at a different job. That's not fair."

"His opinion of me will change when he hears what happened."

Maia hadn't considered that. "I won't let him fire you," she insisted.

"He may not have a choice if Darla insists."

"She won't." *Would she?*

Maia wanted to break down and cry. The ripple effect from their mistake just kept increasing and increasing. All because of a single kiss.

One minute, she'd been soaring among the clouds, in Brent's arms and talking about their future together. The next, she'd dropped to the ground, hitting like a ton of bricks.

Darla wouldn't be mad at Maia forever. They'd make up eventually. Particularly if no bad reviews surfaced. But they might not return to where they had been for a long, long time.

"Here's our ride," Brent said.

Another new ripple appeared and hit Maia like a tidal wave. She and Brent wouldn't survive this disaster unscathed. They might not return to where they had been before, either, for a long, long time. Maybe never.

BRENT WAVED TO the approaching red Honda. When the driver reached the curb, Brent opened the door for Maia, and she gratefully climbed inside. He was glad the driver—a middle-aged woman wearing a hat resembling a Christmas tree, complete with a star on top—had cranked up the heat. Maia shook from head to toe. His suit jacket was worthless in thirty-two degree temperatures.

"Merry Christmas, ya'll," their driver chirped.

"Same to you," Brent mumbled, not feeling the least bit merry. How had the night gone from fantastic to disaster in the blink of an eye?

"Let's see—" the driver said, tapping the phone mounted on her dash "—129 North Cypress Road? That's right?"

"Yeah."

He and Maia buckled their seat belts. She

leaned back, closed her eyes and sighed, appearing to luxuriate in the warm air gusting from the heater. Suddenly, she sat up.

"Where did she say?"

"Books Galore. That's where my truck's parked. Where I met Olive."

"Hmmm." She nodded.

"I'll drive you to your car."

The reminder of their evening quieted them both. Their driver must have sensed her passengers weren't in the mood to chitchat, for she turned up the radio. Christmas music filled the car's interior, allowing Brent and Maia to talk softly without being overheard.

"I'm sorry, Maia."

"Me, too. About a lot of things."

How many apologies in total would be uttered before this was over and done with?

"I shouldn't have gotten involved with you," he said. *Not kissed you, not held you, not let myself imagine a future together.* "I should have put a stop to it when I had the chance. Instead, I encouraged you."

"We need to quit playing the blame game."

She was right. They'd both made mistakes, were both responsible. Brent attempting to assume the lion's share was his way of appeasing his guilty conscience. What he deserved was to drown in it.

"If your dad fires me, I'm going to leave Payson. I may anyway, even if he doesn't."

"Leave?" She twisted to confront him. "Where did that come from? And like I said before, he won't fire you."

"Me staying will make things difficult for you. I'll be a constant reminder." And *she'd* be a constant temptation. Brent had already demonstrated the magnitude of his weaknesses where Maia was concerned.

"What about Channing and your plans to become a rodeo judge?"

Brent had yet to think that far ahead. In fact, thinking was getting harder and harder by the minute. The black cloud had zoomed in from where it had been hiding these recent weeks and hovered directly over his head. The air inside the car grew heavy, and the familiar weight bore down on him.

He resisted. Pushed back. But the cloud would win eventually. He was fighting a losing battle.

"I'll talk to Channing," he said. "Explain what happened. Turn down the sponsorship."

"So, you're running away."

"I'm not."

He was. Running hard and fast. As usual. Some part of him reasoned if he changed locations, then perhaps he could somehow change and repair his broken self.

What was the old saying about the definition of insanity? Doing the same thing over and over and expecting a different result? Brent was living proof. Except this time the result was not the same. He'd hurt others besides himself. People he cared about and who mattered to him.

"With me out of the picture," he continued, "you can mend your relationship with Darla. She'll hire you back."

"Ahhh. You're leaving for my benefit. Not yours. How noble of you."

He didn't flinch at the snap in her voice. "I don't want to cause more strife between you and Darla."

"Whatever. Leave. Just stop making yourself the villain in a bid for pity."

Okay, that stung. "You're mad at me. Nothing less than I deserve."

"For Pete's sake, Brent. I'm not mad at you." She pushed ruthlessly at her hair as if it were responsible for her annoyance. "I'm mad at myself and at life in general. We're two nice people, two deserving people, who happened to meet at the wrong time. That stinks, frankly."

"I agree. Life is seldom fair."

"But here's the problem. Rather than accept our circumstances or wait until the time was right, we threw a stick of dynamite into a crowd."

She groaned.

"We're not kids or ignorant or stupid," he continued. "We knew the risks when we left that reception. Shame on us."

Brent could see that his remarks hit home. He would have liked to reach for Maia's hand. He didn't. That would send the wrong message, give her hope when there wasn't any.

"We were wrong," she said. "But is that reason enough to destroy all possibility for potential happiness? For you to up and leave behind everything you'd built here? Throw away the progress you've made? When are you going to stop punishing yourself for walking away from rodeo?"

Was that what he'd been doing? Punishing himself?

"I wish I'd met you two years ago," he said. "Then I might not have left rodeo or at least had an exit plan before I did."

She touched *him* then. Taking his chin in her fingers, she turned his face toward her. "Don't leave. Not yet. Let's see what happens first. Tomorrow's Christmas. You're not working. Take the morning to think. Make an appearance at Cash's wedding in the afternoon. You don't have to stay for the reception. Then spend the rest of the day mentally regrouping. We can talk later, if you want. I'll be home by six."

Her advice was good. Sensible. Thoughtful. Brent rejected it anyway.

"I won't leave right away," he said.

"Promise?"

"I told your dad I'd feed the horses and clean the corral in the morning so he and Rowdy could have the day off."

"That's nice of you."

He could tell by her expression, she'd misinterpreted his remark and assumed he wasn't leaving until they'd had a chance to talk. Brent didn't correct her. He figured he could be on the road by noon at the latest.

"Dad said you were volunteering at the shelter tomorrow before Cash's wedding."

He'd forgotten. His plan had been to take his suit with him to the shelter and change there. "I doubt your dad will want to see me."

"Are you canceling?"

"Yeah."

"Brent—"

"I'm not going."

She hunkered down in her seat. "Fine. I won't push. A little time apart might not be a bad idea."

He'd be skipping Cash's wedding, as well. No big deal. He wouldn't be missed.

"Let's meet on Monday. You, me, Dad and Darla. We'll explain our side."

He'd be long gone by then. "We don't have a side."

"We'll express our regret. Make amends. Maybe we should say we've decided not to see each other for a while. Dad will come around. And Darla. When you think about it, this could wind up being for the best."

"You're kidding."

"You'll have more time to judge the bull-riding practices at Rim Country and obtain your certification. Three months from now, no one will remember."

The black cloud had affected Brent's ability to think clearly. In an effort to clear the fog, he put what Maia had said into bullet points.

Express regrets. Make amends.

Brent had that down. He'd been doing nothing else for the last two years. Expressing regrets, anyway. Not so much making amends. He'd only started that after coming to Payson and working for the MacKenzies.

Ansel would come around. Darla, too.

In three months? Nope. Maia was fooling herself. And if Brent ever screwed up again, this disaster would be dragged out and paraded around as evidence he hadn't deserved a second chance.

I'd have more time to judge bull-riding practice and obtain my judging certification.

A whole lot more time. Brent would be out

of a job again. If Ansel had a lick of sense, he'd fire Brent like Darla had.

What was that last one?

"Maybe we should say we've decided not to see each other for a while."

"Temporarily," Maia said. "Take a step back until this blows over."

Brent hadn't realized he'd spoken out loud. "No." He shook his head. "Not temporary. Permanent."

"You can't mean that."

"We're here!" their driver announced.

Her voice sounded the like a snowy owl's screech. That happened when Brent started his descent into the darkness. Sounds were amplified and distorted. Retreating into himself was the only way to muffle them.

The small Honda rocked as they went over a speed bump at the entrance to the strip mall parking lot. Brent's truck sat in front of the bookstore. Blinking lights from the store's window reflecting in the windshield created a surreal effect that matched his mental state.

"There," he said. "The Ford pickup."

"You got it!" Their driver pulled up behind Brent's truck. "Merry Christmas, you two. And happy New Year. Stay safe."

"I'll tip you in the app," Brent said and opened his door. It weighed a ton.

"Thanks! And cheers."

A moment later, he was opening his truck's passenger door for Maia. She hadn't spoken since he'd refuted her statement about a temporary separation.

He hoped she wouldn't resume their conversation. Fate, for once, accommodated him. Silence hung between them the entire drive to where she'd left her SUV. She unbuckled her seat belt before Brent had come to a complete stop and opened the door the instant he shifted into Park. To his surprise, she hesitated rather than jumping out.

"We can get through this, Brent."

"Define *get through*."

"Everything's going to be all right. For us. For Darla. For Your Perfect Plus One."

"People don't easily recover from screwups like this."

"But they do recover."

"Your dad and Darla gave me a chance, and I repaid them by breaching my employee contract and causing a scene."

"I have faith."

That word again. Brent was starting to wonder how Maia could be so naive. She'd had her share of hard knocks and in some ways was still coping with them.

"There's a difference between having faith and sticking your head in the sand."

Maia bristled. "Is that what you think I'm doing?"

"You focus on the positive and ignore the negative."

"Is that so wrong?"

"It's unrealistic. You're setting yourself up for hurt and grief."

"Why are you acting like this?" She stared at him in puzzlement.

"Like what?"

"A pessimist."

"Pessimism and depression go hand in hand. Let's be honest—the world is a pretty bleak place. You and I—" he chuckled dryly "—we don't stand a chance. Even if we get through this, as you say, nothing will go back to the way it was before. Don't believe me? I have some scars to show you."

Her eyes flashed with pain.

Brent wished he wasn't the cause of her anguish, but he refused to mislead her with false optimism. Remaining in Payson and continuing to see Maia every day at work would intensify her anguish. Him leaving was the only sensible solution.

"Better a clean break now," he said, "than a messy and miserable break later when we're more invested in each other and have more to lose."

"Are you sure that's what you want?"

"Don't do that, Maia."

"Do what?"

"Keep fanning a dying fire. Your family comes first. And your sister's business comes next. You and I are at the very bottom. We're the most expendable."

She shivered despite the warmth. "I could love you if you let me. If you were willing to try. Give us a chance."

Her admission was no doubt intended to soothe. It had the opposite effect. Brent felt like a first-class heel. He was abandoning her. Same as her ex.

"That's what happens when you love someone who doesn't love themself. They disappoint you. They can't help themselves."

"You can," Maia said, her tone a blend of anger and sorrow. "You just won't."

For a moment, Brent was hurled back in time to a conversation with his dad. He'd said the same thing to Brent, nearly verbatim.

"You're right."

She flung open the door. After stepping out into the cold, she hurried to her SUV. Brent waited until he was certain her vehicle had started without problem and then followed her down the road for the next mile where she turned left, and he continued out of town to Bear Creek Ranch.

He arrived at the bunkhouse without remembering how he got there. That happened sometimes. He drove on automatic pilot, as if in a hypnotic state. Actually, he went through entire days on automatic pilot without remembering anything.

His bunk mates weren't home, either spending the holiday evening with their family, friends or girlfriends. Brent had the place to himself.

Wasting no time, he removed his boots and belt and clothes, trading them for sweatpants and a T-shirt—his favorite outfit for sinking into the murky depths. Under the bedcovers, the blackness opened its jagged arms, welcoming him like an old friend.

I've missed you.

Why had he taken the jobs with Mountainside and Your Perfect Plus One? Forget about himself. He'd caused a rift between Maia and her sister. Possibly between her and her dad. Gotten her fired from a lucrative part-time job. Potentially damaged her sister's business. He wasn't just making himself the villain or attempting to appease his guilty conscience. He was a wrecking ball demolishing everything in his path.

The darkness pulsed and throbbed as it sang its siren's song. Brent stopped thinking about Maia and listened, letting his mind go blank.

CHAPTER SIXTEEN

"TJ, SWEETIE. Come back here."

Maia had spent the last ten minutes chasing her son from one end of the house to the other. She'd mistakenly thought it might be fun letting him open a present or two from Santa here before they went to her parents' house where there'd be more gifts and a big family brunch.

Because she hadn't had a bag large enough to hold the plush stick pony that made "realistic" galloping and whinnying sounds, she'd simply taped a giant red bow on the pony's neck and laid it beneath the tree. TJ had gone wild with excitement the second he laid eyes on the pony. He'd ignored the rest of his gifts and played only with Windy, the name printed on the side of the halter, riding him up and down imaginary mountains while mimicking the sounds the pony emitted.

Giving up, Maia let TJ play a while longer. She was in no frame of mind this morning to engage in a battle of wills.

Bits and pieces of scenes from last night had

been returning at frequent intervals. Was Brent all right? He'd been upset when they parted, which could trigger one of his funks. Should she call or text him?

Given a second chance, there were at least ten things she'd say or do differently. She tried telling herself her worry was a waste of time and energy. He was attending Cash's wedding later today, and then on Monday, they'd meet with her dad and Darla, who'd have calmed down by then.

Except Maia couldn't quite remember Brent agreeing to the meeting.

She'd call tonight if she hadn't heard from him by…six. Six thirty. No, seven.

With that conundrum settled, she readied her food contribution to brunch—a tangy fruit salad and banana-nut bread—and tried desperately to get some food into TJ.

"Sweetie," she coaxed on his next gallop past her. "Have some milk and a cookie."

Not a cookie, an oatmeal bar. More a snack than breakfast. She reasoned he wouldn't starve before they got to her parents and had a real meal.

TJ stopped long enough to grab the sippy cup and oatmeal bar and give her a quick kiss. Then he set off, eating and drinking as he rode Windy from room to room.

Maia sighed and then smiled. Seeing her son having fun eased some of her worry. For a total of ten seconds.

Perhaps Brent had been such a pessimist because he didn't care for her as much as she cared for him. She'd maybe read too much into his declarations at the reception because that was what she'd wanted to hear.

Maia's stomach knotted. He hadn't purposefully deceived her. If anything, he'd been excruciatingly honest, insisting more than once he wasn't ready for a relationship.

With a sinking feeling, she forced herself to admit the truth. She'd unfairly pressured Brent, disregarding her many claims to the contrary. Why? She wasn't a needy or insecure person.

This answer hit her like a knock to the knees. Luke. His cheating on her, his abandonment when she revealed her pregnancy and his turning his back on TJ, had left a crack in her strong, independent woman armor. Without her realizing it, insecurities had snuck in and affected her relationship with Brent.

If only she'd waited a few weeks to talk to Brent and reveal her feelings for him. A few days. Heck, a few hours. One snap decision. One wrong step. One little mistake, and a future with Brent had gone from promising to bleak.

"Whee, heee, heee," TJ shouted as he rode

his stick pony down the hall—his version of whinnying. Next came the galloping. "Gum, gum, gum, gum."

Finished with her food prep, Maia resumed chasing after him. "Sweetie, we've got to get ready to go to Grandma and Grandpa's."

Was she seriously attempting to reason with a sixteen-month-old?

At last, she cornered him in the kitchen and then wrangled him into the bathroom. Of course, he refused to go in the tub without the stick pony. They compromised, and Maia propped the pony's head over the side of the tub. After his bath, riding imaginary mountains resumed while she dressed.

Loading the food cooler, gifts and, of course, the stick pony, into the SUV, they left for Maia's parents' home. TJ neighed and galloped during the entire drive. The constant noise didn't distract Maia from her continued ruminations about her and Brent. Had he called her dad about canceling his volunteer shift at the shelter today? When did Darla plan on telling their parents about what had happened at the wedding? Before or after brunch?

By the time Maia and TJ swung into the driveway, she was physically and mentally exhausted. Seeing her sister's car there launched a fresh wave of anxiety. Maia had wanted to arrive first and run a little interference with her parents. So much for that idea.

After removing TJ from his car seat, Maia set him on the ground. "Here, sweetie. Help Mommy. Take this, okay?" She handed him the diaper bag.

He whinnied and pointed a pudgy finger at the car.

The pony. How could she forget?

Carrying the stick pony in one hand, he dragged the diaper bag across the ground to the front door with his other hand. Maia tried not to cringe, envisioning the scuffs and scratches. She grabbed the food cooler and the large plastic bag of gifts for her family and started for the house. TJ had already rung the doorbell. And rung it and rung it.

"Hello! Look who's here," Maia's mom gushed when she answered the door, not at all perturbed at her grandson's annoying antics. "And what's that? Did Santa bring you a present?" She tweaked the stick pony's ear.

"Puh!" TJ shouted and held up his prize.

"Such a beautiful horse." She straightened and enfolded Maia in a hug. "Where's Brent?"

"Brent?" Maia's heart faltered.

"I thought he was coming with you."

Impatient, TJ galloped into the house.

"Why would you think that?" Maia asked, covering her disconcertion by shifting her load. Darla must not have told their parents yet.

"Well, I guess I assumed. Your dad mentioned Brent was going with him to the shelter today and I…" She relieved her of the food cooler and stepped back. "I thought you two were getting close. Am I wrong?"

"Yes!"

"You're not wrong, Mom," Darla said, joining them in the living room, a dish towel tucked into the waistband of her pants. "Maia and Brent *are* getting close. Maybe little too close."

Maia sent her sister a look and waited for Darla to say more, only she didn't. Was she granting Maia a reprieve?

Her mom's glance traveled from one daughter to the other. "I don't understand."

"Let's head to the kitchen," Maia said, changing the subject. "This fruit salad needs to chill."

Her mom didn't fall for the ploy. "Are you two squabbling again? Honestly, it's Christmas."

"We're aren't squabbling," Darla answered.

"Then what?"

"We're having a disagreement. About work."

"Can this wait until Monday?" Maia asked as they walked past the family room to the kitchen.

"I know you're angry, and you have every right to be…"

Darla glanced away, but not before Maia saw the pain in her sister's eyes. Her heart sank. Her broken promise and impulsive actions had hurt her sister. If Darla was put out, she had good reason.

Maia tried again, her voice soft. "Brent and I are planning on talking to you and Dad then."

"Talk about what?" her mom asked. When no one answered, she insisted, "Girls. Please. What's going on?"

"We might as well tell her," Darla said with a resigned sigh. "She won't quit pestering us until we do."

"You're right, I won't."

Maia really didn't want to have this conversation. If only she could find an excuse to stall.

"Honey," Darla called to Garret. "Can you please watch the girls for a while. TJ, too. Maia, Mom and I are going to be busy."

His head popped up from where he knelt in front of the fireplace, stuffing balls of crumpled newspaper into the spaces between logs in preparation for lighting a fire.

"Okay." He searched the room as if conducting a silent head count. Satisfied, he returned to the fireplace. "Will do."

Had Darla told her husband about what happened? Maia assumed yes, and her cheeks warmed from embarrassment.

"Where's Dad?" Darla asked their mom.

"He's in the bedroom. He'll be out any second."

Maia supposed she should be thankful for that. She wouldn't have to see the expressions of disappointment on both her parents' faces, just her mom's.

"MAIA AND BRENT were at the same wedding last night," Darla said once she, Maia and their mom were standing at the kitchen island.

"Together or with different dates?" their mom asked.

"Different."

"Don't you usually avoid sending coworkers to the same wedding?"

"I do," Darla said. "This was an emergency."

Suddenly, Maia's dad burst into the kitchen. Maia couldn't recall ever being happier to see him, though she knew her reprieve was short-lived.

"Brent just called." He held out his phone as if to support his announcement.

Maia glanced away. Brent was calling to inform her dad he wouldn't be at the shelter today. This was her fault, too.

"Did you invite him to dinner?" her mom asked.

"I didn't get the chance. He quit!"

"Quit?" Maia squeaked.

"Quit?" her mom echoed. "Why on Earth would he do that?"

"Just said the job wasn't for him." Maia's dad shoved his fingers through his silver hair, leaving tufts standing up in places. "I was sure he liked working for us. The men all speak highly of him."

"I think I know why he quit," Darla said.

"You don't know," Maia countered.

"All right. Then tell us."

She hesitated.

"Maia?" her dad pressed.

"He thought you'd fire him. I guess he was beating you to the punch."

"Why would I do that?"

"Because of what happened last night." She met her sister's gaze.

"Somebody needs to tell me what in blue thunder is going on," her dad demanded.

"Yes," her mom seconded.

In the background, TJ whinnied and galloped back and forth in front of the Christmas tree. Maia's nieces whispered and giggled as they examined the many wrapped presents. Garret succeeded in lighting the fire. He closed the screen and stood to inspect his handiwork.

"Well," Darla started.

"While Brent and I were at the wedding last night," Maia said, "we left the reception briefly, to talk outside in the hall. My date discovered us, and the situation got a little messy after that."

"Why would he care that you and Brent were talking?" her dad asked.

"Because they weren't just talking," Darla said and filled their parents in on all the gory, ugly details.

When she finished, Maia's dad speared her with a look—the same one he'd used when she and Darla were young and pushing the boundaries.

"I like Brent," he said, "don't get me wrong. But you shouldn't have abandoned your dates like that. Not at a wedding when you were there as representatives of your sister's company."

"I know, Dad." Maia stared at the floor. Her shame and regret had been hard to bear before her parents were involved. Now it was unendurable.

"Don't be so hard on her," Maia's mom interjected. "She and Brent have feelings for each other."

"They also had an obligation to Darla. She's not wrong for being upset."

"But they're sisters."

"Maia is also Darla's employee." Her dad put an arm around her shoulders. "I love you, sweetheart. However, I'm going to support Darla on this." He nodded at his oldest daughter.

"And you should support her." Maia barely held back her tears.

"I get that you think I'm the wicked witch of the west," Darla said.

"I don't."

"I am sorry that I was gruff last night. I was surprised. And shocked. And upset, yes. Very upset."

"I'm sorry," Maia said, still fighting for control. "We were wrong. Really wrong."

"What are you going to do about it?" her dad asked.

"Darla's refunding the two clients' fees and taking the money out of my and Brent's pay. I'll issue a written apology, although neither of the clients was that mad in the end."

"Not them. What are you going to do about Brent? Now that he's quit, he's likely to leave town. Frankly, I don't want him to go. You don't want him to go, either, or you wouldn't have gone out into the hall to do more than talk."

"We agreed we aren't going to see each other."

She'd said temporarily. Brent, permanently.

The bits and pieces of that scene returned to Maia, hitting her like tiny daggers. She must have been in denial, refusing to accept that another man would choose to walk away from her, and had put the memory from her mind.

"He needs this job," her dad said. "It's giving him a purpose."

"I'm sure he'll find another job," Darla said. "I've read his résumé. He's landed on his feet before."

Maia's dad looked at her with concern. "Have you told him how you feel?"

"Yes," she murmured.

"And he doesn't return your feelings?"

"Yes. He said he does. But he argued that staying would make things awkward for me and cause a rift between me and Darla."

"Will it?"

All eyes turned to Maia's sister.

"We're going to make up, sis. We always do. I am going to need a day or two to process. Put things in perspective."

"Fair enough," Maia's dad announced.

"Not to be a Debbie Downer," Darla continued, "but I have to ask. Is Brent staying what's best for everyone, him included? The fact is, he has some issues. Mental-health issues. That's no secret. He told me when I interviewed him. He didn't come right out and say depression, but I got the gist."

"Which is why he needs a job and a purpose," Maia's dad said. "Those are crucial for healing what ails his soul."

"He needs professional help, too," Darla said. "I'm not sure he's ready to accept that. Or ready for the commitment holding a steady job requires. People with depression often struggle with fulfilling their responsibilities. They can be unreliable. Irresponsible."

"That's pretty judgmental of you," Maia snapped. "It's not like Brent's a criminal or a liar or a degenerate. He has a common illness a lot of people suffer from. He deserves our compassion and our understanding."

"He *did* lie," Darla said sadly. "He promised to avoid you at the wedding, and then he didn't."

"Because I asked him to talk."

She stood straighter. "I'm looking out for us. For the family. Brent is very likable and charming. He has a ton of good qualities. He's kind. Nice. Polite. That's the reason I hired him. And he may, someday, once he's better, be the guy of your dreams. Before then, he has to deal with his issues. This wasn't the first time he ran into difficulties at work. And not the first time he was fired."

"You *fired* him!" Maia's mom asked.

"Yes, I did."

"She fired me, too," Maia said. "All right, deservedly, though I wish you'd given us a chance to explain first."

Her mom gasped. "You fired your sister?"

"Mom." Darla visibly struggled for composure. "She signed an employment contract. No fraternizing between coworkers. What happened last night is exactly the reason I have those clauses in the contract. If I let her slide, I have to let other employees slide or I risk being sued."

"She needs that money to pay for her saddle."

"Don't give Darla any grief," Maia's dad told her mom. "She a business owner, and sometimes business owners have to make difficult decisions."

"It was a mistake. People make mistakes. And family should get more breaks than other employees."

Maia wasn't sure about that.

"Fine," Darla pushed her fingers through her hair. "Maia, you can have your job back. But not Brent."

"I don't want it back. The saddle's mostly paid for, anyway."

"In all honesty, maybe that's for the best."

Maia's nieces and TJ chose that moment to burst into the kitchen.

"We're hungry," Darla's oldest exclaimed.

"Wanna open presents," her youngest demanded.

"Let's talk more about this later," Maia's dad said. "These young'uns are expecting a happy Christmas morning, and I for one want them to have it. Darla, I know you and Garret are leaving for his parents' after brunch. Why don't we all get together tomorrow and pick up where we left off?"

Maia and Darla both nodded, Maia glumly. They opened the gifts after that, the children in a chaotic frenzy. TJ abandoned his stick pony for the toddler push tricycle his grandparents had bought him. He then tried to ride the tricycle while balancing the stick pony across the handlebars. The girls squealed with delight at the identical baby dolls with matching wardrobes from Aunt Maia.

She tried to muster enthusiasm over the cashmere sweater from Darla and ruby earrings from her parents. Her heart just wasn't in it.

She had to find a way to talk to Brent. Later today. Tonight. In the morning. He may have quit Mountainside Stables, but he hadn't left town yet and might not for a few days. There was his final paycheck to process. Plus, he was attending Cash's wedding this afternoon.

What if she showed up at the bunkhouse?

Or waited outside Wishing Well Springs after the wedding for him to appear. How would he react? Surely she could reason with him. Assure him that her dad wanted Brent to stay on and convince him to remain.

Maia picked at her food rather than eat, her appetite having abandoned her. Darla wasn't eating much, either, though the food was delicious. Their mom was pouring a second round of coffee when Darla's phone rang.

She stared in bafflement at the display before answering. "This could be work. I forwarded the office phone to my cell." She placed the phone to her ear. "Your Perfect Plus One. Darla speaking." As she listened, the creases in her brow deepened. "No. I understand. Take care of your son. He comes first. I'll call the client. Let me know how it goes." Frowning, she disconnected.

"Problem?" her mom asked.

"It's Lindsey. She has to cancel. Her son fell off his new skateboard and, she thinks, broke his arm. She's taking him to the emergency room. Now I have to inform the client his date is a no-show."

"Don't you have someone else available?"

"Normally, I would. But it's Christmas Day. And the wedding's in a few hours." Darla buried her forehead in her hand. "Just what I need on top of everything else."

Maia sat up, excitement coursing through her. She believed in signs, and this had all the makings of one.

"I'll do it," she blurted. "I'll be his date. If Mom's willing to watch TJ."

"No." Darla shook her head. "This is for Cash's wedding. Brent will be there."

"I won't talk to him. He'll be invisible to me. I swear."

"Absolutely not."

"I owe you. Big time. Let me make it up to you by covering for Lindsey."

"Give her a chance," their mom pleaded. "This could be an opportunity to mend the rift between you."

Darla looked to Garret who shrugged. She closed her eyes and moaned. "I must be out of my ever-loving mind."

"Is that a yes?" Maia sprang to her feet.

"Yes. But don't make me regret my decision."

Maia hugged her sister's neck. "I won't. Scout's honor. I'll be the best wedding date ever."

"Talk to Brent," her mom said as Maia was leaving a couple hours later, her cheek sticky from TJ's kisses.

She had every intention of talking to Brent.

After the wedding. Long after. If he avoided her, which he might, she'd track him down at the bunkhouse.

Brent had been ready to give up on them without a fight. Well, Maia had enough fight in her for the two of them and the determination to go after what she wanted.

CHAPTER SEVENTEEN

AT HOME, MAIA CHANGED as fast as she could into one of her standard wedding outfits. Freshening her hair and makeup, she read the bio for her role and their fictional backstory on her phone. Sam was a former calf roper. Maia styled her hair and chose her outfit accordingly, wearing her flashiest Western boots and a striking turquoise necklace.

No sooner was she in her SUV and on the road to the prearranged meeting place when Darla phoned. Maia hit the Answer button on her car's display.

"You have your work cut out for you," her sister said. "The client is less than thrilled about the last-minute change."

"Understandable. I'll be all smiles and win him over with my wit and sunny personality."

Sam had once competed professionally with Cash and Channing back in the day. Did Brent know him, too? Possibly. Sam's longtime girlfriend had recently dumped him. According to the notes Maia had read, he didn't want to arrive at the wedding single and stand out like a sore thumb from his cohorts who were there with their gals.

Maia sincerely doubted his friends would think poorly him. But Sam was nursing a broken heart and was entitled to feel sorry for himself.

"Don't blow it," Darla told her.

"I won't."

"Check in with me the first chance you get."

"Want me to text you a picture?"

"This isn't funny."

"I'll call," Maia promised. "And Darla? Thanks."

She sighed. "Talk to you later. After I get a glowing report from Sam," she added with a hint of warning.

Once Maia hung up, she wondered if she should warn Brent she'd be there? That way, he wouldn't mistake her for a regular wedding guest and attempt to talk with her. She decided yes and, pulling into an empty bus stop, fired off a text ending with Sorry about last night. Hope you're doing okay.

Brent didn't respond. In fact, he still hadn't responded by the time Maia was in her date's car and on their way to Wishing Well Springs. Was he busy getting dressed? Was he out of cell range? She decided he must already be at the wedding and had shut off his phone to prevent it from going off during the ceremony.

She did her best to concentrate on her date. Sam seemed like a nice guy, other than he rambled on endlessly about his ex-girlfriend during the twenty-minute drive. Maia was no relationship expert, but she'd bet money he was still hung up on this gal and that their breakup had been nasty.

Honestly, she felt bad for him. More so, perhaps, because of what she and Brent recently went through.

"Crummy way to spend Christmas," Sam commented while parking the truck. "Not that I had any other plans. I did until a couple weeks ago when Ellie decided I wasn't paying her enough attention. One missed anniversary." He snorted. "Who keeps track of the day they met, anyway?"

"I'm sure Cash appreciates you coming today and giving up your holiday plans. He's a great guy. His fiancée, too. I've met her a couple of times."

"Ellie likes her. They met at a barbecue last summer."

Once again, Sam had brought the conversation back to his ex-girlfriend. Definitely hung up on her, she decided, noting his hound-dog expression.

Wishing Well Springs was decorated much the same as it had been last night. The Christmas tree greeted them when they entered. The giant wreath hanging from the wall waved at them with its long gold ribbons. On closer inspection, Maia noticed a billowy, fibrous material resembling snow covered the floor at the altar and silver fairy lights adorned the arch. The effect was lovely and very festive.

She started searching for Brent the second she and Sam sat in a pew near the back. Brent was nowhere in sight, and she tried not to let Sam notice her disappointment. She needn't have bothered as he completely ignored her.

The reason became obvious when he said, "There's Ellie," and glowered at a pretty auburn-haired woman two rows ahead and six seats over.

"She's here?"

"Yes." His stare intensified.

"Did you know she was coming?"

"Yes," he repeated.

Maia forgot about Brent and observed Ellie. The young woman sat with an attractive cowboy and flashed him what Maia considered an exaggerated smile. All of a sudden, she flicked a glance back at Maia and Sam. Then, dialing up her smile another notch, she returned her attention to her date.

Okay, thought Maia. Here's why Sam hadn't wanted to attend the wedding solo. He'd known Ellie would be here with another man.

She supposed she could help the poor guy out. The next time Ellie glanced back at them, Maia made sure to gaze attentively at Sam.

He didn't notice, but Ellie did, and her brightly lipsticked mouth flattened.

More guests arrived, filling the remaining pews. None of the people squeezing into the last vacant seats was Brent. Maia's anxiety increased, and she discreetly checked her phone. No reply to her text. No missed call from him.

Where was he? She sent a second text, this one a GIF of a penguin waving hello.

He could be with Channing and Cash, lending moral support to the best man and groom. Though Brent and Cash were only casually acquainted, Brent and Channing were good friends.

Yes, that made sense. In which case Brent would be the last one seated before the start of the wedding. It would also explain why he'd turned off his phone.

Maia remained optimistic right up until the first bridesmaid walked up the aisle, resplendent in her vibrant maroon dress. On her heels came four more bridesmaids, a flower girl and then the ring bearer. No sign of Brent. He wasn't here and, evidently, not coming.

Sam remained fixated on Ellie. Maia was able to sneak in several quick peeks at her phone with him being none the wiser or appearing to even care what she did.

The ceremony felt like the longest one in the history of weddings. When it finally ended, Maia had to prevent herself from shoving her way out of the pew and hurrying to—where? The entrance, she supposed, where she could call Brent.

Except she couldn't, shouldn't, do that. One, she owed Sam her full attention. Two, she'd promised her sister she wouldn't screw up again. Maia had no choice but to wait.

An image of Brent loading his truck sprang to her mind and sent a surge of alarm coursing through her. Her breath quickened.

What if he'd been packing when he called her dad this morning and quit? Why hadn't she tried to reach him earlier instead of waiting? She'd been so sure he would be here, take one look at her and realize the two of them belonged together.

There had to be another reason he wasn't answering her texts and had missed the wedding. A dead battery, in either his phone or his truck. He was embarrassed he didn't have enough money for a gift. He'd forgotten. He'd confided what happened last night to Channing, who then told Brent to stay away.

By some minor miracle, she survived the next fifteen minutes without having a meltdown. As the wedding party gathered to form a receiving line, she spied Channing nearby speaking with his parents.

"Excuse me just a minute, will you?" she said to Sam.

He grunted a reply, his attention riveted on Ellie and her cowboy companion twenty feet away.

Maia rushed over to Channing.

"Channing. Hi. I'm so sorry for interrupting." She acknowledged his parents. "I won't keep you, but have you seen or heard from Brent?"

"No. He was supposed to be here, but he didn't show."

"I've tried texting him, and he's not answering."

"Did you call?"

"No. Not yet. I'm here with a date. A Your Perfect Plus One date," she clarified.

"Are you worried? Did something happen?"

Maia considered before answering. "We had a fight." A simplification but true. "He called my dad and quit this morning. What if he left town?"

Channing exhaled a long breath. "He wouldn't leave without calling me."

"Then where is he? Why isn't he answering me?"

"I'm sure he's okay. Probably hiding out. That's what he does when he's having a rough time."

"Maybe you're right." She glanced back at Sam. "I have to go. Let me know if you hear from Brent."

"You do the same."

She hurried back to Sam, aware she'd pushed the boundaries. They entered the receiving line, and when their turn came, expressed their congratulations to the newlyweds.

Just like last night's wedding, the reception was being held at Joshua Tree Inn next door. It would be quite the affair as the bride's parents were rumored to have pulled out all the stops.

Outside the wedding barn, Maia and Sam waited for…well, she wasn't sure what. She suspected he was hoping to run into Ellie.

A nearby family of four with two teenage boys engaged Maia in congenial conversation while Sam pouted. She knew the instant Ellie exited the barn, for he stiffened, and his brow furrowed.

"Are you from Payson?" the wife asked Maia.

"I am. Born and raised."

Sam muttered something unintelligible and took off before Maia could reply.

"Is he okay?" the woman asked while their dad admonished the bored and restless teenagers to quit picking on each other.

"I think he spotted someone he knows."

Between Sam's behavior and her anxiety over Brent, Maia had trouble concentrating. She didn't immediately realize the raised voices were people arguing and not celebrating. Or that one of the two voices belonged to Sam.

"Look!" the younger teenager said and pointed. "That dude who was here is yelling at some lady."

"Oh, no." Maia watched in horror as the argument between Sam and Ellie escalated.

People literally stepped away, leaving the pair in the center of an open circle. Where were Cash and his bride? All Maia could think of was how awful to have a scene like this at a wedding.

"Should you, maybe, go over and say something?" the wife asked Maia.

Sam and Ellie fired curses and insults at each other like cannon shots, some Maia wouldn't dare repeat. Sam's face burned a bright red. Ellie gestured wildly, her hands slicing the air.

Maia caught sight of Ellie's date off to the side. Like everyone there, he stared in confusion and annoyance. He didn't much like his companion causing a scene. No one did.

"I'm not sure I want to get in the middle of that," Maia told the wife.

What would she say, anyway? She hardly knew Sam.

Luckily, one of his rodeo buddies intervened. He pulled Sam aside and spoke to him in a low voice. Ellie spun around. Spotting her cowboy friend, she went over to him, straightening her coat, which had become disarrayed during the intense exchange.

He backed up at her approach, raised his hand and shook his head. Maia didn't blame him. She didn't want to get near her date, either. But she supposed she had no choice.

"Enjoy the reception," she mumbled to the family and checked her phone again as she walked away. Nothing from Brent or Channing. Darn it.

Sam's rodeo buddy whisked him away to a secluded spot by one of the tall pine trees. When the buddy spotted Maia, he mouthed, "Give us a minute." She was more than happy to comply.

Waiting, she sensed the stares of everyone gathered outside or strolling to the parking area. They probably felt sorry for her, thinking her date had made a fool of himself. They'd be wrong. Maia couldn't care less. She'd not met the vast majority of people here today and would likely never see them again.

At last, Sam and his buddy separated. Maia readied herself, assuming Sam would meander over, shamefaced, and offer her an apology. A quick survey of the gathering outside the wedding barn revealed Ellie and her date had left. Presumably together. Maybe not.

Instead of coming toward her, Sam changed direction and made a beeline for the parking area. No *See you around* or *Are you okay*?

What? Seriously?

His buddy came over. "Hey, sorry about this. Sam left."

"So, I see."

"I think he may have forgotten you were here."

"Apparently."

Maia watched Sam weave back and forth between vehicles. A few seconds later, the headlights on his truck flashed.

"Bye-bye," she murmured.

"Can I give you a ride to the reception?" the pal asked.

"No. Thank you, though." She smiled.

"You sure?"

"Very. I have somewhere else to be. Merry Christmas." Maia hurried down the walkway to the edge of the parking area where she phoned

Darla and relayed the details of Sam's abrupt departure.

"He's gone?"

"He hightailed it out of here five minutes ago. Call him if you don't believe me."

"What kind of jerk does that?" Darla groused. "Argues in public with his ex and then deserts his date? Yeesh."

"He's in love with this gal and went a little nuts when he saw her with another man."

"I'm really sorry you had to suffer the likes of him."

"Is it okay if I leave?"

"Sure. Unless you want to go to the reception. You can. You were invited."

"No. I'd rather not, if you don't mind." *I have to find Brent.*

"I'll pay you the full amount. You've earned it."

"That's not necessary." Money was the least of Maia's concerns at the moment.

"Hey, sis." Darla paused. "Thanks. A lot."

"Well, I owed you."

"About this morning. The argument…"

"I'm really sorry," Maia said.

"Let's talk later, okay?"

Relief washed over her. She and Darla would be okay. "Sounds good. I love you."

"Love you, too."

The instant she hung up, Maia opened the ride service app on her phone and ordered a car to take her to where she'd left her SUV. The driver arrived fairly promptly. Twenty minutes later, she was in her own vehicle and on her way to Bear Creek Ranch.

She phoned her mom to check on TJ. He was napping soundly on the carpet near the Christmas tree, his stick pony and tricycle beside him. Maia's mom hadn't had the heart to move him and had just put a pillow beneath his head and an afghan over him.

"You're the best, Mom. I won't be too long. Five, six at the latest."

"Take all the time you need, honey. My fingers are crossed you and Brent work this out."

Maia drove as fast as the legal limit allowed. Once at Bear Creek Ranch, she headed straight for the bunkhouse, saying a silent prayer that she'd find Brent.

"Yes," she whispered when she spotted his truck behind the bunkhouse. "Thank you, thank you, thank you."

She didn't stop to consider what she'd find. Jumping out of the SUV, she ran to the bunkhouse door.

AN INSISTENT BANGING penetrated the dense layer of cotton batting surrounding Brent. Was someone hammering outside his window? That made no sense. A woodpecker on the roof? Fireworks?

He tried ignoring the noise to no avail. Each sharp report caused an excruciating pain inside his head like a series of small explosions. He cracked open an eye and encountered a dull blackness.

What time was it? What day? Where was he?

The banging continued. Brent rolled over onto his other side and covered his head with his pillow.

"Brent! Hello. I know you're in there."

Someone was at his door. He lifted the pillow and squinted at the wall as if that would provide an answer.

"Brent. Come on. Answer the door."

Maia? He covered his eyes with the blanket and willed the wheels of his muddled brain to start turning.

Bear Creek Ranch. He hadn't left yet. The day of the week and the time continued to elude him. Last he recalled, it had been Christmas morning. Who knew now? Brent had slept away entire days before, at his lowest points.

Christmas Eve had been one of those low points. When the memory of Maia's anguished eyes floated to the forefront of his consciousness, he shoved it back to the recesses where it belonged.

Bang, bang, bang.

For crying out loud. When would that infernal racket stop? How was a body supposed to get any sleep?

He burrowed farther beneath the covers, pulling the blanket past his ears. If he concentrated, he could block out the noise and the disappointments and regrets.

"Brent! Please. If you don't answer the door right now, I'm coming in."

Maia again. Brent was certain he'd locked the door. He always did before he sank into the murky depths.

"I have a key."

A wave of déjà vu poured over him like cascading water. He'd been here before. No, not here. In this same situation. Him trying to shut out the world and someone trying to push through his defenses. His mom? Channing?

"Brent!"

Maia wasn't taking the hint. Hmmm. There probably was a hidden spare key, and she'd use it.

Slowly, one inch at a time, he peeled back the bedcovers. His arm felt like a dead weight and functioned only marginally. Cold air penetrated the fabric of his T-shirt, causing his muscles to contract. As if rising from a coma, he sat up. His head spun. Wavy lines appeared before his eyes. His stomach lurched.

"I'm not leaving," Maia called and jiggled the doorknob.

"Okay, okay. Cool your jets," Brent said, his voice hoarse and unrecognizable.

With tremendous effort, he swung his legs over the side of the bed. The icy floor sent a jolt through the soles of his bare feet. By now, his eyes had adjusted to the darkness. None of the other beds were occupied, which meant he was alone. It must still be Christmas Day. Or it was the day after Christmas, and his bunk mates were at work.

"Brent?"

"Give me a minute", he said, his voice louder and stronger.

Spying his discarded socks on the floor, he donned them with fumbling fingers. Reaching for the old hoodie lying at the foot of his bed, he shoved his arms through the sleeves. The zipper defied him, and he abandoned the effort.

Standing wasn't for the faint of heart. His knees wobbled like they had the first time he'd ridden a bull at thirteen. Then, his unsteadiness had been the product of exhilaration and adrenaline flooding his veins.

Not now. Must be hunger and dehydration.

Brent hadn't eaten or drunk any water in a while.

One step. Two steps. Three. He ran his fingers through his hair on the way to the door and scrubbed the last remnants of sleep from his bristled face before letting Maia inside.

"My God, Brent." She gaped at him, her brown eyes wide with shock. "Are you all right?"

He must look pretty awful. "I was sleeping."

"I've been knocking on the door for almost ten minutes. I thought something had happened to you."

"No such luck."

"Don't say that." She reached for him, but he sidestepped her.

"I'm okay. A little out of it is all."

He went over to the refrigerator and removed a bottled water and downed the entire contents in six swallows. The cool liquid jump-started his system. His knees were already steadier. Seeing the plate of Christmas cookies Syndee had baked for the guys, Brent fished one out from under the plastic wrapping and ate it in three bites. The sugar infusion hit him instantly.

What would caffeine do? He eyed the coffee maker on the counter. Naw, too much effort. He settled for a second cookie and closed the refrigerator door.

"I thought you'd left town," Maia said.

"What day is it?"

"Saturday. Christmas. You called Dad this morning and told him you quit."

Brent dug through the cotton batting and found the memory. "What time is it?"

"Around four thirty."

He'd slept for almost sixteen hours, except for the ten minutes this morning when he'd woken long enough to call Ansel and resign. "Why is it so dark outside?"

"The sky's overcast. It's supposed to snow again." She glanced around the bunkhouse. "And you have the curtains drawn."

Brent wiped his mouth with a paper napkin and considered this information.

"I was expecting to see you at Cash's wedding," Maia said.

"I didn't go."

"I texted you. Channing did, too. We were concerned when you didn't answer."

Brent cast about for his phone. Must be in his pants pocket among the pile of clothes on the floor. "I was sleeping soundly."

She studied him with cautious uncertainty. The way people reacted to someone gravely sick or—go on, say it—someone with a mental illness.

Face facts. Normal healthy people didn't sleep

for sixteen hours straight. Brent suffered from depression. Not a funk. Not a black cloud. Not *issues*. He had an illness that, if left untreated, could destroy his life and drive away every person who cared about him. He could deny it all he wanted, pretend he was fine, hide his condition and hope no one noticed, but he'd never improve without treatment.

Difficult to get that treatment when he didn't have a job and a place to live. Might as well get used to living out of his truck or on the streets. Pete and the others at the shelter could give him tips.

"Brent?"

"Yeah." He shook his head. "I was just thinking."

"Me, too," Maia said.

"About what a mistake it was getting involved with me?"

"No. The opposite, actually."

He almost laughed.

"Darla and I told Dad what happened last night."

"Bet that went over big."

"He doesn't want you to quit. He wants you to stay and keep working for Mountainside." She paused, her demeanor tender now. "I want you to stay, too."

"Are you two gluttons for punishment? Look

at me. I'm a mess. A walking disaster. Darla's the only one of you who has any sense. She isn't offering to rehire me, is she?"

Maia shook her head.

"Smart woman."

"She hired me back. I filled in today at Cash's wedding when another employee had to cancel at the last minute."

"That's good. I'm glad." Brent sat at the kitchen table, his energy level not yet restored.

Maia dropped into the chair beside him and repeated, "Stay, Brent."

"There's no chance for us."

"You need a job and professional help and a support system. You can get all that here."

She was right. And without gainful employment, Brent wouldn't be able to continue paying off his credit card debt and the loan to his friend.

In hindsight, calling Ansel this morning had been a rash response to guilt and remorse. He'd decided he wasn't worthy of a good job and a fair shot from his boss.

"You've made so much progress this past month," Maia continued. "Your job at Mountainside. Judging the bull riding. The online support group. The shelter. Don't throw it all away. Which you would if you left."

She reached for his hand. The gesture took

him by surprise. How could she look at him, touch him, in his current disheveled and emotionally weak state? He must disgust her.

He'd seen it before on the face of his friend from Tucson who'd booted Brent out right before he came to Payson. On the face of his former supervisor at the BLM. On his dad's face.

"Why are you really here?" he asked Maia.

"I told you. To convince you to stay."

"Is that all?"

She gazed at him with heart-tugging sincerity. "And to convince you that what we have, could have, is worth fighting for. But that can come second. Your mental health is more important."

He didn't flinch when she said the words *mental health*, as he had when others spoke them. Was that because of the progress he'd made recently or because of Maia?

"I think my mental health and what we have, what we *could* have, are related. You've been my motivation, Maia. Losing you could cause me to backslide."

"Then why did you end things so abruptly?" she asked.

He let out a long sigh. "That's what I do. What I've done these past two years. I leave before I'm kicked to the curb."

"I would never do that."

"Maybe. I have a way of wearing thin."

"You can change." Maia's fingers tightened on Brent's. "Break the pattern, if you want."

"Why are you wasting your time with a guy like me? You have everything going for you. A family who would move Heaven and Earth for you. A terrific son. A job you love. A successful business you'll take over one day from your dad. A dream that drives you."

"Why not a guy like you?"

"I have nothing to offer you. Zero. Zilch."

"First of all, I don't need you to offer me anything more than your commitment, your loyalty, your help, your time and—okay, I'll say it—your love."

"Maia." Did she have any idea what she was saying?

Her gaze remained steady, and sincerity shone in her eyes. "I think I'm falling in love with you, Brent Hayes, and I'm pretty sure you're falling in love with me. Tell me I'm wrong."

Love. Just hearing her give voice to his growing feelings caused the dam inside his heart to burst. He'd been heading toward love since the moment he'd laid eyes on Maia at that first wedding.

"Besides," she added, still staring at him with that incredible sincerity. "You have a lot going for you, too, when you think about it. A job you love. Not working for Mountainside. Judging rodeo. And can't that also be your dream?"

Brent sat back in the chair and closed his eyes. Climbing out of the murky depths was a slow process. But he was climbing out. Out and toward a goal. Toward Maia.

"Being with me won't be easy," he said. "Not initially. Maybe not ever. Mental illness is something I'll be managing for the rest of my life."

"Nothing worthwhile is easy."

"That's not true."

"Stay," she whispered. "We can do this. Together. I'm here for you."

Brent couldn't believe his ears. No one had ever said that before. He was used to hearing *You're more trouble that you're worth* or *Man, you are one messed-up guy*.

"I need to see a doctor. Talking to Pete at the shelter and the people in the online support group has helped me finally accept that I can't get better on my own."

"That's a really big step. I'm glad for you."

"Will you come with me?" he asked, expecting her to say no.

"Of course. Whatever you need."

Brent swallowed the huge lump that had formed in his throat. Maia was sitting there, offering him everything in the world he could possibly want. Still, he hesitated.

"I'll have setbacks. Mood swings. I'll disappoint and frustrate you. What if I shout at TJ because I stepped on one of his toys?"

"You'd be human. And we'll talk about it. Learn coping techniques. For both of us."

"You say that now. Just wait."

"I have my own baggage. A toddler son who's ten kinds of trouble. A pushy, meddling family—Darla, especially. I guarantee you they will be constantly sticking their noses in our business."

Maia wasn't going away, Brent realized, or kicking him to the curb. She truly wanted him to stay.

"You're crazy, you know," he said. "And I'd be crazy to agree. This could end badly. It will end badly. I'm unreliable. At loose ends. Rock bottom."

"Then we have nowhere else to go but up." She smiled, her entire face radiating joy. "And it won't end badly if we're patient and considerate of each other and willing to put in the work." She squeezed his hand again. "Are you, Brent? Willing to put in the work?"

Here it was. One of those defining moments like in a movie or that people wrote about in their memoirs. He either walked through the door Maia held open or he packed his bags and left town, relegating her to the role of someone in his past. There was no in between. No hanging in limbo. In for a penny, in for a pound.

Was Brent in? For better or worse?

"I'm a catch." Maia pretended to preen. "You'd be a fool to turn me down."

Brent released her hand and pushed to his feet. "I'm a lot of things, Maia, including a fool. On more than one occasion."

The joy drained from her.

"But not today. If you're willing to take a chance on us, then so am I."

Leaping up from her chair, she then skirted the table, threw herself into his open arms and found his mouth with hers.

"I am falling in love with you," she said, her lips brushing his, the sunshine returning to her face. "Make no mistake."

"I'm going to get better, Maia. I promise."

They kissed and kissed again. An optimism Brent hadn't experienced in too many years lifted him from the depths and into the light. He had a long way to go. With Maia beside him, the journey would be an adventure.

Several minutes passed before they broke apart. Brent lost track.

Maia cradled his cheeks with her palms. "Let's spend the rest of Christmas with TJ. If you want to and are up for it. He's had a big day and will be impossible. Fair warning."

"I need to shower first."

"I'll wait. Maybe fix us some coffee."

"That'll hit the spot. And give me a boost. I'll need one before talking to your dad about getting my job back."

"No worries. He likes you."

"Will he like me as the man dating his youngest daughter? Dads can be funny about that."

"He'll approve. Mom, too."

"What about Darla? She hates me."

"She doesn't. She is overprotective," Maia conceded. "But all she really wants is for me to be happy. And I am. Very happy."

Brent pulled Maia close. "Me, too. More than I thought was possible."

When they stepped outside a while later, it was to a robust snowfall.

"A little late," Maia said, "but we're having a white Christmas."

"How about that."

She punched him teasingly in the arm. "You're not even looking."

He'd been staring at her, unable to tear his gaze away.

"We should make a wish," she said and closed her eyes.

Brent did, too. But his Christmas wish had already come true, and she was standing right beside him.

One Year Later

EPILOGUE

"WANNA SEE SANTA!" TJ announced from the back seat of Maia's SUV in what was definitely not his inside voice.

"We will, sweetie. Soon."

His vocabulary over the past year had increased at a remarkable rate. Of course, she credited his above-average intelligence. In reality, it was the result of his outgoing personality, an active social life and the village of people who helped raise him.

Besides Maia, there were his grandparents, his aunt and uncle and cousins—Maia's nieces loved teaching TJ new words—his teacher and playmates at Little Tykes Learn and Grow, and his best buddy Brent.

Maia loved watching the two of them together. Not only did Brent have an abundance of patience, he was one of the few people who talked to TJ. Really talked to him. And TJ responded by listening. *Really* listening.

"You excited?" Brent asked Maia.

He reached across the SUV's console to

straighten her crooked stocking cap. They were all three decked out in holiday garb, though Brent's only concession was a red-and-white woolen scarf. He did look dashing in it.

A burst of warmth filled her, and she took her eyes off the road for only a second to offer him a smile. "I am excited. I love the Cowboy Christmas Jamboree."

"You seemed a little tired at dinner."

"Well, I did work from six to three and then went *s-h-o-p-p-i-n-g*," she spelled out the word, "with Mom and Darla."

Her extremely bright son would ask what she'd purchased if he realized she'd been to the store. Maia was having enough trouble as it was keeping Santa's stash of goodies hidden from him.

They were meeting Maia's family at the event for an evening of holiday fun and entertainment. As usual, the highlight would be a visit with Santa. TJ had learned, mostly from his older cousins and playmates at class, what Santa was all about. He couldn't wait to meet him in person to recite his wish list. A big change from last year when he'd cried and then wanted down from Santa's lap.

"I thought you were going to get another practice session in today," Brent said, as they

turned onto the road that would take them to
Rim Country Rodeo Arena.

"Didn't happen. Too busy. I was thinking
Saturday morning if you're available."

"I don't have a rodeo until mid-January, so
all my free time is yours until then."

"All?"

"Every second." He grinned.

He'd recently returned from the National
Finals Rodeo in Las Vegas where he'd once
competed for a championship title. This time,
his purpose had been to watch and learn and
shadow a seasoned bull-riding judge.

Brent had earned his certification this past
August and had landed several judging jobs
at small rodeos in addition to Rim Country.
He worked most weekends. Weekdays, when
his schedule allowed, he led trail rides for
Mountainside Stables and helped Maia's dad
with horse care and maintenance.

He no longer resided in the bunkhouse. Once
he'd started rodeo judging, and Rowdy hired on
with the forest service, the two of them moved
into a cabin belonging to Channing's family.

Javier and Syndee remained a couple. Sadly,
Rowdy's romance with his girlfriend had run
its course. He'd been ready for a change when
Brent mentioned the cabin was newly available to rent, and having a roommate kept Brent

on track. Both he and Rowdy volunteered at the shelter regularly. Brent attended a weekly men's support group and private counseling sessions with a therapist.

Getting the help he'd needed and finding his passion had made all the difference. Brent flourished, professionally and personally. His mom had visited not once, but twice this past year. She and Brent talked regularly, and he often included Maia and TJ in the video calls. Maia liked his mom very much. How could she not? The woman loved and supported Brent one-hundred-percent. Plus, she adored TJ.

Six months ago, Brent had reached out to his dad and half-siblings. He'd felt he couldn't move forward until he resolved his past. With his therapist's coaching, Brent was able to better understand his dad, how his strict upbringing had shaped him, and choose the right words to say when they conversed. He and his dad weren't the best of friend, but they were making progress. Brent had recently mentioned a possible trip to see his dad and half-siblings.

Maia snuck another peek at Brent, and her heart filled to bursting. The person she'd glimpsed deep down had fully emerged, and she'd fallen more in love, if that was possible. Every day she discovered something new about him and herself, too, because she was also flourishing.

Darla often teased Maia, saying she wore rose-colored glasses. She didn't care. A little positivity never hurt anyone. And while Maia was ready to take her and Brent's relationship to the next level—to start discussing a lifetime commitment—she was content to wait until he was ready.

"I'm glad you're free," she said, "because Snapple's been acting a little temperamental lately."

"His scar again?"

"Not that. He's developed a stubborn streak. We're having constant arguments about who's in charge."

Problems of this nature frequently arose with highly athletic, strong-willed horses like Snapple. Along with the good qualities that made him an outstanding competitive trail horse came a few bad ones: stubbornness and skittishness, for instance.

Maia hadn't won the Diamond Cup in April, but she'd finished twelfth. Not too terrible. There was always this coming April, and she had her sights on placing in the top three. Snapple had the ability, as the numerous ribbons and trophies in less-prestigious competitions had demonstrated. If Maia could just correct this recent crop of pesky little quirks.

"We need your expert training," she said. "Again."

"Might cost you this time," Brent teased.

"Oh? What did you have in mind?"

"You and TJ come with me to the Gila Bend Rodeo in January."

"Hmm. You drive a hard bargain, Mr. Hayes."

He didn't drive a hard bargain at all. Maia had been wanting to see Brent occupying the judges' booth at a rodeo other than Rim Country. Now she'd have her chance.

"Wanna go," TJ shouted from the back, apparently understanding the part of the conversation that involved a road trip.

"We will," Maia said, though she was answering Brent and not TJ.

Arriving at Rim Country, they parked and walked toward the entrance, Brent holding TJ's hand. Maia phoned her mom for an update. The rest of the family was already there and waiting by the concession stand.

Maia's dad had decided out of the blue three days ago he wasn't giving the pony-cart rides. Instead, Rowdy would be in charge with Pete's help. The change in plans had surprised Maia. When she'd questioned her dad, he'd vaguely alluded to spending the evening with his family.

Okay, she supposed. His choice.

"Santa this way," TJ said. "Hurry."

"Don't you want some hot chocolate first?" his grandma asked.

"See Santa first."

"We want to see Santa, too," his cousins echoed.

"TJ," Maia cajoled. "Don't be bossy."

"I not bossy," he argued back and tugged hard on Brent's hand.

Brent gave her a wink. "Let's see Santa. It'll be fun."

Maia's dad led the way, which seemed kind of funny to her. He usually lagged behind, letting the grandkids charge ahead. "Lois, do you have your phone?" he asked. "We need to get some pictures."

"Let Darla. She's better at it."

On cue, Darla plucked her phone from her purse. Well, she was the designated family photographer.

She and Brent had become good friends since the Your Perfect Plus One fiasco last Christmas Eve. It wasn't just that Brent treated her little sister right. Darla also respected Brent for his valiant effort battling his depression and for obtaining his judging certification. Both had required hard work and dedication. Two qualities Darla valued as a successful business owner.

"Hurry," TJ urged.

Brent laughed. Maia groaned. They and the family followed TJ to the arena where the maze had been set up. Once again, animated reindeer pointed the way and, once again, TJ begged to ride them.

Maia noticed Brent becoming quieter and quieter as they traversed the maze, and she tried not to worry. His last episode had been seven months ago and mild compared to others.

"I know TJ and the family are overwhelming," she said. "You coming tonight means a lot to me."

He reached for her hand and brought it to his lips. "Nowhere else I'd rather be."

There. The smile she adored bloomed on his face. Maia did more than relax; she lost herself in his eyes and reveled in the incredible way he made her feel. This was surely another Christmas in what would be a lifetime of Christmases together.

Waiting to see Santa was no easy task for three rambunctious and excited children. TJ and his cousins jumped up and down, twirled, squabbled and tugged eagerly on the coat sleeves of the nearest adult. As they neared the front of the line, Maia's dad paid the donation for photos of each child with Santa, sitting atop his makeshift throne.

Darla readied her phone. Maia, too. She wanted a few of her own shots.

The girls went first, much to TJ's consternation. Maia's efforts to quiet him were in vain. "Manners, TJ."

"My turn, my turn," he protested.

At long last, Santa finished with his cousins. TJ bolted forward, only to stop short in front of Santa, abruptly shy.

"Go on," Maia coaxed.

TJ shook his head.

"Come on, young man." Santa beckoned. To be correct, Channing beckoned. That was him beneath the long white beard and hair. His new wife Kenna played the role of elf helper and photographer.

TJ spun and ran to Brent, hugging his leg. Brent knelt and took TJ by the shoulders. She missed hearing what Brent said, her attention distracted by the pony cart pulling up to the arena fence and stopping. Rowdy and Pete waved, grinning from ear to ear.

"What are they doing here?" Maia asked her dad.

"Just watching your young'un."

Whatever Brent said to TJ must have worked

because her son slowly approached the throne and let Brent lift him onto Santa's lap.

They all watched, and Maia snapped pictures while TJ shyly whispered his list in Santa's ear. His elf helper took the photo. Darla videoed the entire exchange.

Maia laughed, expecting her son to jump off Santa's lap. Except that didn't happen. Instead, Santa reached into his coat pocket and pulled out a small gift bag. Odd, he hadn't done that with the other kids. He then put the bag in TJ's hands, pointed to Maia and said something to TJ she couldn't hear.

With an exaggerated nod, TJ clambered down and scurried over to Maia, holding out the gift bag. "For you, Mommy."

"What's this?" She automatically accepted the gift bag, exchanging glances with Brent.

He shrugged. "Open it and find out."

"Open it," TJ parroted.

Darla, Maia noticed, continued to video. The remainder of her family had moved closer as if jockeying for a glimpse of what was in the bag. They were certainly acting strange. Brent, too.

"We're waiting," her mom encouraged.

Maia stuck a hand into the gift bag and felt a small jewelry box nestled in the tissue. Her heart beat faster. Her breath quickened. Her nerves tingled.

Slowly, because she wanted this moment to last forever, she lifted the box from the bag.

"Brent?" She swallowed. "Is this from you?"

"Maybe." He gazed at her with both expectation and trepidation. "That depends on your answer."

The gift bag fell from her fingers to the ground.

"Mommy." TJ bent down to retrieve it. "You dropped this."

"Hold on to it for me, okay?"

She ran her fingers along the top of the velvet box. Could it be…? She cracked the lid, just enough to peek inside. Her world came to a standstill.

"Maia MacKenzie."

Brent was suddenly standing before her. He took the velvet box from her trembling fingers and opened it all the way. A gorgeous diamond-and-emerald ring twinkled in the moonlight.

"You're like no one I've ever met," he said, a catch in his voice. "You pulled me out of a dark place and into the light. You encouraged me to repair bridges I'd thought burned and taught me the importance of family and forgiveness. You gave me a dream and supported me every step of the way while I achieved it. You had faith in me when others didn't."

He cleared his throat, and she noticed his

eyes had gone a little misty. How sweet. Her own eyes filled with tears as well. Then, he removed the ring from the box and held it out to her.

"Will you marry me, Maia? I'll always be a work in progress, but I promise to do my best to make you happy and be a good father to TJ—"

"Yes." She didn't let him finish, "Yes, yes, yes."

"Yes, yes," TJ repeated and raised his arms in the air.

Maia watched, a lump in her throat, as Brent slipped the ring on her finger. "It fits!" she exclaimed.

Cheers erupted, and Maia looked around to see the faces of her family and friends filled with joy for her and Brent. They'd known all along, of course. How could she have seen the clues and not put them together? Her dad taking the lead on the walk here. Darla continuing to video. Rowdy and Pete in the pony cart. Brent's silence, which was likely a case of nerves.

As if he had anything to be nervous about. There wasn't a chance she'd have turned him down.

"I love you, Maia."

She flung her arms around his neck and

kissed him on the cheeks and his lips and even his forehead. "I love you, too. We are so going to have the best life ever."

She barely heard the hoots and hollers and congratulations. Maia had eyes only for Brent.

"Wishes do come true," she murmured and claimed another kiss. Especially Christmas wishes.

* * * * *

HARLEQUIN SELECTS COLLECTION

19 FREE BOOKS IN ALL!

From Robyn Carr to RaeAnne Thayne to Linda Lael Miller and Sherryl Woods we promise (actually, GUARANTEE!) each author in the Harlequin Selects collection has seen their name on the *New York Times* or *USA TODAY* bestseller lists!

Get 4 FREE REWARDS!

We'll send you 2 FREE Books plus 2 FREE Mystery Gifts.

FREE Value Over $20

Both the **Romance** and **Suspense** collections feature compelling novels written by many of today's bestselling authors.